Being Sawyer Knight

by Nicola Haken

Being Sawyer Knight

Copyright © 2014 Nicola Wall

Cover Design by reesedante.com

Edited by Holly Baker

ISBN-13: 978-1499670028
ISBN-10: 1499670028

"The best way out is always through."

~ Robert Frost

*Dedicated to my oldest friend and very own
fairy-boy, Paul 'Luap' Horrocks.*

CONTENTS

PROLOGUE

~Sawyer~

"*I* can't believe you're really leaving," I said, almost mournfully to Jake. We've been best friends since primary school. We've always done everything together. When we were younger we'd team up to make fun of the girls, we'd hang out after school to play with our Power Rangers and drive our mum's mental. Then when we got older we'd hide behind the school bike sheds together to grab a smoke at break time, join forces on the Nintendo when we should be doing homework, chase the girls... Or rather I'd chase the girls, and he'd stand aside while I had my fun.

But this morning everything changed. His dad has landed himself a dream job in Australia and Jake and his family are leaving. Tomorrow morning.

"And you'll miss the party next week," I added, as if my eighteen birthday would be reason enough for his dad to change his mind and stay - give up his career all for the sake of my party.

"It's shit I know. But hey, you'll be fine. You've got the guys and that chick in your maths class who's been coming on to you since you started sixth form." By 'the guys' Jake was referring to Kip, Jacob and Mike. We've been buddies since high school, Kip and I even longer, and last year decided to start up a band together. And the chick? That would be Elle. She's been helping me out in the library at lunch with my maths assignments, but I haven't told Jake because he'll just assume I want to screw her. And I don't. She's smart, pretty and funny as shit, but she's more like a sister to me. "You'll be too busy being famous and getting laid to miss me," he joked.

"Yeah right," I said, dismissing him. I'm not stupid enough to think the band will go anywhere, but I play mean guitar, I love singing and have a decent enough voice to play the local pubs and clubs every weekend. That's why I'm taking maths and English A levels too. If the music doesn't work out, I'm guaranteed a decent job with those qualifications behind me. "It's just gonna be weird. We've been mates forever."

Fuck I was sounding like a complete pussy, but I couldn't help it. He was my best friend and I was going to miss him. I supposed I'd taken him for granted all these years and I didn't know how big a part of my life he was until I discovered he wouldn't be in it anymore.

"Want to grab a pizza? A last supper so to speak?"

"Sure," I agreed as we neared the college gates. "What about your A levels? Will you be able to carry that on over there?"

"I don't know. Think they're called something different over there but that's my dad's plan, for me to finish my education and be something smart."

"I've no doubt you'll be something smart, mate. You always did beat my arse at tests."

"Only 'cause I copied off Danny Henderson," he fired back. He was talking shit. Jake is a smart arse - quicker

than anything and smarter than Carol fuckin'
Vorderman.

Hooking the strap of my bag across my body, we
made our way to the bus stop before hopping on the
419 into town. After wandering the shopping centre for
a while, talking shit and taking the piss out of the
cleaners in their bright blue tabards, we ventured into
Pizza Hut and ordered our usual Meat Feast to share
between us.

"I'm gonna miss you, Sawyer," Jake said before wiping
the corners of his lips on a napkin. For the first time in
forever we both stayed quiet while we ate our pizza.
What was there to discuss? We couldn't plan anything,
talk about what game we were gonna play tomorrow or
where we were going next weekend. He wasn't going to
be here, so what was the point?

"We should get going. Jerry will go ballistic on my arse
if I'm out much longer." Jerry is my stepdad, and the
biggest arsehole in the world. He married my mum
when I was seven and didn't show a shred of interest in
my existence until my band started getting gigs at local
pubs. Now all of a sudden, he's really proud of me and
wants to be our manager. I couldn't refuse him because
I knew it would upset my mum - she hates it when we
don't get along. But I also knew the fucker only wanted
in to take a cut of the money I earned.

Looking at my watch I noted we still had another
twenty minutes before the bus was due, so instead of
taking the direct walkway to the station, we killed some
time by walking the long way, past the shops and
through the alleys. It was getting late, the shops were
closing and it was dark above us. An old woman walked
past us and when she neared us, she took one look at
the hoody pulled up over my head and picked up her

pace. I couldn't help snorting a laugh - some people are so judgemental.

"Saw, wait up," Jake called. I was walking a few steps in front so I stopped at the sound of his voice and turned around.

"What's up?" I asked with a cock of my head. He just stood there - staring at me. I walked curiously towards him, worried something was wrong. He wouldn't quit with the staring and it was starting to freak me out. When I reached him he started walking forwards towards me and instinctively I stepped backwards before he bumped into me. But he kept coming, so I kept retreating… until my back hit a brick wall.

"Mate, what the fuck is wrong with you?" I asked nervously, suddenly feeling a little breathless. He was right in front of me now. He pulled down his hood and the streetlight above us lit up his face, making his blue eyes sparkle as they bored into mine. "Jake?" I pressed again. He was just… *staring*. Like he didn't know whether to punch me or… *kiss* me? No. No fucking way. "Jake you're freaking me out. For fuck's sake, say something!"

The weirdest part of this whole thing was that even though I felt confused, a little scared and wholly uncomfortable… it didn't even occur to me to push him away. Not even when he placed his hands on my shoulders.

"Sawyer," he whispered, his voice strained like he was in pain. "I'm going to miss you like crazy."

"Uh… yeah I know. You said."

Christ, I was practically panting. What the fuck was going on?

"No, Sawyer. You *don't* know, and I can't leave until you do. I'll be on the other side of the world soon, so I guess that means I've got nothing to lose." I opened my mouth to speak but all that came out was a rush of breath. "I love you, Saw. I've loved you since we were fourteen."

What. The. Fuck.

"Jake... quit fucking around," I said, forcing playfulness into my voice. What the hell had gotten into him? Ignoring me, he pressed his chest against mine and I gulped. "Seriously, mate." He needed to back the fuck off... so why was I suddenly nervous that he might actually do just that?

"I'm not fucking around, Sawyer," he said calmly... *seriously*. Then he brought his palm up to my cheek and my breath caught as his fingers moved down and smoothed over the light stubble along my jaw. *Now would be a good time to deck the fucker.* "You must've noticed the fact I've never had a girlfriend. Or seen the way I look at you when you shower after P.E? Or the way my breathing gets heavy when I smell that body spray you wear?"

Of course I'd noticed the no girlfriend thing, but to be honest I put it down to him being a geek who was too busy studying to be arsed chasing girls when he could just have a wank instead. As for the shower and heavy breathing thing? No fucking way did I ever notice that.

"Jake..." His name came out as a breathy whisper. To my ears it almost sounded like a *pleading* whisper. Obviously I'd misheard, so I pulled my hood down too so I could hear myself properly. *Push him away now, Sawyer.*

"I love you, Sawyer Antony Knight." When his other palm cupped the other side of my face, my eyes wandered down to his wrist, following the trail up his arm until they landed on his face, meeting his gaze.

Seriously, push him away. Punch him. Beat the living shit out of him for pulling this kind of stunt on you! "I'm going to kiss you, Saw." *Like fuck you are! Move, body...WALK AWAY!* "I'm going to kiss you and take that memory with me to treasure for the rest of my life."

Cautiously, never taking his eyes from mine as if he were assessing my reaction, his face inched closer to mine. When his breath swept over my face, I started breathing so heavily I felt like I was going to die from the pressure in my chest. No matter how hard I tried to force it out with each breath, it wouldn't leave...

Until his lips touched mine and I stopped breathing altogether.

He planted soft, careful kisses along my bottom lip, pulling away after each one and studying my expression. When I didn't react, he kissed me again - only this time he pulled me into him with his hands cradling each side of my head. I didn't want to look at him - didn't want to believe this was really happening, but no matter how hard I tried to close my eyes they refused. Jake dipped his tongue into my mouth and I gasped, almost choking on the taste of him. Suddenly I was ravenous. This time I *did* close my eyes and forced myself to concentrate on the amazing feeling against my lips, the intoxicating taste on my tongue... and the sound of his soft, barely there stubble grazing against my own. Unconsciously my hands wound around his back, pulling his body against mine. I could feel his hard dick straining against the denim of his jeans, and when I found myself wanting to reach down and cup it, I pulled away - disgusted with myself.

"Jesus, Sawyer. If I'd known you'd react like that I would've told you three years ago."

"I...I didn't... I mean I don't..."

6

"It's okay, Saw. I'm leaving remember? I won't tell anyone you're g-"

"I'M NOT…" I couldn't even say the word. "You shouldn't have done that, Jake! What the fuck were you thinking?"

"I was thinking that I'd wanted you for the last three years, and I couldn't leave without tasting you."

"You're out of order. Why the fuck would you pull this shit on me? I'm not… I'm not *like* that."

"*This* tells me otherwise," he said with a cocky smile, cupping my dick through my pants.

"GET THE FUCK OFF ME!" I yelled at him. Then I shoved him off me with so much force he stumbled, saving himself on a lamppost. "You had no right to do that to me!" I growled in his face. "I'm fucking glad you're leaving," I spat.

"Sawyer," he muttered pleadingly. "Mate, come on…"

"You lost the right to call me 'mate' about ten fuckin' minutes ago. Get the fuck out of my life, Jake, and don't ever contact me again."

"Sawyer," he called after me when I started jogging towards the bus station. "Sawyer I'm sorry!"

And those were the last words I ever heard from my best friend.

CHAPTER ONE

~Sawyer~

Ten Years Later...

"*So* tell me..." the journalist whose name I'd already forgotten began with an eager smile. Leaning forward in her chair she continued... "What's it like being Sawyer Knight?"

Oppressive.

Tiring.

Lonely.

"Awesome. Of course it is. I'm a very lucky guy." I gave the same robotic answer I've been trained to give, but feeling the lie coat my tongue made me remember why I don't usually agree to do interviews. It's all bullshit. They ask the questions the world is apparently dying to know the answers to, but they only want the 'right' answers. They're only interested in the fame, the money and the glamour of it all. Not *me*. They don't give a flying fuck about *me* - Sawyer the human being.

"And how are you feeling about being back in the UK?"

"It's great. Good to be home." I kept my answers short and evasive, flashing her the wink that seems to make every female on the planet squirm on the spot.

"Will you be visiting anyone special while you're here?" she asked with a raised eyebrow. What she meant was, am I seeing anyone, who is she and when are we getting married. Crossing my ankle over my knee, I had to try really hard not to roll my eyes and walk the hell out of there.

"We'll be too busy with the tour to take time out for ourselves. But I hope to catch up with my friend while I'm here."

It's not really a 'hope'. I've already seen Elle and will see her every single day while I'm here, but I don't need the pond scum, known as the paparazzi, following her every goddamn second. Not that my silence will make much, if any, difference, but I've still got to try.

"That would be Elle Wilson, right?"

"Right."

"And she's really *just* a friend?"

"No. She's my *best* friend." The interfering journalist sighed and I could tell she was getting frustrated at the fact her attempts to drag some dirt out of me were futile.

"And what about the guys? What are their plans?"

"I imagine Kip will take a day to visit his family and the other guys their friends, but really you'd have to ask them." Except she couldn't because the arseholes didn't turn up this morning, leaving me to deal with this shit on my own. My fist was already itching to punch each one of my band mates in the face. Twice.

She went on to ask me a couple more simple questions with hidden meanings but I think the impressive yawn I let out gave her a clue as to where this was heading and

9

she flipped her notepad closed. So, after using just ten minutes of her allotted twenty, she gave up.

"Well Sawyer," she said, drawing the interview to a close. "It was a pleasure meeting you today."

"Likewise," I completely fucking lied.

I shook her hand, because she offered hers, then stood up and walked towards the door.

"Oh, before you go!" she called after me. I stopped and turned my body to face her, trying very hard not to groan. "Would you like to address the rumours about your-"

"Time's up," our PR manager, Claire, interrupted. I shot first the interviewer, and then Claire, the deadliest glare I could summon and then literally stormed out of the room like a pissed off teenager.

"Sawyer!" she called after me, her heels clicking furiously against the floor as she tried to catch up with me. "Sawyer, wait up!"

"Front or back?" I asked Jim, our temporary head of security, when I approached - ignoring Claire completely.

"Back. There's a mob of girls out front and we don't have the numbers to get you through there safely," he replied. Our security team has gone to shit since Billy got fired a couple of weeks ago so public appearances have been limited. Hopefully the new guy they're bringing in to head the team will sort that shit out.

I hurried through some double glass doors, down some stairs and then out through a back door marked 'Staff Only' with Jim and Neil flanking me either side. Our drivers were waiting for us just a step away from the exit and I ducked inside the back of the car, welcoming the privacy of the blacked out windows. Jim climbed in beside me, and Neil got in the car behind with Claire. I knew I'd have to talk to her eventually but right now I was too pissed off. She arranges all this godforsaken interview shit and she knows how I feel about it, which is why she should have made sure the other guys were there to take some of the heat.

Jim tried to make small talk on the way back to the hotel but seemingly thought better of it when all he got in return was a huff. I texted Elle en-route to ask if she had time to meet up later and when she replied with a 'hell yeah', my mother of a bad mood instantly started lifting.

"Do you ever get used to seeing that kinda thing, mate?" Jim asked, directing his gaze towards a giant billboard with our picture on it. I'd seen several on our way here this morning, all announcing the tour dates.

"Don't really notice 'em anymore," I clipped, still drowning in my bad mood. Honestly, after all these years, seeing my face lit up on a billboard is no stranger than seeing a framed picture of myself up on my grandma's living room wall. At least that *would* be the case, if she were still alive.

For once, getting into the hotel unseen was relatively simple. We used the back doors and were escorted to our suites on the top floor by hotel security. A shot of whiskey and a sleep – that's what I wanted. But of course I wasn't fucking lucky enough to get it.

"Where the fuck were you guys?" I blasted when I waltzed into my suite and found the rest of the guys lounging across my furniture.

"Um, yeah… sorry about that, dude," Matt sniggered, rolling a joint filled with fuck knows what.

"Daz?" I pressed, ignoring Matt as usual. Believe me, there's a reason we call him Matt the Twat. But the guy plays drums like no other, and as far as I'm concerned that's the only reason I haven't kicked his ass into next year yet.

"We were never supposed to show up," he explained, each word making my blood grow a little hotter. "They only wanted you, mate. Claire said you wouldn't have turned up if you knew that."

"Damn right I wouldn't!" I yelled, balling my hand into a fist so tight my knuckles ached. "Devious bitch!"

"Chill out, mate," Kip interrupted. Kip and I have been friends since primary school. His real name is Isaac but he earned the nickname 'Kipper' because he looked so similar to the kid in the Biff, Chip and Kipper books you're forced to read as a child. Same blonde hair, red cheeks and crooked nose. I've known the guy for twenty years and he still looks the same, only bigger and with ninety percent of his body covered in ink. Out of all the guys, Kip and I are the closest. We started this band back in college with a couple of mates who went their own way before we hit it big. Daz, Matt and Gavin joined the team a year later, just as we were getting ready to throw in the towel. "It's done now."

"Yeah, well maybe I am too," I spat. Matt rolled his eyes at me. Of course he knew I wasn't serious, but fuck if this life isn't what it's cracked up to be.

"Well," Kip continued. "She'll be here in an hour so I suggest you go take a breather before she gets here."

"Yeah," Matt joined in. "Smoke a joint, take a shower and rub one off…"

Being Sawyer Knight

"What's she coming for?" I asked Kip, once again continuing as if Matt didn't exist. Matt's a nice enough guy don't get me wrong, he's just a huge fucking idiot with one of those faces it takes all your inner strength not to punch. "There's nothing scheduled for today."

"She's bringing the new head of security to meet us all. He's from Australia apparently."

"I don't give a fuck who he is as long as he can do his job properly."

Billy had been our head of security for the past two years. He and I never saw eye to eye. He was lazy and incompetent and my point was proven when Gavin found a random groupie hiding in his bunk on the tour bus last month. It was Billy's job to make sure that kinda shit didn't happen, and so just ten minutes later he was given his marching orders.

Without saying another word I stomped off into the bedroom. I went straight to the mini bar and took out two miniature bottles of whiskey before downing them straight in quick succession. Once the burn in my throat had eased, the warmth of the alcohol travelled through my veins, settling me instantly. Next I practically threw myself onto the four-poster bed, rolled onto my back and silently cursed my life before drifting off to sleep.

"Saw!" I thought I heard the faint sound of my name but it wasn't strong enough to make me open my eyes. "Yo, Sawyer!"

"Ugh," I grumbled into my pillow. It was Matt calling me, and when that didn't get a response he started knocking too.

"Sawyer, dude. Claire's here." *And I should move, why?* "Right, Saw I'm giving you five seconds before I'm coming in, so if you're jerkin' your junk you better put that shit away."

"Fuck you, arsehole! Gimme two minutes." *And why the fuck are you all still in my suite?*

"You got *one*!"

Seriously, was one fucking day off too much to ask for? Just *one?* Apparently so. Sighing, I dragged my weary ass out of bed and rubbed my eyes. Then I headed out to meet the guys and our new head of security. I walked into the room with a disinterested look on my face, purposely refusing eye-contact with Claire because I'm an immature twat like that.

"Sawyer," Claire began. "I've already introduced the other guys, well except Kip because he's, um, *entertaining* in his room, and now I'd like you to meet our new head of security." Out of courtesy, and because it wasn't the new guy's fault I was pissed off with Claire, I raised my head and looked over to where he sat. My eyes began at his feet, and then travelled up his body…

And then they met his face.

My chest tightened and all traces of moisture evaporated from my mouth– in surprise, panic or regret I'll probably never know.

"Long time no see, Sawyer."

Jake.

Jake Reed.

Jake Reed, my ex-best friend. A friend I'd shared everything with growing up and a friend I'd pushed away saying I never wanted to see again. Now he was here, right in front of me, dressed impeccably in a sharp black suit with enough buttons undone on his white shirt to show the world he was ripped, and the only thing I could remember about him was the way his lips felt on mine.

I'm fucking screwed.

CHAPTER TWO

~Jake~

Sawyer Antony Knight. It'd been ten years since I last saw him, in the flesh at least, and yet he still managed to take my breath away.

"What are you doing here?" he asked me, sounding almost pissed off.

"I'm your new head of security."

"I know that. But why are you *here*? You moved away."

"I came back," I stated simply, shrugging nonchalantly. He was unsettled and I'd be lying if I said it didn't turn me the hell on knowing I had that affect on him. My dick swelled, straining against the restrictive fabric of my pants, the second my eyes landed on Sawyer's body. It was unexpected, but not necessarily a surprise. I didn't come here to win him as my lover, but the man sitting in front of me had plagued my every conscious thought since the day he left me outside the bus station ten years ago, so the physical response I was experiencing was only natural.

I accepted this job because it's an amazing opportunity. After spending my entire adulthood working for my father's security firm, this is the kind of end-goal some people can only dream of. I get to travel the world, front what - on paper - sounds like an impressive team, and of course the money is off the fucking charts. But most of all, I'm good at what I do. I'm the best. Sawyer Knight has always deserved the best, and if he won't let me take care of his heart, I will at least make sure I protect his life.

My father's company expanded into personal security and bodyguard services about five years ago. I quickly worked my way up the top – not because I'm his son, but like I said, because I'm the best. For the past two years I have been in charge of protecting one of Australia's top soap opera stars, Chad Willis. I was all set for accompanying him to LA after he landed himself the leading role in Quentin Tarantino's latest movie… but then I heard about this job and neither my mind or my heart could turn it down.

I found out during my first meeting with the band's manager, Philip Sinclair, that they have been receiving death threats, aimed mainly at Sawyer. As far as I'm aware the band haven't been informed about this issue yet, and for now at least, I agree there is no point. They are no doubt from some deranged fan with too much time on their hands. This series of threats is likely not the first the band has received and I'm certain it won't be the last. It's part of the package when you're in the public eye – people hate you as much as others adore you.

"Wait... are you…" Ah, Isaac. He walked into the suite with one arm wrapped around some tits on a stick, pointing at me in recognition. "You went to school with me and Saw, right?"

"Right," I answered, forcing a smile. I didn't like him back then and from what I'd seen of him in interviews, I don't like him now. He's cocky and arrogant and has seemed to believe from being only thirteen years old that he was put on this earth purely to *service* the female population. "Jake," I offered. He scratched his head as if searching for the memory of my name, but in order to remember it he'd have had to have known it in the first place. Back in school, he hung around with Sawyer a lot, but wouldn't give me the time of day.

"Jake! Of course!" he beamed as if he suddenly remembered. He was a lying shit. "How've you been, mate?" he asked, practically tossing the stick woman aside to come and shake my hand.

"Good," I answered curtly. "Great to be back on home soil," I added with a smile when I realised I was behaving like a jerk.

"So is there anything else, Claire? Only I've got some, um, *business* to attend to," Isaac said, tossing a suggestive and slightly nauseating look towards Tits on a Stick.

"No, Kip. That's all," she replied, rolling her eyes. *Kip?* "I just wanted you all to meet Jake." Without needing a second word of encouragement Isaac, or *Kip*, had disappeared with his piece of pussy. From the way he looked at her it was obvious she was a 'one night' thing. I'd be surprised if he even knew her name. "Okay, guys, well that's all for tonight. We'll meet before rehearsals tomorrow to discuss the new plans Jake is proposing."

Being Sawyer Knight

"What kind of new plans?" Sawyer asked dubiously. His voice danced into my ears and spread to my veins, warming my whole body.

"I think we, meaning your security team, need a little more structure," I began. "A designated guard for each band member, a new system for…"

"I'm happy with how things are," Sawyer cut me off. I had to bite the inside of my lip to stop me from grinning. He was being purposefully awkward and I couldn't help find it amusing. I was affecting him, and I liked it.

"Well we'll discuss it further in the morning," Claire interrupted. "Jake has had a long few days spent travelling, I'm sure he'd like to get to his room and rest."

"I feel fine. In fact, if you want me to stay behind and explain things a bit more, Sawyer, that's no problem."

Please say yes.

"Nah, mate. I'll wait till the morning like the others."

Fuck.

"Well how about we just have a drink? Catch up on the old times?"

Sawyer's hazel eyes narrowed as my question swirled around his mind. His expression screamed unease, doubt… maybe even fear.

"Sure. Sounds good," he said flatly, refusing to give me just a hint of how he was truly feeling through his tone. "That means the rest of you can fuck off to your own suites. I don't get why you've been hanging round here all day anyway."

"Yours is the biggest," Matt – who according to the press, the other guys call 'Matt the Twat – chipped in. "Therefore you have a bigger minibar."

"What the fuck ever," Sawyer said, shooing him off with his hand. "You want more liquor you call room service. No need to hover round my ass all day."

"What the hell is wrong with you today, man? You get your period or somethin'?"

"Fuck you, Matt."

"Is this still about the interview? It's over, dude. Forget about it."

"You're still here."

"Fine. Whatever. Come on, guys." The other two, Darren and Gavin, got up to follow Matt out of the room. "Hey, Jake... when he starts to piss you off, there'll be beer in my room!" Matt called back to me. I raised my palm in acknowledgement, even though I had no intention of taking him up on his unappealing offer. And then there were three...

"I'll get going too," Claire said, standing from her chair and smoothing her skirt with flattened hands. "And Sawyer, snap out of this mood you've gotten yourself into. It was one interview, and you know how important these things are for publicity. It's part of the deal. Don't let it ruin rehearsals tomorrow."

"Sure," he said, sounding sincere. "Sorry I've been such a jackass. I've had a headache all day, I guess that made things worse."

"Get an early night in that case. We've only got two days before the first show, and we have a lot to get through before then. Oh and Philip will be joining the meeting in the morning too, so don't be late."

"Wow. How nice of him," Sawyer spat sarcastically. "I'm honoured."

Claire had opened the door and was hovering in the open space. With her hand on the doorknob, she drew in a deep breath through her nose before squinting her eyes and opening her mouth. "There's another interview tomorrow with all five of you. Don't lose your shit." Then she was gone, with the door closed firmly behind her before Sawyer could even open his mouth to respond.

"Bitch," I heard him mutter under his breath. Then he closed his eyes and sucked in a deep breath through his nose. He stayed in that position, relaxed into his chair, legs apart, head back, for a couple of minutes. I just stared at him – devouring the image of him and committing it to memory. My eyes honed in on his strong neck and I absently licked my lips as I watched the thick vein there throb in rhythm with his heart. God, how I wanted to lick that vein. How I wanted to taste his salty skin, inhale the sweet scent of him, feel his pulse against my lips…

"So you don't like interviews?" I broke the silence, needing to hear his deep, gravelled voice.

"Why are you really here, Jake?" he asked, sounding exasperated, and maybe confused, as he finally made eye contact with me. "After the way we left things…"

"We were just kids then, Sawyer. I'm sure we're both mature enough to move on from that."

"But you moved so far away – the other side of the world. Why did you come back? Leave your family? Your friends?"

"I came back because this is an amazing opportunity. And... because I've missed you." His brow furrowed and tiny sparks of panic literally flickered in his eyes. "We were best friends for a *long* time, Sawyer. I missed being that close to someone. I missed the fun we used to have. Because we did, remember?"

"Yeah," he agreed, smiling fondly. "Remember that time we filled Dennis Lawson's locker with dog shit?"

"Oh yeah! Fuck, we were evil little shits."

"Nah. The prick deserved it. That kid was so full of himself you'd think he shit diamonds or something." I nodded, smiling at the memory. "Drink?"

"Sure," I agreed, loosening my tie. Sawyer stood up and strolled towards the minibar. His jeans were so tight I could see every flex of his arse with each step. He was good looking back in high school, but now... now he's beautiful.

Conversation was a little awkward at first. We stuck to 'safe' topics, talking about our childhood and everything leading up to – but not including - the last time we saw each other. Soon enough, the rich whiskey started taking effect, visibly relaxing him. Three shots in and I saw a genuine smile... not a forced one he'd only put on for my benefit. The curve of his lips illuminated his entire face, making his caramel eyes sparkle under the wisp of dark brown hair that couldn't seem to keep itself from falling over his face.

"So, how are your parents?" I asked casually in an effort to keep the conversation flowing. I didn't want this night to end.

"Jerry fucked off a few years back. He was our first manager before we got signed, got us a few gigs here and there… but then I found out he'd been knocking my mum around, so after beating the living shit out of him, I told him he either disappeared or I'd call the cops."

"Jesus," I barely whispered, shaking my head at the image he'd put in my mind. "How's your mum now?"

"Good, last time I heard."

"You don't see her?"

"Not often. She doesn't exactly approve of my lifestyle. Got to do what's right by her church buddies, ya know."

"Wow. Sorry, mate." Sawyer shrugged casually, feigning indifference. His eyes told a different story though. Evident discomfort forced his eyebrows together slightly and when he blinked, it took his eyes a couple of seconds longer than necessary to open again. "So who do you go to when you need to escape all this shit?" I asked, motioning my hands around the opulence surrounding us.

"Elle," he said simply. Just the sound of her name tugged on the corners of his lips, making him smile.

"Maths girl?" I already knew the answer. The whole world knows about Elle Wilson – best friend and possible secret girlfriend of the hottest singer this decade has ever seen.

"Yeah," he agreed, still smiling as he nodded. "After you… *left*," he started to explain, the word 'left' cracking on his lips. "I spent more and more time with her. She helped me with my maths, gave me her old papers to study, that kind of shit. I still fucking failed," he added with yet another smile. I liked Elle already. So far, she's the only person who seems to make Sawyer happy. "But seriously, she's the only person who's ever been there for me. If it weren't for her… I don't think I'd have survived this life very long."

Wow.

"Sounds lonely," I said, picking my glass up from the table and taking another sip of whiskey. The burn ceased after the second glass, and so now, four glasses in, the rich liquid trickled smoothly down my throat like silk. "Are you lonely, Sawyer?"

His eyes widened just slightly and he stuttered on his response. I stared intently into his eyes, trying to catch a glimpse of his soul hiding behind them. I could almost see the debate taking place in his mind – whether to be honest with me, or lie.

"No. Course not." He went for the option of lying. "I'm surrounded by people every day."

"But they don't know you," I stated cautiously, the end of my sentence coming out slightly higher as if it were a question. "Not the *real* you."

"How the fuck would you know? You don't know me," he spat. The anger in his voice halted the rhythm of my heart for a brief second while I considered what I was doing. I *should* back off. I *should* be professional and keep a safe personal distance. I *should* apologise for riling him.

Being Sawyer Knight

But I knew immediately I wasn't going to do any of those things. Despite what he might think right now, I *do* know Sawyer Knight – the *real* one. I grew up with him, I loved him… I *still* love him. We might have spent the last ten years apart but I've never stopped following him. I've watched his career go from strength to strength. I've studied him in interviews, TV appearances and even went to watch him play when the band's last tour landed in Australia. Each time I watched him I was drawn to his eyes, and not once had I ever seen the sparkle in them that I used to fantasise over as a teenager. He never smiles – not genuinely. He never talks about his private life. Never discusses himself unless prompted, and even then the discomfort is evident by the slight squirm of his body.

Sawyer is hiding from the world.

He's hiding from himself.

And I'm going to find him.

Chapter Three

~Sawyer~

"*I'm* sorry, Sawyer," Jake apologised. "I didn't mean to upset you. I just imagine this life can get pretty lonely at times."

Damn right it can, but I didn't want him of all people to know that. Why? I'm not really sure. Maybe because it always did annoy me that he could read me so well, and I don't want *anyone* having that kind of power over me.

"Forget it, man. I shouldn't have snapped, been a long day, that's all."

"You sound different," he said, stroking the stubble on his chin between his thumb and forefinger. I tried to reply but found my lips were so suddenly dry that they'd stuck together. I licked them slowly, unable to take my eyes off his fingers caressing his strong chin. Clearly, I'd had too much to fucking drink. "Your accent," he added. "You've got an American twang to it. You use American words."

"Well, my base is in L.A. When we're not touring I spend all my time there. Guess some of the lingo must've rubbed off on me. *You* sound just the same." In

26

fact if I were to close my eyes and listen to him speak, his voice could easily take me back to when we were seventeen.

"I *am* the same, Sawyer. And so are you." I pursed my eyebrows, confused by the obvious hidden meaning in his tone. "You're still afraid."

"Afraid?" I questioned, my voice breaking as it fought past the lump in my throat. "What the hell are you talking about?"

Jake stood, stepped around the glass coffee table and perched on the end of it so our knees were almost touching. My heart stopped, my head swam, and my mouth was coated in sandpaper.

"Admit that being this close to me is affecting you," he challenged.

"Don't do this, Jake," I croaked – my voice weak and uncertain. "Not again."

Just when I thought he was about to lower his hands onto my knees, my breath hitched and he stood from the table.

"I know you, Sawyer. Always have, always will." Bizarrely, I didn't doubt that, and it unnerved me. "I'm not letting you go a second time."

"You can't be serious. This is a fucking joke right?" Anger forced me to my feet and Jake followed. He is an inch or two taller than me so I straightened my back, forcing my eyes to his level. "And did you tell my team about your little obsession with me, huh? When you applied for this job? You'd be out on your ass by sunrise if I told them."

"But you won't," he said confidently, and I wanted to punch the smug bastard for being right. We were just inches apart – so close I could feel his breath swim over my face. I had to swallow down the nonsensical lump of emotion swelling in my throat before I could respond. He was right – he *was* affecting me. And damn if that didn't make me hate my own fucking guts.

"No, I won't. If you stop this shit now, keep things professional, then there should be no problem."

Why did he have to start this shit up again? He'd ruined our friendship once before and now, just as I started to believe we could get that friendship back, he decides he's intent on ruining it again.

"You *will* be mine, Sawyer Knight. The faster you try to run the quicker you'll fall to your knees. Then, Sawyer… then you'll be too weak to resist."

"You're drunk." He *had* to be. No sane or sober person would say shit like that on the first day of a new job…or *any* day, ever. "We've had too much to drink. Go back to your room, Jake."

"Yes, I *am* drunk," he admitted. *Thank fuck.* "But the only factor that plays in this, is that it's given me the courage to speak my sober thoughts out loud."

"Jake…" it came out as practically a whimper. I wanted to beg him, *plead* with him not to keep pushing this, pushing *me*. I'll never be who he wants me to be. Everyone wants something different from me and I gave up trying to please them all a long time ago. Am I hiding the *real* me? Maybe. I wouldn't even know who the real me is anymore. Whoever he was, he died the day my career was born.

"Goodnight, Sawyer," he breathed, leaning in to whisper straight into my ear – so close his soft stubble grazed mine for just a second. It was long enough to take my breath away, and then I closed my eyes, refusing to open them until I heard the door close after him.

I can't deal with this shit now. Trying almost destroyed me once before and so I'm sure as shit not going to put myself through that again. Flopping back onto the plush couch, I didn't have a fucking clue what I was going to do.

"Hey, Jim," I greeted, pressing the phone to my ear.

"Blonde or brunette?" he interrupted. Of course he knew why I was calling. There was only ever one reason I called him so late at night, and that was when I needed to distract myself for a couple of hours. I'd barely opened my mouth to say 'either' when there was a knock on the door to my suite.

"Never mind," I snapped down the line before hastily ending the call. Then, getting up from my seat and fixing my robe in place, I walked over to the door, sucking in a breath as I prepared to rip whoever it was a new asshole.

"You didn't text," Elle scolded, brushing past me and waltzing straight over to the plush couches. Pete, another member of our security team, and the one who'd clearly escorted Elle to my room, gave me a firm nod before disappearing down the hall.

"Sorry," I muttered, sighing as I kicked the door closed behind me.

"Come sit with Aunty Elle," she cooed with that bright smile of hers as she patted the couch next to her. She wore her long, blonde hair up today. Perfectly styled of course, which is why she is the band's head stylist on our UK tour dates, and the occasional European leg if she can leave the salon. Elle went into hairdressing on a whim after leaving college. It sparked an interest in her she didn't know was hiding, and within just two years of getting her NVQ she opened her own salon in London.

Hair Design by Elle, began as a small backstreet shop offering cheap cut and blows to old ladies. It didn't take long for her to make a name for herself once the trickle of younger clients started coming to her. They spread the word, telling their friends who told their friends who told their friends... you get the idea. Six months later she moved to bigger premises on the high street, and six months after that, she was booked a month in advance at a time.

She's cut my hair since before she even qualified – I was her 'dummy'. So naturally when the band took off, so did Elle. Suddenly *everyone* wanted their hair styling by the same woman who dressed the hair of Sawyer Knight, and within weeks Elle Wilson was a prominent name in the world of fashion and beauty. Of course, some people challenged her, accused her of living off the success of the band, but her work speaks for itself.

She's worked her way up in the industry by working her tiny ass off. She attends, and even co-organises some, fashion and beauty events, and is now a well respected and admired member of her profession. That has *nothing* to do with the band, that's all on her.

"What's up with my muscle man, huh?"

An involuntary smile crept onto my face. She began calling me muscle man when I started hitting the gym when I turned eighteen. Elle is the only person who can get away with calling me shit like that and she knows it, too.

"I met our new head of security today," I confessed, getting straight to the point. There was no point trying to lie to Elle. Sometimes I think she knows me better than I know myself. Fuck that, she *definitely* knows me better than I know myself.

"Aaaaand?" She drew out the word, clearly failing to see the importance.

"It's Jake."

"Jaaaake?" she pressed, confusion forcing her eyebrows together. Then it hit – the realisation. "Wait, Jake? Jake Reed? Jake, best friend until you kissed him, Jake?"

"I didn't kiss him," I snapped. "He kissed *me.*"

"Whatever. Let's not go over the specifics again," she said with a teasing smile. "So how do you feel?"

"I don't know."

"Sure you do. Tell me."

"Pleased. Confused. *Angry.*"

"Angry?"

"He seems to want to pick up exactly where we left off. He… he told me I would be his. Can you believe that shit?"

"Wow. Ego much?"

"Exactly. I don't know why he even thinks I'm… *that* way."

"You can say the word, you know. It's not contagious."

Ignoring her, I continued. "I've never given him any reason to think I'm, I dunno, *into* him. Why does he have to keep fucking everything up? I didn't think I'd ever see him again and now I feel like I'm seven-fucking-teen again."

"Sawyer," she said quietly, *seriously*, and I knew what speech was coming. "Why are you so against being who you are?"

"Please don't start this bollocks, Elle." Why does everyone seem to know 'who I am' when 'I' have no fucking idea?

"Don't you dare get pissed off with me. It's the truth and you know it. When we left sixth form, when you started-"

"That was a mistake. I don't want to rake over that crap."

The truth is, Jake *does* affect me – just like he did all those years ago. I'd had 'thoughts' about other guys before that day, but I put it down to haywire teenage hormones. A phase. I convinced myself it was normal. Then, when he kissed me… and my body responded in a way it had never done before with a girl, it confirmed what I'd always suspected but refused to admit.

I thought I was gay. 'Thought' being the operative word. So, after leaving sixth form, I experimented a little. It wasn't hard to meet willing guys in some of the clubs we gigged in, and I *needed* to prove my suspicions wrong. So I did. Over the course of a few months I accepted the odd blowjob from a couple of guys I barely knew. While they were the best orgasms of my life, I also realised if I closed my eyes it was really no different to fucking a girls mouth. Therefore, decision made. I wasn't gay. I'm *not* gay. I can get whatever I need from a woman and that has served me okay this far.

"You were happy then, Saw."

"I'm happy now," I countered.

"Bullshit. You're afraid."

"DAMMIT, ELLE!" I yelled, jumping from the couch and stomping over to the minibar. Plucking out a full-sized bottle of whiskey, I took an eager glug straight from the bottle. "People need to quit making out like they fucking know me!"

"You're saying I don't know you? You're my best friend, Sawyer. I *do* know you."

After another swig of my medicine of choice, I twisted the cap back on sighed heavily.

"I'm going to have to see him every damn day and I don't know how to deal with it. If he keeps it up, I'm going to have to get him fired."

"You won't do that."

"Stop it, Elle! I mean it. You don't know how far I'd go and neither does *he*."

"Have you told him where to go? That you're not interested?"

"Of course I have."

"Then he'll get the message and back off. Don't worry about this, Saw. If you're not interested then it's really no different to the hundreds of groupies who lust after you every day. Just ignore him, and he'll give up."

"I don't have to see the same groupies every day. I don't have to talk to them. They don't get to come into my personal space. This is different."

"Only if you let it be. If he keeps harassing you when you've told him he's out of line, that's just creepy. Thinking about it, he always was a weirdo in school. No one ever hung around with him. I always thought he would turn out to be a murderer or a paedo or something."

"Don't say shit like that," I snapped. "He's nothing like…" I trailed off when I saw her plump red lips turn up into a smirk. She only said those things to get a reaction out of me and I stupidly fell for it. "You barely knew him at school. I don't think you guys ever even spoke to one another."

"Busted," she said, winking at me. "But it hurt you didn't it? To hear bad things being said about him?"

"I'd feel uncomfortable hearing bad shit about *anyone,* Elle."

"Bollocks. One thing you don't do, Sawyer Knight, is empathy."

"Are you saying I'm heartless?" I shot back, jerking my neck to the side in surprise.

"No. I'm saying you don't let yourself feel."

"Ah, come on now. This is all getting a bit too philosophical for my taste. What's next? You want me to fall to my knees and start thanking God for his guidance?"

"Fine. You don't want my advice? Deal with this shit on your own." Fuck. She was pouting. Elle is the only woman in the world who can pout like that and make me feel like the biggest jerk on the planet.

"Sorry," I muttered genuinely, settling back onto the couch beside her and putting my hand on her knee. "Today's been intense. It went to shit the minute I turned up at that fucking interview."

Welcoming the subject change, I told Elle all about the interview which Claire, the PR manager from hell, had arranged for me to do solo. Except I don't *really* feel that way about Claire, she's like a mother to me. To all of us. The conversation involved lots of swearing, huffs and eye rolls, but by the end of I felt a lot less agitated and ready to face tomorrow.

"You staying here tonight?" I asked Elle when I heard my bed calling my name.

"Can't. I've got to pack my things for the shoot tomorrow."

"Oh fuck. I forgot about that."

I hate photo shoots almost as much as I hate interviews. They involve people, and as a general rule, people piss me off.

"You're getting so bloody miserable in your old age," she chided with a playful nudge to the shoulder. "Go and sleep off this foul mood. Then rehearse your arse off in the morning and I'll see you at the studio in the afternoon."

"Sure. I'll call Pete to come take you home."

"Thanks," she said as I reached for the phone. I told Pete what I wanted him for and he said he'd be straight round. "Call me in the morning," Elle said before kissing my cheek, hovering in the doorway as she waited for Pete. "And fucking smile! It doesn't hurt I promise."

"Love ya, gorgeous girl."

"Love ya back, muscle man."

Pete was at my door within one minute. We were taking up the entire top floor of the hotel and security staff were positioned in rooms in between each band member.

Jake's room was next to my suite – literally touching it. We probably shared the same walls. Fuck.

I felt the stirrings of an erection before I'd even loosened my robe to look down at myself. Yep, there it was. My rigid cock stared up at me, mocking me, enticing me. "Damn him!" I cussed out loud. This is the response my traitorous body has at the simple knowledge Jake is in the next room.

No.

This had nothing to do with Jake. This was a normal bodily reaction to the fact I hadn't had any pussy action in several days. As soon as I'd relieved the pressure, any thoughts of Jake would disappear and I could go to sleep.

That's what I told myself as I flopped back onto the bed, letting my robe fall to the side as I gripped my throbbing cock in my hand. I started with gentle strokes, forcing myself to remember the girl I fucked three nights ago in New York. I didn't pay much attention to her face, but she had golden hair that spilled over her shoulders, tits so huge Matt said he would be wanking to the memory of them for years to come (he had her the next night), and a pussy so tight I wondered if she'd ever let anyone fuck her before.

Remembering the sight of me entering her from behind had me stroking myself harder. I had my fingers wrapped so tightly around myself it almost hurt, then I yanked them away when the memory of Jake's hand pressed against my jeans-clad cock, over ten years ago, infiltrated my thoughts. I was too frustrated to stop. I needed this release. I needed to get rid of the sexual tension so I could look at Jake as just my friend.

So, with that in mind, I allowed myself to think of him. Just this once I would let my mind wander to the place I always stopped it from going. I would think of him only until I'd come, and then I would put this inexplicable draw to him away for good.

I ran my thumb over my tip, circling the tender head before smoothing a drop of pre-cum down my shaft, making it glisten beneath the light shining down on me. I let myself remember his kiss as I locked my fingers around my length and started moving them up and down. It was ten years ago, but if I closed my eyes I could still taste him. I could still *feel* him. I could still *smell* him.

I imagined him as the man he is now, not as the boy he was then. I pretended he was right here with me, kissing me with the same tender lips I'd experienced just once before. I cupped my balls with my free hand, slowly rolling them between my fingers and imagining it was Jake who was doing it. I groaned at the thought, biting my lip as I imagined him replacing his wandering hands with his tongue.

Strokes turned to rough tugs and my back instinctively arched into the mattress, forcing myself further into my hand. I pumped at the same speed Jake's mouth was going in my imagination and when tingling heat started building in the base of my spine, I tore my hand from my balls and gripped the sheets, squeezing them as pure pleasure started attacking my body.

My hips bucked, thrusting me faster and harder into the image of Jake's mouth etched on the back of my eyelids. I saw his blue eyes looking up at me, twinkling with pride and satisfaction. It spurred me on and I tugged harder, moaning into the empty air. I looked past his dark cropped hair and imagined what the muscles on his back would look like as they flexed with the movement of his head bobbing up and down.

The heat soared through my hips, surging straight to my balls and drawing them up inside me. I was almost there. My cock was twitching in my hand begging for more friction. The red tip glistened, encouraging me… and in one last moment of defiance, I allowed myself to breath his name.

"Jake," I whispered into my shoulder, before gently biting the firm muscle to mask my moans. The feel of his name on my lips, the sound of it in my ears… it undid me completely and I came hard, a powerful jet of warmth shooting across my stomach.

I lay there for a moment, building up the energy I needed to clean myself up, and then it hit me. That was supposed to fix things. So why was I now imagining what Jake would look like if he released himself all over my stomach?

Shit.

Chapter Four

~Jake~

Straightening my tie, I sat back in my chair and addressed the rest of the team sitting around the solid walnut conference table.

"Have there been any more threats since we last spoke about them?" I was told about the death threats after I'd accepted my position and signed the various paperwork and non-disclosure agreements. Since then, I was left to tie up my loose ends in Sydney and we hadn't had much contact again until my arrival yesterday.

"Just one. Hand delivered to the hotel the guys were staying at in New York."

"I need to see that."

"Of course," Claire agreed. "We'll meet back here after the shoot this afternoon and I'll give it to you. Seems amateur to me – letters cut out of newspaper clippings. The only thing that's concerning us is the fact they seem to have knowledge of our itinerary."

"I'm not sure I feel comfortable lying to Sawyer about this," a woman, sitting opposite me with her arms folded across chest said. She was younger than me, mid-twenties at the oldest. She wore her thick black hair loose down her back and she scowled at me when I questioned her response with a raise of my eyebrow.

"And you are?" I asked curtly. Out of everyone in the room, hers was the only unfamiliar face.

"Laurelin Beckett. Sawyer's PA."

PA – a fancy word for dogsbody.

"Well, *Laurelin,* you're not lying to him. You are simply not alerting him to the problem. There's no need to panic any of the guys until we know if this is a serious threat." She shrugged at me and averted her gaze. That one move told me everything I needed to know about her. Immature. Naïve. Incapable and untrustworthy.

"Okay, I want to be first point of call if we receive any more. I also want the original copies of those previously sent, and a full list of anyone who has official knowledge of the band's schedule."

""Don't you think we've already looked into that?" Laurelin piped up. This chick was going to be a pain in my arse.

"But it hasn't got us anywhere, has it?" Claire interrupted. "Jake is head of security now. He calls the shots regarding the boys' safety."

"Thank you, Claire. I'd briefly like to announce the changes I'm implementing now, and then we'll go over them thoroughly when the guys arrive." After removing the printouts from my briefcase, I passed them around the table. "These are just for reference. Claire is having new contracts drawn up as we speak," I told my team while they looked down at the paper in their hands.

"I think it's best to assign a guard to each member of the band, rather than whoever's available. To be honest, considering Souls of the Knight are one of the biggest bands of this decade, I can't actually believe this shit hasn't been taken care of before. A good security team needs structure, consistency. There can't ever be a moment where one of us doesn't know what he's supposed to be doing. This team has been running like a fucking playground and it ends, now."

"Totally with you, boss," Jim interjected. The other guys nodded their heads. "I lost count of the amount of times I said this shit to Billy. If it weren't for the guys themselves, I would've jacked in this shit a long time ago."

"Jim, I want you with Darren. Pete, you're with Matt."

"Lucky me," Pete muttered under his breath. Part of me was looking forward to getting to know Matt for myself. He definitely had the worst reputation of all the guys. They can't call him Matt the Twat for nothing.

"Dave, I've paired you with Isaac, and Sayid you're with Gavin. Sawyer seems to be the target of these threats so for now, Neil, you shadow him along with me until I find a replacement for myself. I'd like two guys on him permanently and obviously one of those can't be me. I'll have other stuff to tend to as well. So I'd also like to arrange interviews for another seven men. It literally baffles me how a band of this stature hasn't got enough men to offer complete twenty-four hour watch."

"Someone *is* with them *all* the time," Claire said, shrinking back in her chair a little. I scanned the rest of the eyes at the table and every set had grown slightly wider, like I'd offended them.

"But someone is not *awake* with them *all* the time. Sleeping on the same floor, on the same bus, on the same street, just isn't good enough. Someone needs to be alert at *all* times, and not just because of these threats, because in all honesty they're probably meaningless pieces of paper from a fan with an overactive imagination. I have never seen such a shoddily put together team. I'm not questioning your abilities here, I *know* you guys are good at your job otherwise you wouldn't still be here. You've been poorly managed, so poorly in fact that if the press got wind of this, they would be all over it like flies on shit. I've been brought in here, no expense spared, to protect this band, so I hope you'll all join me in this and respect that I know what I'm doing."

"I'm in," Jim was first to say. Sayid followed, then Dave, Neil and then Pete. Claire nodded encouragingly and unsurprisingly Laurelin remained silent with a juvenile look of annoyance on her face.

"Great. Time to get the guys down here and go through it with them. Sayid, Pete, go and fetch them."

"I'm guessing we'll need reinforcement, especially with Matt and Kip. It's a four man job getting either one of those assholes out of bed before noon."

"Fine. I'll come too," I said, rolling my eyes. If you want something doing right, do it your goddamn self. "Oh, Claire?" I called back, holding the conference room door open with one hand. "Can you call the arena and let them know we'll be an hour early for rehearsals?"

"They won't like that," she replied.

"I don't give a fuck whether they like it. *That* is what's happening. Until we know for sure if an outsider has access to the schedule, we need to keep things fresh. Add some spontaneity."

"Things don't work like that…" she tried to argue.

"Things work however we *say* they work. Call them."

"Okay," she said, raising her palms in the air.

Now, time to go and drag the guys' arses out of bed.

Being Sawyer Knight

As expected, staff at the O2 Arena weren't happy with the change in schedule, but also as expected, they couldn't afford to fuck with a band who were bringing them so much damn money, so of course, they backed down. I hadn't been able to take my eyes off Sawyer since the second I met him in his suite this morning. Not *just* because I had to keep him in my line of vision to protect his safety, but because his jeans hugged his arse so tightly every time his back was towards me my dick twitched in my pants, because the white t-shirt he was wearing had deliberate rips slashed across the front, exposing the beautiful firm lines of his chest, because his dark fringe kept falling down across his forehead, revealing his soft caramel eyes every time he swept it back in place with his fingers...

I hadn't been able to take my eyes off him... because he mesmerized me.

Staff and technicians scurried around the stage, the tension dripping from their skin in the form of sweat, as they hurried to get everything ready for the live rehearsal. While the final sound check was being carried out I issued my team with positions, making sure each side of the stage was manned and then sending Pete and Dave to guard their dressing rooms. I situated myself on the arena floor, keeping centre to the stage with my body straight and alert and my arms folded firmly across my chest.

"Hey, boss," Sayid said, leaving his position to quickly run over to me.

"What is it, Sayid? You're supposed to be by the stage."

"Laurelin told me Sawyer is planning a night out with Elle. He always runs that kind of stuff past us, but not this time. Just thought you should know."

"Thank you, Sayid," I replied curtly, nodding once. "We'll discuss who'll escort him after the photo-shoot this afternoon."

"Sure," was all he said before hurrying back over to his position. What was he thinking? Sawyer knows he can't go out as and when he pleases without adequate protection. And don't even get me started on the fact Laurelin went to Sayid and not me. I'm in charge here and I made that perfectly clear at the conference table this morning.

I rolled my shoulders, trying to dispel some of the tension that had suddenly crept up on me. When I saw Claire give me the signal from where she was standing by the emergency exit, I scanned the area one last time and asked the guys to do the same over my radio. When the all-clear was announced by all, the band slowly filtered onto the stage, and when Sawyer hopped onto his waiting stool in front of me, hitching one leg up onto the bar as he slid the strap of his guitar around his strong neck, my breath faltered.

I wonder if he knows how beautiful he is with all those lights shining on him? He will later, I decided... because I was going to tell him.

Being Sawyer Knight

After a silent cue from one of the sound guys, Bez I think he's called, the intro started playing, bellowing through the speakers. They were starting with their biggest hit of 2013 - Twisted. Each band member joined in at their designated spot in the song, playing their instruments and humming. Then Sawyer rested his strategically positioned fingers against the strings of his guitar, and the song *really* began.

Sawyer's voice came first. The lyrics dripped from his lips in the deliciously deep, gravelly voice that could only belong to Sawyer Knight. His eyes were closed, enabling me to ogle him. Not once did I take my eyes off his face. I stared at the soft lines framing his eyes when he squeezed them closed a little tighter, at the two day old stubble coating his strong jaw, at the way his plump lips curled around every word he sang.

So beautiful...

I didn't realise how firmly I was biting my lip as I watched him until his eyes opened, immediately locking onto me. His gaze made my jaw drop slightly, hopefully so slight it was unnoticeable, and it felt like my dick was trying to lurch towards him. A sharp intake of breath resounded through the speakers, and although it occurred at a pause in the song where he needed to draw air for the next line, I knew it was more than that. I knew it was *me*.

"Jake?" Claire's voice snapped me back into the arena and my head jerked around to face her. "Everything okay?" she asked quizzically, wrinkling her eyebrows. Shit. Had my gawping been that fucking obvious?

"Sure," I answered confidently. "I was just deciding how to deal with the crowd I saw gathering outside earlier."

"We'd usually ask the guys. Most of the time they're willing to stop for a few photos and autographs, although Sawyer's been in a stinking mood since yesterday so I don't know if he'll be up for it."

"Leave Sawyer to me." Claire looked at me curiously, obviously wondering how in hell I thought I had a chance getting through to him when he was famous for not listening to anyone except Elle. "We go back a long way, remember? I know how to break the stubborn shit down into a human being capable of reason and rational thought." At least, I hoped I did.

"Good luck with that," she teased, clearly believing I was taking on the impossible. Good job I like a challenge… otherwise I wouldn't even be here right now. "Anyway, I've just been talking to the studio and they can't accommodate us any earlier for the shoot."

"No problem. It will give the guys time to hang out with the fans outside before we go."

Appeased, Claire sauntered off to wherever she came from, giving my eyes permission to hone in on the man I have adored since I was fourteen years old. When Sawyer caught my gaze again I expected him to look away, or maybe close his eyes like he did when he began his first song. But instead, his eyes bored into mine and he stared straight back. He watched me so intently, so penetratingly, that it felt like we were completely alone in this gigantic building… like he was singing just for me, singing *to* me.

I needed to get out of here. For the first time in my life I had been rendered incapable of doing my job effectively and I needed out so I could think of a way to make damn sure it doesn't happen again. Anyone could have walked right past me in that moment and beelined straight for the guys and I wouldn't have noticed a thing because I couldn't look anywhere else but at Sawyer.

"Pete, I need you to switch positions with me," I spoke firmly into my radio as I gave the order.

"Ten-four, boss. On my way."

I forced my gaze away from the stage while I waited for Pete, all the while silently begging my dick to calm the hell down. This man, Sawyer Antony Knight, has the power to either complete me, or destroy me.

"I need to talk to you," was how I greeted Sawyer when he opened the door to his dressing room. We had an hour to wait before the stylists and makeup artists were available to prepare the guys for the shoot, so they were all chilling back in their respective dressing suites.

"Um,'kay," he said nervously, backing into the room. I followed him inside and then turned back to the door, locking it behind me. That move caused his Adam's apple to bulge as he swallowed nervously. "W-what's up?"

"You looked beautiful on that stage," I said, advancing towards him. Instinctively he backed away, but I kept moving forward until he was pressed against the wall. "My dick was so hard for you, Sawyer. It's been hard for you since I got here."

I flattened my palm against his heaving chest and his own hand quickly reached up to move it away, but instead it lingered, his fingers curling around my own.

"Please, Jake. You're messing with my head. I can't take it much longer. You were my best friend and I've missed that. Please don't fuck that up."

"But I don't want to be your friend, Sawyer. I want to be your everything."

"You can't be serious. You don't even know me anymore." His voice was faltering. I was winning.

"I *do* know you. I know you better than anyone. I know you better than you know yourself. If I didn't, how would I know that you want me to do this?" I breathed, sliding my hand down his chest until it reached the waistband of his jeans. He swallowed forcefully and then opened his mouth, to protest I assumed, but when my hand dipped inside and took hold of his cock, all that came out was a moan.

The risk I was taking was either going to be a monumental breakthrough, or the biggest mistake of my life.

"Jake… please… I don't…"

"Shh," I whispered into his ear as I fumbled with the button on his jeans, allowing his stunning fucking erection to spring free. I almost came in my pants just from the feel of him against my fingers. "Don't overthink this. Close your eyes if it helps."

"Jake…" Ignoring him and his weak attempt at protesting, I dropped down to my knees. My mouth watered at the sight of his rock hard cock and when a single bead of pre-cum oozed from the tip, begging me to lick it off, I ran my tongue across my lips. "What are you doing?"

"I'm taking what I want, and giving *you* what you need," I answered, never looking up at him in case eye-contact frightened him away.

"Someone might come in."

"I locked the door."

"They might hear."

"You'd better be quiet then."

I paused for just a second while I waited for his next concern. When it didn't come, I wasted no time in tasting him. After licking that glistening drop of pre-cum from the end of his beautiful cock, I swirled my tongue around the head until he started nudging at my mouth, desperate for me to take him deeper.

"Easy, boy," I groaned against the hard flesh. Then I tormented him further by running my tongue slowly upwards from base to tip while cupping his sac with my hand. His hips squirmed impatiently and although I wanted to drag this out, savour him, show him how good it could be… I was too desperate. I'd been imagining the feel of this man in my mouth, and other places, for so many years, and my own dick was on the verge of coming from the mere thought of tasting him as he exploded down my throat.

Unable to wait any longer I wrapped my wet lips around his thick length and took him all the way to the back of my throat. He gasped in what seemed like a mixture of surprise and pleasure, and then I heard a gentle thud as he threw his head back against the wall. One of my hands rolled his already tightening balls between my fingers, while I gripped the base of his cock with my other, sliding it up and down in my mouth's trail.

God he felt so good – even better than I'd imagined. I'd dreamt of this moment so many times, too many to count, and when I felt him push deeper into my mouth, my knees almost gave way.

"Fuck…Jake…" If I didn't have my lips curled so tightly against his rigid dick I would've smiled knowing I was pleasing him so much. Taking it a step further, I removed my hand from his balls and slid one of my fingers inside my mouth along with his throbbing erection.

After gathering some moisture I trailed my finger lower, below his balls, and massaged my way across the smooth and sensitive flesh of his perineum. When my finger stopped against his rim, Sawyer tensed, his back stiffening.

"Jake, I-I…" Ignoring his doubts once again, I slowly pushed my finger inside his puckered hole, causing his cock to start pulsating against the back of my throat. "Ah, *fuck*," he groaned. He was close, and it made me feel like a fucking king. After letting his arse adjust to the intrusion, I slowly worked my finger in and out while continuing to suck him harder and faster. When I entered a second finger, he started falling apart. "Jake stop. Stop, I'm gonna, I'm gonna come…"

Being Sawyer Knight

Of course I ignored him. I had fantasised about tasting every last drop of him too many times to give up now. So, pumping my two fingers in and out of his tight hole in line with the same fast rhythm of my mouth on his cock, I worked him until the end.

"Jesus, *fuck!*" he growled through clenched teeth, as hot spurts of the most delicious fucking nectar I'd ever tasted shot towards the back of my throat. Easing my fingers out of him, I stroked his balls one last time while I licked his cock completely clean. Climbing to my feet, I stared at Sawyer, watching as he panted with his eyes closed.

"You taste so fucking good," I whispered against the throbbing vein in his neck, before kissing my way up to his ear.

Then it came…

The regret.

The doubt.

The fucking denial.

He pushed me off him with two hands pressed against my chest and when I looked into his eyes, bursting with what looked like shame, I knew I'd lost him. Again.

"You need to leave," he said, his words swamped with guilt.

"Don't do this Sawyer. You can't tell me you didn't want that. That you didn't *enjoy* it? The taste in my mouth is proof that you fucking *loved* every damn second of what I just did to you."

"Please," he practically begged, shoving his semi-erect cock back into his pants. "Leave. Now."

"I'll leave," I surrendered. "But I'm not *leaving*. I won't give up on you, Sawyer. You mean too damn much to me and I *know* you feel the same. You're just scared."

"Fuck you!" he spat, anger making the vein in the centre of his forehead pop out. That vein has reared its ugly head for as long as I can remember. If he got into a fight back in high school, it would protrude so much I used to worry it might explode. "You've not seen me in fucking years, Jake. So whatever you *think*, you don't know me at all! Now get the fuck out of here before I do something I regret."

"Funny, I thought you just did that," were the last words I said before straightening my tie and turning my back on him.

This is going to be harder than I thought. But *not* impossible. He was right about one thing. We *have* changed - we've grown up. Back then I was his follower, I'd have done anything he'd asked because I was so fucking in love with him. But now, I'm in charge. He's still living so far back in the closet if he were to stumble he'd end up in fucking Narnia. He's still afraid, scared to go after what he wants.

Good job I'm not. I've grown into a determined man – a confident man. I get what I want, always. And I *will* be getting Sawyer Knight.

Chapter Five

~Sawyer~

Damn him! Why is he doing this to me *again?* I'm *not* gay. I can't be. I refuse to be! If what he's insinuating got out, it would ruin me. The backlash from the public would be unbelievable. My mother would disown me. The guys in the band would never forgive me. Our manager would probably find a way to sue me and make damn sure I never worked again.

"Fuck this!" I growled, ramming my fist into the wall. I knew as soon as I pulled my hand away and noticed bubbles of blood erupting on the surface of my knuckles I would be in the shit with our makeup artist. Camouflaging cuts is practically impossible when they're still bleeding.

"Sawyer?" I heard Laurelin calling through the door. I like my P.A. She's only been with me twelve months but we get along pretty great. She reminds me a lot of Elle – she's got that same sassiness to her, the same smart mouth. Of course, she doesn't, and never will, know me as well as Elle does, but she knows where to find the best bagels in town no matter which city we travel to so that makes her a pretty perfect assistant, to me.

"What's up, Lin?" I asked, opening the door to her.

"Wardrobe are ready to go through some outfits for you."

"Well wardrobe will just have to fucking wait," I snapped. "Sorry," I immediately tacked on.

"Everything okay?" she asked, brushing her fingers along my forearm. In all honesty I'm not too comfortable with how touchy feely Laurelin is, but she's the same with everyone so I just tend suck it up.

"Sure," I lied. I'd never been more *not* okay. "I think I just need a decent coffee. Could you head out and get me one? The stuff in the machines here tastes like piss."

"Of course," she agreed. "I might even pick you up a Danish pastry if you're lucky."

"Ooo, you're spoiling me," I said, forcing a smile. "Have you seen Elle?"

"Yeah, she's outside talking to Jake." She said his name with such distaste, as if she were afraid it would coat her tongue with a deadly disease. "Do you want her?" Her question snapped me back into the room. For a second I'd forgotten she was still here, too busy worrying about what Jake was saying to Elle.

"Nah, doesn't matter. Now run along, Lin," I teased. "That coffee isn't going to magically appear."

Not seconds later, Kip appeared at my door.

"Mate, wardrobe want us."

Nodding my head, I replied, "Sure. Be out in two secs."

After stretching my neck and trying to erase the last hour from my mind, I nipped into the bathroom to rinse the blood from my knuckles. Luckily Laurelin didn't notice, but I knew Elle would. I huffed to myself, knowing I would be under her interrogation soon.

When I walked out of my dressing suite I smacked straight into Jake, whose eyes zeroed straight in on my grazed hand.

"What happened?" he asked, genuine concern saturating his voice.

"Leave me the fuck alone, Jake," I barked at him.

"You know I can't do that. I'm your bodyguard."

"Yeah? Well maybe we'll just have to rectify that situation." Just the thought of replacing him made my chest ache, and that right there was what I needed to rectify. The confident expression Jake's face always seemed to hold these days didn't falter for even a second. It was like the smug bastard *knew* I wouldn't get rid of him, and I genuinely didn't know if that comforted me or pissed me the hell off.

I walked quickly to the wardrobe department, ignoring any kind of eye or vocal contact with Jake the whole way. When I got there, the rest of the guys were already dressed in their first outfits for the shoot.

"About time," Elle grumbled. The simple knowledge she was here instantly made me feel at ease. "I've still got to style yours *and* Kip's hair."

"Sorry, gorgeous girl," I said smiling as I picked her up and twirled her around. I mainly did that to annoy her, because I'm an ass like that.

"Put me down, Saw," she scolded, twatting my shoulder. "Now hurry up in here so I can get started on your hair," she added when I lowered her down. Then she leaned in so only I could hear and whispered, "We *will* be talking about what the hell is wrong with you later."

Anger caused my fists to clench by my sides.

"What the fuck has he been saying to you?" I hissed back.

"*Who?*"

I straightened my back, eyeing her up suspiciously. I didn't know if she genuinely had no clue what I was talking about, or if she was trying to trip me up so I would unwittingly admit what happened with Jake earlier.

"Never mind. I won't be long here. I'll meet you back in my dressing room."

"Hmm. You're hiding something from me and you're going to tell me what it is."

"Love ya, gorgeous girl," I said, before bending down to kiss the top of her head.

"Whatever," she argued. "Your charm doesn't work on me."

Ain't that the damn truth?

I'm pretty much a creature of habit when it comes to clothes – t-shirt, designer jeans, studded belt. So, as expected, it didn't take long for me settle on three different outfits for the shoot. I was back in my dressing room with Kip and Matt trailing behind me (and Jake of course, but I was trying to forget he existed), in under thirty minutes. Elle was already waiting for me with what looked like a whole suitcase full of styling products scattered across the place.

"Hey, Saw," Matt muttered, bumping my shoulder with his and nodding towards the lobby outside my room. "See that chick? Big tits, firm ass, red bikini?"

"Um, yeah."

"She's got the tightest fuckin' pussy, man. Had her bent over the couch in my room less than an hour ago, and she said she'd be happy to go for round two with you when we're done here."

"Jesus, Matt," Elle said, rolling her eyes.

"What's her name?"

"There's my boy!" Matt said, practically congratulating me as he clapped my shoulder. "Her name's Candi, and I'm telling you, man, that chick is up for *anything*."

"Okay, guys. Out. All of you," Elle ordered. "I've got work to do here and you're distracting me." Saluting her, Matt and Kip left, but Jake lingered a second longer.

"I'll be right outside," he told us. *Of course you fucking will.*

"Sawyer, what the hell are you playing at?" Elle blasted the second we were alone. "That skank is probably riddled. You're not seriously considering it?"

"My sex life is none of your goddamn business, Elle."

"Hey, you might get away with speaking to other people like shit but you can't with me. What the fuck is wrong with you? It's *him* isn't it? Jake?" She hushed the last part, probably in case he could hear on the other side of the door.

"What's he said to you, huh?"

"Nothing! He's never even mentioned you to me! Just tell me what's going on with you guys, Saw? Because I know something is."

"Nothing's going on."

"Bullshit."

"I swear it, Elle. We're not *together* if that's what you're thinking."

"That's not what I asked. Something is happening, and it's more than him just coming on to you. If that was it, and you weren't interested, you'd just laugh him off. So, do you *want* something to happen between you?"

"Fuck, Elle," I sighed, flopping down into the leather chair in front of me. "He sucked me off in here earlier."

"What the…" Her jaw literally fell wide open. "And… you didn't want him to? I'm confused."

"That makes two of us. It was fucking amazing, Elle. Everything about it. The way he smelt, the way he spoke to me, the feel of him wrapped around my cock…"

"Yeah, you can spare me the specifics, hun. You're practically my brother."

"Sorry," I muttered, exhaling a soft laugh. "But I swear, the second he'd finished… I *loathed* myself for giving in to him."

"That's absurd, Sawyer. Why the hell would you hate yourself for wanting sex with someone?"

"Because… I'm not gay, Elle! How many times do I have to tell you that?"

"You let another man suck your dick, and not for the first time I might add. Sounds pretty gay to me."

"Don't, Elle," I warned.

"I was just teasing. But you know how I feel about it all, Saw. This isn't the first time we've had this conversation. Why won't you let yourself be happy?"

"Happy? You think coming out would make me *happy*? Elle, I would lose all my fans, therefore my career. The guys would never speak to me again. My mother would condemn me to the pits of hell. That wouldn't make me happy, it would destroy me."

"This isn't the 1950's anymore for Christ's sake. There are tons of gay singers out there!"

"Oh please. Maybe in the prissy boy bands, but not in our world. Besides, when Jake went down on me, I closed my eyes. I didn't touch him *once*. It could've been anyone giving me that blowjob – any *woman*. I know what's going on; I've thought about nothing else since he got here. Fucking men is a fantasy, that's all. People have all kind of fantasies but that doesn't mean they act on them."

"Who are you trying to convince? Me or *yourself*?"

"Shooting in ten!" Gavin called through the door. I'd never been more thankful for an interruption.

"Shit!" Elle hissed. "Come on, I've got ten minutes to turn you into the knicker-soaking rock star the world wants to see in this magazine."

"Gorgeous girl, I can make women drip for me with just a wink. My hair doesn't matter."

"That's quite an ego you have there," she joked, whipping out the little pink pouch that contained her comb and scissors from her pocket. "This conversation isn't over, Sawyer. Just on hold."

"Hmm, I thought as much."

The photo shoot was long and monotonous, just like they always are. The only good thing is, I didn't have to force a smile. People have come to know me as the brooding, mysterious member of the band, so for the most part I can just sit around looking miserable as shit, and people think I've done a great job.

Posing with my guitar for an individual shot, I decided Elle was right. I didn't need to fuck that Candi chick to prove a point. But then I caught Jake staring at me like he wanted to fucking devour me, and I knew I did in fact need to prove to both him *and* myself, that I wasn't who he thought I was.

So that's how I came to find myself in my hotel suite, lying on my back with my dick balls-deep in Candi's mouth after cancelling my night out with the guys, knowing Jake was standing right outside my door. I looked down at her, watching myself slide in and out of her mouth. I could *see* what she was doing to me, but I could barely *feel* it. It was then I realised I was talking shit to Elle before. It *couldn't* have been anyone else sucking me off before. Only Jake has ever made me come as hard as I did in my dressing room just hours ago.

And that pissed me off.

"On your knees," I ordered. Offering me a lopsided smile as she bit her lip, Candi scrambled to her knees on the bed, ass in the air, just how I wanted her. I crawled up behind her, and after rolling a condom down my waning erection, I wasted no time in nudging at the entrance to her pussy. I needed this. Being inside her would prove a woman could provide everything I need. "Now, Sawyer. I need you to fuck me."

"Put your head down on the pillows," I told her after catching her looking behind to study my face. From behind was always my position of choice. I don't like eye-contact during sex – it makes it too personal. I don't want or need any kind of mental connection. I eased in slowly, and then stilled while her body got used to me filling her.

"Please," she begged. "Fuck me, Sawyer. Fuck me real hard."

Slowly, I started moving. I rocked my hips, pushing myself deeper with each thrust. She wasn't as tight as I'd have liked. Unable to get the friction I needed, I stared down at my cock entering her body, hoping the visual would speed things up. When it didn't work, I closed my eyes.

And I imagined Jake.

Soon enough I was pounding her hard and fast. She was a screamer, but I tried to ignore the moans coming from her mouth as I pretended it was Jake's hips I was grabbing on to. Gritting my teeth, I fucked her like my life depended on it. Then, the second I allowed myself to think of Jake's mouth wrapped around me this afternoon, I exploded, my body shuddering as my orgasm ripped through my body.

"Fuck," I said, exhaling and immediately withdrawing so I could collapse onto the mattress.

"Mind if I take a shower before I leave?" Candi asked, thankfully understanding the fact she was only here for a quick fuck, nothing else.

"Sure," I said, draping my forearm over my eyes so I didn't have to look at her. I'd just used her completely. I fucked her for no other reason than to prove to myself I was straight.

I failed.

The only thing that got me off was the memory of Jake's mouth around my cock and the image of his naked body, a body that I had to imagine. I'd seen Jake naked before – back in our teens, but even through his clothes I could tell he doesn't have the same body I remember. His shirts didn't used to cling to his firm chest like they do now. If he wore a jacket, it wouldn't grip his broad shoulders causing the material to strain with every flex of his muscles.

Damn him for coming back here!

When Candi got out of the shower, I took one myself while she was fixing her clothes and hair and all that other shit women do. She was just about ready to leave when I'd finished, picking her bag and jacket from the floor as I made my way into the bedroom with just a towel wrapped around my waist.

Being Sawyer Knight

I walked her to the door, seemed like the least I could do, and of course Jake was standing right outside. He probably heard everything. Funny, because that was my intention, yet now, looking into his blue eyes that seemed to run deeper than the ocean, I just felt like a prick.

Candi waltzed off down the grand corridor without so much as a goodbye. Jakes eyes wandered after her for a short second before switching to me.

"Was she for my benefit or yours?"

"Don't start, Jake."

"Feel better?" he asked condescendingly as if he knew *exactly* why I brought her here. His confidence never faltered, and it intrigued me. He was never so sure of himself back in school. More often than not he was happy to just follow me around like a lost puppy. Was this an act? Or did I really just not know him anymore?

"Can you arrange for a driver to take me to see my mother tonight?" I asked, ignoring his question. If Candi didn't work, maybe some good old-fashioned preaching would.

"Shouldn't be a problem. Does she still live on the Mount Hill estate?"

"You remember?"

"Of course I remember. I haven't forgotten a single thing about you, Sawyer."

"Umm, well… yes she does," I choked out, feeling a little breathless all of a sudden. "I'd like to go around seven – it will be dark then."

Spring is almost over and as usual I will miss it. I like the dark nights; they make it a little easier to live unnoticed – to hide.

"Neil and I will take you."

"I'd rather you didn't," I said, and immediately felt like a jackass.

"As you wish." I was going to take back my ridiculous comment but he spoke before I could continue. "I'll send Jim for you instead."

"Uh, sure. Thanks. Um, that'll be all," I added, again feeling like an utter douchebag. 'That'll be all'… what the fuck was I saying?

"I'll just *run along* then shall I?" he teased with a wicked grin that dove straight to my cock.

"Sorry. Long day. Catch you later."

"Wait…" Jake grabbed my forearm, pulling me back as I tried to retreat into my room. "We should talk about what happened earlier."

"There's nothing to talk about. It shouldn't have happened."

"We both know that's not true," he countered, his voice deepening as his body started closing in on me.

"You need to stop this, Jake. It's not going to happen. I'm not... *like* you. I'm straight."

"So is spaghetti until it gets hot," he whispered against my neck. Then he nibbled gently along the tender flesh, his coarse stubble grating against my own, and everything I've ever forced myself to believe started disappearing against my will. His presence affected me more than I liked or wanted and I needed to get away from him before I became incapable of coherent thought.

"You need to forget this afternoon," I said, immediately wanting to punch myself in the balls for allowing my voice to crack. "It will *not* happen again."

Then, shoving him away, I stormed back into my room and slammed the door behind me.

Jim knocked on my suite door bang on time. Pulling on a shirt after finishing some push ups, I answered immediately, as usual feeling the need to hurry up and get my time with my mother over with.

"Neil's downstairs. We're taking Sayid too, there're crowds front and back of the building."

"Press or fans?"

"Both."

Nodding in understanding, I hooked my jacket onto my finger and threw it over my shoulder. We decided to go through the main hotel entrance seeing as there were crowds at both exits anyway. The sound of camera shutters flooded the air before I'd even fully stepped out of the revolving doors. I've learned to tune out the sound over the years, and I also learned quite early on that if you look towards the ground while surrounded by the press, you don't get blinded by the incessant flashes…but I don't think it would ever be possible to ignore the screams and chants of excited fans. Not that I'd want to – I wouldn't be where I am today without their passion and support.

"SAWYER! SAWYER!"

"SAWYER, OVER HERE!" Girls yelled and sang my name, bouncing up and down and trying to reach out to me. I stopped by a couple of them, draping my arms around them while their friends took pictures on their phones.

"OMG I love you! Thank you so much!"

"I love you, too! All of you!" The reaction to my voice never failed to overwhelm me – especially when some girls literally cried.

"Sawyer, is it true you're dating Elle Wilson?" The waiting journalists and photographers didn't waste any time calling my name either.

"Are you glad to be back in the UK?"

"Sawyer, do you want to address the rumours about your sexuality?"

"What rumours?" I snapped, going against everything I've been trained to do and immediately wanting to punch myself in the head for not ignoring them.

"That's enough for today, guys," Jim intercepted, putting one hand on the small of my back and slowly pushing us through the crowd towards the waiting car.

"SAWYER!" they continued to yell. "Have you seen today's article in The Sun? Want to respond?"

Being Sawyer Knight

Jim covered my body with his while I slid into the back seat of the car, and the second the door closed next to me, the most welcome silence descended.

"What article?" I barked when Jim climbed in the other side.

"We're heading round the back where it's gated off to switch cars. Should make sure we're not followed."

"Jim? What fucking article!"

"I dunno, mate," he said, sighing. "You need to ask Claire."

"I'm asking *you*."

"If Claire kicks my arse for telling you this I'm saying you forced me."

"Fine by me. Hell, tell her I had you by the throat if you want. She doesn't scare me, dude."

"Apparently some guy has sold a story saying you two had a... *thing*... going on between you in college."

"What the *fuck?*"

"Hey, come on, mate... you know the press is full of this shit. If you make a big deal out of it they'll just assume it's true. We all know it's not, so don't beat yourself up about it."

"I want to see that paper."

"Claire, and I think Jake too, have copies. But honestly, it's not worth it. Those damn papers are filled with all kinds of shit and lies every bloody day. Just shrug it off. It'll all die down soon enough."

"You're right," I agreed, forcing a look of indifference onto my face. He *was* right about one thing – I couldn't afford to get worked up about it. If it'd been a woman I wouldn't have given a damn, so I needed to act the same right now – especially in front of the guys.

As planned, we quickly swapped cars and waited back for a few minutes until the original car had passed the photographers. As expected, some of them quickly jumped in their own cars to follow, then Jim radioed Pete to come and distract the others by asking them to leave. We knew they wouldn't of course, but while they were listening to him we had our opportunity to leave unseen.

The familiar balloon of dread inflated in the pit of my stomach when we pulled up onto my mother's estate. I *detest* the place. Everything about it reminds me of a time I wish I could forget – the mass of flats all cramped together in tall blocks, the metal railings surrounding the brick walls that are filled with graffiti (and not the artistic kind, more like 'Kev fucked Kerry 2012'). Not to mention the fact you can smell the stench of stagnant piss coming from the stairwells before you even get out of the car.

The place is a dump – always has been, always will be. I've tried to talk my mother into letting me buy her a nice detached house, wherever she wants in the world, over the years, but she refuses to have anything to do with money earned from my 'sinful' career filled with vile music and starstruck whores.

Jim and Neil accompanied me to my mother's door while Sayid waited in the car with the driver, whose name I still hadn't leaned. Opening the door, she greeted me with the same surprised gasp followed by a look of disappointment as she always does when she sees me.

"What are you doing here?" she asked, ushering me inside before anyone saw me. "Can't they go somewhere else?" she whispered, referring to my security team.

"No, Mum. They can't."

"So why are you here? You *never* come home. Is everything alright?"

She was right. I never come home because I hate the damn place. Usually, I arrange for her to be picked up and brought to wherever I'm staying.

"It's been, what… ten, eleven months since we saw each other? I just wanted to see you."

After an awkward, one-armed hug, I headed into the tiny living room while my mum made up a pot of tea in the kitchen. The flat hadn't changed at all since I was a little boy. An involuntarily look of disgust crept across my face as I weighed up the peeling floral wallpaper, the stained brown carpet and the electric fire with metal bars across the front.

"So," Mum began, joining me in the living room with a tray holding a pot of tea and two cups and saucers. "What do I owe the pleasure?"

"We'll be heading to Manchester after tomorrow's show. Just wanted to check in before I left."

"Well it's always good to see you, darling." She said it with such disinterest I knew it was a lie. "How have you been?"

"Busy," I replied robotically. Conversation between my mum and I has always been a little formal.

"I don't suppose you've thought about finding a nice young woman and settling down yet have you? I see Elle around here quite often," she said with a raised eyebrow. Mum was elated when I started hanging around with Elle. I think in her head she had me calmed down and married off to her within a few months of us becoming friends.

"Elle is my *friend*, Mum. You know that."

"A mother can still hope," she said, sounding a little dejected. "She's a lovely girl. The things she has to put up with from that mother of hers are despicable."

Yeah, Elle's mum is a bitch of the highest order – you won't find me disagreeing with that one. She spent Elle's childhood drunk most of the time, offering them a new stepdad every two weeks and leaving Elle to practically raise her much younger sister, Kylie, by herself. She's sponged money off Elle ever since she got her first job as a Saturday girl in a salon. Now, the more money she earns, the more her mother takes. She won't refuse her because Kylie is only fifteen and still living at home. That's the excuse she uses anyway – I still think she'd keep bailing her out even if Kylie were out of the equation. She's her mother, and Elle feels some bizarre sense of loyalty towards her based purely on the fact she gave birth to her.

Then again, who I am to talk? I never leave my mother without passing her quite a hefty cheque.

"You look different," my mum continued, eyeing me up curiously.

Being Sawyer Knight

"I have a few new tattoos since you last saw me," I said, shrugging. Possibly the skulls and roses added to my left arm a few months ago.

"It's not that," she dismissed, shaking her head. "You've met someone haven't you? A mother can tell these things."

I hesitated for a moment before deciding to be honest. Hell knew I needed advice from somewhere because all I was succeeding in doing was driving myself fucking insane.

"Yeah. Yeah I have."

"And what's she like?"

"I can't stop thinking about her." Okay, so when I said I was going to be honest, that wasn't *entirely* true. "I mean, *all* the time. She never leaves my head, and everywhere I go she seems to be there."

"That's great!" she beamed, her eyes full of hope. "So why are you unsure? Does she not feel the same?"

"Yes. At least she *says* she does. I'm just worried about people's reaction I guess."

"Oh my… What's wrong with her? Does she have tattoos?" She said the word tattoos like it was a terminal illness.

Judgemental as ever I see, Mother.

"No, Mum, she doesn't have tattoos." I sighed, exasperated. But wait, *does* Jake have tattoos? I haven't seen him naked in over ten years, Hell, I haven't even seen the flesh of his forearms since he's been back in my life. "It's complicated. She works with us. She's part of our team. I don't think it would go down very well."

71

"Hmm." Her face wrinkled a little like she was slightly repulsed – no doubt about the fact I'd fallen for someone in the industry. She wants me to settle down with a nice girl from the countryside who never fails to attend Sunday mass at the local church. "You can't live your life by what others might think, darling. You're the only one who has to walk in your shoes, no one else." Whoa… was that my mum being… *human?* I almost choked on my tea. "Besides, you haven't put others thoughts first in the past now, have you?" Ah, there we go – a dig at how I ignored her pleas for me not to live this life full of sin. Everything was right with the world after all.

"Maybe you're right." Turned out, being 'honest' was pointless, seeing as I was *actually* spinning her a web of bullshit. Truth be told, this wouldn't be an issue if Jake were a woman. My mum was right… I've never put anyone's thoughts before my own, and if the only issue were that Jake worked for me, I wouldn't even have to think about it. "So how are you? I'm sorry I haven't been in touch much lately."

My mum and I exchanged formal and polite chitchat for twenty minutes or so. As usual, she told me about the latest church gossip and I told her jack shit. She said she had no idea I was even back in the country at one point, but I knew she was talking crap. My face has been plastered over every magazine over here for weeks now, talking about the upcoming tour. Fair enough, she wouldn't read any of those 'trashy' magazines, but you can't walk through a damn supermarket without seeing it on the shelf.

"So Marjory is taking over the organ until we find Helen's replacement," my mum continued. I switched off for a little while, but thought I'd better make the effort for the last few minutes before I left.

"Helen Davison?" I asked, feigning interest. If it was the Helen I remembered from being a kid, she's a toffee-nosed bigot with an ass the size of London.

"Yes. Did you know her son decided to become a *homosexual?*" I swear, she actually shuddered at the word. "And then she seriously thought she could keep her hand in at the church after that? She thinks she can mock God by strolling into his house as if nothing was wrong!"

"Well… it's hardly Helen's fault," I tried to reason, but really I just wanted to get the fuck out of there.

"But she is standing by him! She is supporting him even though she knows he's going against God's will – against our faith, against everything we believe in. It's unnatural and the whole situation disgusts me. She won't be welcome at my door again, that's one thing I'm certain of."

I'd been brought up hearing things like that throughout my childhood. It used to affect me, because I used to believe in God and I would've been too scared to go against him. Then I grew up and realised religion is all political bullshit. But that doesn't stop me fearing *people*. Rightly or wrongly, being judged *does* bother me. I don't want people to be disgusted by me, and they would. My mother is not the only person who thinks that way.

"I have to go, Mum. We've got sound checks to get through ready for tomorrow." I was lying of course. Final sound checks go ahead on the day of the show, not before.

We said our goodbyes as formally as we said our hellos. Suddenly feeling a little sick to my stomach, I hesitantly wrapped one arm around her and gave her a peck on the cheek before giving her a cheque, which she took without hesitation, and heading outside. Jim and Neil were waiting outside for me, each guarding one side of the door. With a simple nod as my only form of communication, I walked briskly down the concrete steps, flooded with piss and grime, and practically pole-vaulted into the back of the car.

Yeah, that visit was a complete waste of my fucking time.

I don't know how I was expecting to feel after visiting my mother, but it sure as shit wasn't to feel worse. Since the band went global, I've spent the years wading through my life without much thought. I've never taken anything too seriously, too busy being swept along by the glamour and the power. People have always hung off my every word. I'm the frontman – the decision maker. I've always had complete control over everything in my life.

Until now.

I don't quite know what led me to do what happened next. Maybe it was because I couldn't get pissed and risk a hangover from hell the night before a show. Maybe it was because I couldn't call Elle because she was

working at some fashion event in the city. Or maybe...
it was because I just needed to see him.

Chapter Six

~Jake~

"*Sawyer?*" I answered the door to my room wearing only a pair of grey jogging pants.

"Can I come in?"

Wordlessly, I stepped aside. Sawyer walked past me and took himself over to the white leather couch. He sat down, making himself comfortable, and then after locking the door, slipping into my shirt on from the back of the chair, I joined him, sitting just inches away. As usual he looked perfect. His hair was damp, freshly showered I assumed. He had on a short sleeved t-shirt that exposed the impeccable curves of muscle along his arms, decorated with some of the finest Japanese artwork I've ever seen. Then I looked into those rich, caramel eyes, and they were heavy with burden.

"What are you doing here, Sawyer?" My tone was laced with confusion, maybe even suspicion.

"I don't know," he answered. "Can we just... *talk?*"

"Talk?"

"Yeah. Like we used to, you know. Just share random shit. Get to know each other again."

Being Sawyer Knight

"I'd like that," I said honestly. I'd missed more than just his body. I'd missed *him*... His mind, his sense of humour, his passion for music... "I'll get us some drinks."

Conversation flowed slowly, awkwardly even, for a while. Directing the conversation away from himself, Sawyer probed me about my time in Australia. Talking about my family soon led us into a comfortable conversation, and before long, with the help of a couple of glasses of my favourite bourbon, it was just like old times.

"I can't believe Lily is *fifteen*!" Sawyer said, shaking his head in bewilderment. Lily is my baby sister. There's quite a big age gap between us – twelve years. She's a stubborn thing with a masters degree in sarcasm... but I love her, and I am insanely protective of her. "She must've been, what... *five* when I last saw her?"

"Yeah. She's gutted she doesn't really remember you. In fact, I'm pretty sure she thinks I'm bullshitting about knowing you. She said she'll believe me when she sees my picture in a magazine."

"That won't take long."

"No doubt," I agreed. "She'd love to meet you when the tour hits Sydney."

"Yeah?"

"Hell yes! Actually, she'd never forgive me if I didn't introduce you... and the rest of the guys too of course. No offense to you, but I think she prefers Isaac."

"None taken," he said, exhaling a soft laugh. "I'd love to see her again," he added with what appeared to be a genuine smile. Sawyer has a smile I could get lost in – so wide and bright, it illuminates his whole face. "Your parents too. They were pretty cool back in the day."

"They still are."

"Even though you're…never mind."

"Are you asking me if my parent's are okay with the fact I'm gay?"

"No, it doesn't matter. Forget I said anything," Sawyer stuttered before draining his glass of bourbon.

"Well they are," I replied, answering his unspoken question whether he wanted me to or now. "My mum said she'd always known, and my dad just shook my hand and said 'fair enough, son. Now sit your arse down before the rugby starts.'"

"Wow," he breathed, bending forward to pour himself another drink. Leaning across the couch, I put my hand on his shoulder to pull him back.

"That's not a good idea the night before a live show."

"You're probably right," he agreed, shrugging out of my grasp and continuing to pour the drink. "But lately everything seems like a bad idea, so what the hell."

I sat back, watching him curiously as he brought the glass to his lips. His tongue darted out a little, as if getting a sneaky taste before the liquid spilled into his mouth and coated it completely. He winced as the shot went down his throat, then after putting his glass back on the table, he just… stared.

"Sit back, Sawyer," I coaxed, patting the back of the couch. Without looking at me, he did. "Why did you really come here tonight?"

"I just…" He shrugged and then sighed. "Just needed to see you."

"Why?"

"I think you know why."

I knew why I *hoped* he was here, but there was only one way to find out for certain. Scooching closer to him, but not near enough to touch, I leaned forward, my head hovering in the crook of his neck. Inhaling his spicy scent made my dick swell instantly, forcing an involuntary moan from my throat.

"Do you want me to touch you, Sawyer?" I whispered into his ear. "Do you want to feel my mouth on you again?"

"I-I…I don't know," he stuttered, the pain of the decision evident in his expression. Standing up, I started unbuttoning my shirt.

"I'm going for a shower and then bed. Join me, or don't. The decision is yours, Sawyer." Slowly lifting my shirt over my head and tossing it to the floor, I saw Sawyer mulling his options over in his head, and given the fact his eyes didn't once shift from my bare chest, I knew he would be joining me in the shower very shortly.

After folding my pants and stripping myself free of socks and underwear, I stepped under the steaming spray and let it wash over my body. My dick had been hard since the moment Sawyer arrived at my door, and it took all the self-restraint I had not to grab hold of it and relieve the pressure.

I was applying shampoo to my short hair when I heard the door creak open. I didn't turn around - I just waited. After several minutes, curiosity got the better of me, and I turned my body to find him standing in the doorway with an almost guilty expression distorting his beautiful face.

Wordlessly, I stepped back a little and opened the shower door, holding my hand out for him. I saw him gulp, forcing his Adam's apple up and down, and then after taking a deep breath, he slowly began to undress himself. I'd seen him shirtless in magazines, and from afar when I saw the band live last time they were in Australia… but none of those situations gave his body the justice it deserves. In the flesh, just a couple of feet away from me, he took my breath away.

But that was nothing compared to the way my breath caught in my throat when he nervously rolled his pants down and then peeled his tight boxer shorts away from his body. He was already hard for me, just like I knew he would be. He strode cautiously towards me, never taking his eyes off mine, and when he placed his hand in mine, I had never felt so complete.

"You're so beautiful," I told him, pulling him closer and letting the warm water rain down over both of us. His body stiffened when I gently gripped his hips, holding him to me while my mouth inched closer to his. "Relax, Sawyer," I whispered, and then I sealed my lips to his. It took him a few seconds to reciprocate, but soon enough his lips parted enough for me to dip my tongue inside.

I tried to take my time, to savour the taste of him… but I *needed* him too badly. Angling my head to one side,

Being Sawyer Knight

I licked and sucked at his mouth like I was trying to devour him. Then, still digging my fingers into his hips, I kissed along the coarse stubble on his jaw, before settling on his neck and giving the sensitive flesh a soft nip with my teeth.

"I'm going to suck you now," I growled into his neck. "I'm going to be harsh and fast because I *need* to taste you so badly. But when I'm finished, I'm going to take you into the bedroom and take my time with you. Do you want that, Sawyer? Do you want to feel my mouth on you?"

Sawyer's stubble grazed against my own as he nodded weakly. He was still unsure, and I planned to change that by the end of the night. Dropping slowly to my knees, I ran my hands down the firmness of his body. Droplets of water clung to the contours of his sharply defined muscles, before losing their grip and rolling gracefully down his body. Taking hold of his cock in my hand, I swiftly licked the droplets of water from the tip before they had a chance to fall. He groaned in response, making me more impatient than ever.

I took him all the way into my mouth, and immediately got the response I'd been craving this afternoon.

"Oh fuck…" he moaned, twisting his hands into my hair. That simple touch, that purposeful contact, spurred me on and I tightened my lips around him, taking him to the back of my throat. The water continued to cascade over our bodies while I sucked him, creating all the moisture I needed to run my fingers between his firm, toned cheeks and apply pressure to the tight ring of muscle. "Jesus, Jake…"

"One day, I'm going to fuck you so hard here, baby," I said, releasing his cock from my mouth and pushing one finger just barely inside. Again he tensed, but when I took him in my mouth for the last time and wrapped my fingers around the base of his cock, pumping him fast and firm… he instantly relaxed. My own cock was throbbing, *begging* for similar attention, but I pushed my own needs aside, focusing solely on the man I loved, but who as yet, didn't love me.

His fingers wound tighter in my hair, encouraging the movement of my head and increasing my speed.

"P-please, Jake…" he begged, his voice breathless. "I'm so close."

In my head I said 'I've got you, baby' but outwardly, I sucked harder – swirling my tongue around his moist tip with every withdraw. His balls tightened, drawing up into his body. Knowing how close he was, I bared my teeth, grazing them gently along his shaft as I forced him so deep into my mouth I struggled to breathe past the thickness of him.

"Oh, fuck! Fuck! I'm gonna come, Jake…" And he did. Spurts of creamy warmth shot to the back of my throat and I swallowed it down, sucking the last drops straight out of his cock.

I kept him there until he started to soften, then I rose to my feet, sliding my hands up the sides of his delicious body as I did. Frustration set in when my face levelled with his and I saw he was looking guiltily to the floor.

"No," I said firmly, grabbing his chin between my thumb and forefinger, forcing him to look at me. "No regrets, Sawyer. No doubts. Not tonight." I reached out with my spare hand and shut the water off. Then I leaned in closer so my nose brushed his. "You won't think about anyone else but yourself tonight. Do you hear me, Sawyer? You will only think about how *you're* feeling, *what* you're feeling… concentrate on the physical pleasure, baby. Leave everything else until tomorrow."

"This is wrong. You could be fired…"

"Come to bed with me," I said, placing my finger over his lips and ignoring his concerns. "I want you to touch me. I need to *feel* you. Will you do that for me, Sawyer?" I spoke into his neck, and then laid feather-light kisses across his jaw.

"Yes," he breathed. "I'll try."

We dried ourselves off with towels, never taking our eyes off each other as we did. I had my own gown, and Sawyer slipped into the complimentary one hanging on the back of the bathroom door. Then I led him to the bedroom, glancing behind me every few steps to make sure he was still following. He was still so nervous when we reached the bed, I'd never known him be so quiet and I looked forward to calming those doubts that were so obviously running riot in his mind.

"Lie on the bed," I said. He swallowed nervously, he did that a lot lately, and then he did. He lay on the mattress and stretched his body out straight, propping himself up on his elbow and resting his head on his hand. I crawled up next to him, lying on my side so I could stare into those hypnotic caramel eyes of his. "Tell me what you're thinking."

"I'm thinking I shouldn't be here, but also that I don't want to be anywhere else. I feel nervous, excited, satisfied but ashamed. I'm thinking I don't know why the pull I feel towards you is so intense, and I'm thinking I don't have the strength to keep fighting it any longer."

"I'm glad you feel it too," I whispered. "The pull. I've felt it since we were teenagers, Sawyer, and even though we've been apart for so many years, it's only grown stronger."

"I don't *want* to be like this though."

"Like what? Gay?"

"Yes," he said simply, closing his eyes in shame. "All this... I don't know... confusion, it's kid stuff, right? Shouldn't I have been going through all this shit when I was younger? I'm a grown man. I'm too old to be having doubts like this."

"Everybody deals with stuff in their own time. Coming out isn't a race, Sawyer."

"Whoa..." He shook his head defiantly. "I can't- I mean I'll never... no one can ever know about this, Jake."

They have to, I thought to myself. One day, I want to hold this beautiful man proudly on my arm. I want the whole world to know he's mine.

"It's too early to think about that right now. You have to accept yourself before you can expect other people to accept you too."

"I'm serious. You need to know this now. You can't ever expect to have any kind of... *relationship* with me."

"We've gotten off track," I said, dismissing him. "Tonight is about having fun. Let's not ruin it by getting so serious." Closing his eyes briefly, Sawyer nodded.

Being Sawyer Knight

Needing to get him back into the mindset he was in during our shower, I draped an arm over his hip, smoothing my hand up and down his broad back through his robe. "I want you to kiss me again."

Without saying a word, and for the first time without swallowing nervously, he inched his face closer to mine and cupped the back of my neck with his hand. He instigated it this time. His tongue swept over my closed lips, teasing for entry into my mouth. I parted my lips for him, and his tongue delved inside, dancing with mine as he tightened his grip around my neck, urging me closer to him.

Unable to hold back any longer, I started undoing the knot in his robe, teasing it open with deft fingers and pushing the towelling fabric open so it draped behind him on the bed.

"So fucking perfect," I moaned into his mouth, trailing my fingertips along the hard ridges of muscle cocooning his chest, tracing the outlines of what can only be described as exquisite pieces of artwork decorating his skin. Slowly, I worked my way down to his semi-erect cock, curling my fingers around it and smiling as it hardened instantly at my touch.

"No," Sawyer interjected, grabbing my hand and pulling it up to his chest. "I…I want to touch *you* this time."

Sighing in anticipation, I opened my robe and shuffled out of it, tossing it to the floor behind me. Sawyer did the same before bringing his naked body close to mine, pressing our chests together. Placing his hands on my torso, he closed his eyes and let out a heavy, almost pained sigh.

"What's wrong?" I asked gently, wrapping my hand around his and encouraging him to smooth it across my chest.

"I, um, well I've never... *touched* a man this way before," he admitted, his eyes sweeping the mattress in embarrassment.

"You've never experimented before?"

"There were a couple of guys in college," he confessed, shrugging. "But... *they* touched *me* – never the other way round. To touch them would've felt too..." he trailed off, unable to find the word.

"*Gay?*"

"Something like that."

"Are you saying no one has ever been *here?*" I asked, sneaking my hand between his pressed together thighs, encouraging him to part them before circling his puckered rim with the tip of my finger. He shook his head, refusing eye-contact with me. I grinned devilishly at him, and then buried my face in his neck. "I *will* be going there, baby. Not yet. Not tonight. But soon."

Biting his bottom lip, Sawyer's hand slipped free from mine and started wandering cautiously down my body. He stopped just above my pubic bone and inhaled a deep, somewhat anxious breath.

"Just think about how *you* like to be touched, Sawyer. There's no wrong way to do it. Just *feel* me." I sucked in a sharp breath when the back of his fingers brushed against the tip of my rigid cock. I'd dreamt about feeling this man's hands on me too many times to count in my life, yet nothing could've prepared me for just how wonderful it felt – how intense, how fucking *perfect*.

Being Sawyer Knight

"Yes," I hissed, arching myself further into his hand. "Just like that, baby."

Starting slowly, he stroked my cock up and down, his eyes boring into mine as if he were assessing my reaction. Gradually his confidence started to grow, evident by the increasing speed of his hand. My breathing quickened and I reached out to touch him. Palming his cheek with my hand, I poured my emotions out through my eyes – my intense gaze showing how much I wanted him, *needed* him.

"I want to give you what you gave me," he said uncertainly.

"You don't have to do that," I assured him. "This is about relaxing you, Sawyer. Showing you how good things can be."

"I *want* to," he said firmly. "I just don't know if I'll be any good."

"Baby," I began, rolling over slightly so I could take his face in my hands. I ran my thumbs along his jaw in the direction of his stubble, and locked my eyes onto his. "I have wanted you for so damn long, Sawyer Antony Knight. Believe me, I risk exploding into your mouth the second your tongue touches me. It doesn't matter *how* you do it, the fact that it's *you* down there will make it the best fucking blowjob of my life."

Without saying a word, Sawyer shuffled down the bed, positioned himself between my open legs and wasted no time in flicking the swollen head of my cock with his tongue.

Sweet fucking hell...

My hips bucked involuntarily, and I saw a proud smile curl the corners of his lips. I let out a satisfied growl, clenching my teeth together.

"Seriously… I can't hold out long," I breathed, fisting his hair between my fingers. "Not with you… your mouth feels too fucking amazing."

Glancing up at me, he took my whole length into his warm, moist mouth before dragging his lips all the way back up to the top. When he released me, I noticed a glistening bead of pre-cum leak from the tip and without hesitation his tongue darted out to catch it. I caught sight of his eyebrows rise slightly, almost as if he was pleasantly surprised by the taste.

"Please, Sawyer," I whimpered. "Take me all the way, baby."

Closing his eyes, he drew me back into his mouth, circling his thumb and forefinger around the base and gripping me tightly. He worked his mouth up and down along with his fingers, then his free hand cupped my balls, massaging them with his thumb into his palm.

"Yes," I murmured, digging my arse into the bed and forcing myself deeper into his mouth. "Faster, baby…" Doing as I asked, his head bobbed up and down and as I gripped his hair with my fingers, I couldn't take my eyes off his movement. Sawyer Knight, *my* Sawyer Knight – not the one the world thought they owned – was sucking my dick, and he was so fucking stunning it sent me spiralling towards the edge. The violent tingle of my impeding orgasm began in my spine, then it spread to my hips before surging downwards, drawing my throbbing balls up into my body.

Being Sawyer Knight

"If you don't want me to come in your mouth, you need to move away *now*," I ground out through gritted teeth. He didn't move, just sucked harder. "Fuck, Sawyer… God yes…*Fuck!*" I came with a deep moan, pouring myself into his mouth, my cock pulsating against his tongue. Only when I'd completely finished ejaculating did he remove his mouth, and then, wiping the corners of his lips on the back of his hand, he looked up at me with a nervous gaze.

"That was fucking amazing," I said, easing the anxious glint in his eyes somewhat. "Did you enjoy doing it?" I added curiously. Scooting back up to the top of the bed, he collapsed onto his back.

"Yes," he admitted. "And I can't wait to do it again. It felt… right." My heart vibrated in my chest, the reverberations spreading throughout my entire body. I sensed a hint of regret, maybe even fear in his voice, but I dismissed it. I couldn't expect him to be okay with this so quickly – in fact I was still in a state of shock that I'd managed to get him into my bed so quickly. I knew before I even took this job he would resist, and I honestly thought it would take a few months to crack him.

I never doubted that I *would* crack him however. I remember our first kiss like it was ten days ago, not ten years. I *felt* how much he wanted it – wanted *me*. Plus there are the rumours in the media. During the last couple of years a couple of kiss and tell stories have managed to get to print before the band's management have been able to get an injunction against them. There's no smoke without fire, right?

"Tasted better than I thought it would too," Sawyer added with a lopsided smile. "But... I guess I should get going now."

"No, wait," I said quickly, grabbing onto his forearm. "Stay a while? Let me hold you... sleep next to you."

"I can't. Someone might see me leaving your room if I'm still here in the morning."

"I'll set the alarm for a couple of hours time. You can leave while it's still the middle of the night, just please, lie with me for a little while."

"Okay," he breathed. And it was the sweetest word I'd ever heard in my life. Hitching myself up a little and rolling onto my back, I laid out one of my arms for him to snuggle into. Without a second's hesitation, he shifted closer and rested his head on my chest. I closed my arm around him, lowering my head and nuzzling his hair.

"I've waited forever for this moment," I said quietly, squeezing him a little tighter. With my free arm, I plucked the corner of the duvet from the edge of the bed, throwing it over both of our naked bodies. "Promise me you won't run from this tomorrow – run from *us*."

Sawyer was silent for a little longer than I felt comfortable with, but eventually came the words I needed to hear – or at least, the best I could hope for right now.

"I promise to try," he said, his voice weak. "That's all I can offer you right now, Jake. But I meant what I said, *nobody* can know about us."

"That's fine with me." *For now.* "You can trust me. Always." I reached around to the bedside table, setting the alarm for two hours time like I promised. "I can make you happy, Sawyer. Just give me the chance to show you."

Those were the last words spoken between us before I drifted into a satisfied sleep, with the man who owned my heart and soul wound tightly in my arms.

Chapter Seven

~Sawyer~

"*Fuck*!" I blasted, throwing myself out of Jake's bed so quickly I stumbled and whacked my knee on the bedpost. "Double fuck!" I whined, hopping across the room towards the en-suite.

"What's wrong?" Jake asked, rubbing at his eyes.

"It's six o-fucking-clock! I need to get out of here!"

"Shit, Sawyer, I'm so sorry. I set the alarm I swear," he apologised, climbing out of bed after me.

"I know you did. I just... I don't have time for this. Where the fuck did I leave my pants?"

"They're on the dresser. I folded them."

"*Why?*"

"I'm just a tidy guy I guess," he said, shrugging. After pulling my pants on quickly, I turned around to grab my shirt. Then I felt strong arms snake around my waist and my mind was conflicted whether I should melt into them or push him away.

"I need to go," I barely whispered, relaxing into his embrace. He started kissing along my neck and then

92

pushed his hips forward, pressing his obvious erection into the small of my back. "Later," I added, a promise I intended to keep.

"You're not running?" he asked huskily before nibbling on my ear lobe and driving me fucking insane.

"Not today," I teased, but he didn't appreciate my humour.

"Not *ever*," he affirmed, digging his fingers firmly into my hips and pulling me even closer to him. Closing my eyes, I sighed contentedly. How could this feel so right, so natural, when the back of my mind wouldn't quit screaming at me that it was wrong?

"Jake!"

"Fuck!" I growled, grabbing Jake's hands and shoving him off me when I heard Laurelin's voice on the other side of his door. "What the hell is she doing here so early? Shit!"

"Calm down," Jake tried to soothe, but when he put his hand on my shoulder I flinched, shrugging away from him. "Sawyer," he added firmly. "You could be in my room for any number of reasons. I'm your goddamn bodyguard! Stop worrying!"

"At least get dressed before you let her in."

Rolling his eyes, he headed to the closet and quickly pulled on a pair of sweats and a hooded top. I gaped at him for a little longer than I should. Since he'd been back I'd only seen him in suits and business attire. He looked great dressed so casually – younger, more carefree.

"Put the kettle on. I'll just tell her we're discussing arrangements for the tour bus this evening," Jake said, amazingly calm and collected – like he always is. I admire that about him. Nodding, I bent down to drag on my shoes and then headed over to the kitchenette area. I was surprised to see the surfaces looking used. Mine is pristine – untouched. Same goes for the rest of the guys, seeing as we take the easier option of ordering room service for absolutely everything.

"Today's papers," Laurelin snapped, strolling straight into the living area. "There's another story. People are talk- Oh…" she cut herself off, noticing me spooning coffee into the two mugs set out on the counter. "Sawyer," she added, blood rushing to her face when she realised her mistake.

Instantly, I was reminded why I actually came here last night. Jake had completely captivated me, forcing me to forget everything that existed outside of his arms. The rumours. The press. The fucking gossip that no one would tell me about.

"That's why I'm here," I stated, giving up on making coffee and striding into the living room. "To find out what shit is being dished out by the press, and more importantly, why the fuck no one has told me about it."

"It's not a big deal," Laurelin tried to appease. "You know better than to read the papers."

"Don't bullshit me, Lin. If it wasn't a big deal you wouldn't be here right now. Whatever's going on must be holding some weight and I want…no I *deserve* to know what it is."

"I'm not really sure. I'm only the messenger. You should talk to Claire."

"I tell you what, *you* go and talk to Claire and tell her to get her backside to my room *before* breakfast."

"Okay," she agreed, blushing with apprehension. Laurelin didn't like being put on the spot, or me being mad at her. I would apologise later. Right now, I was too pissed off. "I'll call her, see if she's awake."

"You do that," I said acidly, running my fingers through my messy hair. With that, she turned on her heels and scuttled out of Jake's room.

"Bit harsh don't you think?" Jake murmured the second she closed the door.

"What's going on, Jake? And please, don't you lie to me too."

"You know I wouldn't," he said genuinely, reaching out to take my hand. Instinctively, my arm twitched in an attempt to shrug away from him, but his fingers brushed mine and I melted into his touch. "There have been several stories lately. A few blokes coming out of the woodwork and selling stories about their... *relationships*...with you."

"WHAT? I've never had a fucking relationship! How many guys are we talking about here?"

"Four so far."

"Well that's bullshit! I've never been with..." Fuck this was hard, and yet I was only talking to Jake. How the fuck was I supposed to confront this shit with anyone else? With management? With the press? "There were never that many," I tacked on with a heavy sigh.

"You know how it works, baby..." *Baby*...a simple term of endearment I'd been called countless times before, yet for some reason, hearing it from Jake's mouth made my chest tingle. "Someone sees a story, figures it probably paid out well for whoever sold it, and they jump on the bandwagon. They've probably never even met you. But you have lawyers for this kind of stuff, remember? Try and ignore it. It *will* blow over, I promise you," he assured, squeezing my hand as he brought it up to his lips. He planted featherlike kisses on each one of my knuckles and it almost brought me to my knees.

"What are we doing, Jake?" There were a thousand different meanings to my question.

"We're taking it one day at a time. No pressure. Just enjoy us, Sawyer."

"You could lose your job if anyone found out, and I couldn't stop it. They'd say you couldn't protect someone you had an emotional attachment to efficiently. They'd think…"

"I will *never* let anything happen to you. I *can* and I *will* protect you."

"I'm… fuck I don't know what I am anymore."

"Hey," he said softly, snaking his arms around my waist and pulling my body into his. "You're afraid. I know you probably can't imagine it but I've been where you are right now. For years you've been living the only way you knew how, the way you thought you *should* be… and now I've come back into your life and turned your whole world upside in just a couple of days. It's okay to be unsure, to feel scared… but promise me when it feels like it's getting too much, you'll come to *me* – even if it's me that's causing you to feel like this."

Angling my head back, I closed my eyes and forced out a breath.

"*Promise* me, Sawyer," he demanded, sliding his hands up my arms and squeezing my shoulders firmly. "Promise me you won't try and work whatever's going on in your head out alone. Whenever you do that, you only end up pushing me away. I can't do that again, I've waited too long for this."

"You're serious aren't you? When you say you've never stopped thinking about me?"

"Yes," he breathed without hesitation. Then he brought a palm to my cheek and my head involuntarily snuggled into him. "Not one day has gone by where I haven't thought about you... *wanted* you... *needed* you. The closest I could get was to follow your career, and it comforted and tortured me in equal measures."

"You've watched my career?"

"I came to see you last time you were in Sydney," he admitted, a coy smile tugging at the corners of his soft lips. "I have hours and hours of footage of you – interviews, concerts, music videos..."

"Wow."

"I love you, Sawyer. I've *always* loved you."

"Jake I-"

"Shh," he commanded, placing a gentle finger over my lips. "It's too soon for you. I've sprung so much on you in just a few days. I don't need you to say it back. Not yet. I just needed you to know that this isn't some lame attempt to relive my youth, or to mess with your head. I'm back here because I was fucking miserable trying to

live without you, and I owed it to both of us to return to
you and *try*. If you knocked me back, at least I'd done all
I could and I wouldn't spend my life with regrets."

Before I had chance to rethink my decision, I craned
my neck to the side and leaned in to kiss him. His body
stiffened for a brief moment, no doubt from surprise at
my forwardness, but then he relaxed into the kiss,
winding his fingers into my hair and dipping his tongue
into my mouth. Neither of us had shaved yet, and the
sound of our stubble scratching together sent delicious
shivers down my spine. Everything about him felt right.
He's a strapping man – built, strong... yet he has the
most tender touch I've ever experienced. Our bodies fit
together perfectly, our cocks resting at a similar height,
enabling our arousals to rub together.

"I need to go," I whispered, reluctantly pulling away
from his mouth. "How are we going to do this?"

"Work together you mean?"

"Um, yeah," I muttered quietly. The shame I felt
embarrassed me – it felt like I was letting him down.
Even so, going public with this was not, and will never
be, and option.

"Don't worry – I promise not to pounce on you in
front of the guys. We will find a way to do this, baby. I
promise."

"Baby – you can't call me baby."

"You don't like me calling you baby?"

"No I... I, um...I *do* like it. But you need to be careful
you don't slip up when we're not alone."

"I won't let you down, Sawyer," he promised, cupping my cheek. "You can trust me."

I wished I could say the same, but in truth, I didn't know if he could trust me yet. Despite how wonderful his arms felt when they were wrapped around me, I still didn't know if I would run for the fucking hills the first chance I got.

"I've really gotta go," I said. Leaning over and lightly kissing my forehead, Jake nodded.

"Don't be too hard on Claire. You know you've been acting like a complete shit to her ever since I got here?"

"Yeah," I agreed, sighing. "But in my defence she's annoying as fuck at times."

Laughing softly, he rolled his eyes at me.

"Go on, go," he said, shooing me towards the door. As my hand pressed down on the door handle, he gripped me from behind and positioned his lips against my ear.

"If you jack off in the shower, make sure you think of me," he whispered, ensuring that I would indeed be jerking off in the shower.

"You're gonna kill me, Jake Reed."

"But not before showing you the world, Sawyer Knight."

Inhaling deeply and trying to ignore the throb in my cock, I eased away from him and opened the door. After quickly scanning the corridor to make sure no one saw me leave, I practically sprinted to my suite. Once the door was closed behind me, I slid straight to the floor, propping my back up against it and letting my head fall into my hands.

Then I inhaled for what felt like the first time in hours.

"THANK YOU, LONDON – AND GOODNIGHT!" I called out to the twenty-thousand plus people in front of us, screaming our names and waving banners with our faces on in the air. The crowd went crazy, jumping up and down and screaming so loudly the stage vibrated beneath my feet.

The lights dimmed, and after unhooking my guitar from around my neck and pulling out my earplugs, I ran off the stage with the guys following behind me.

"Fucking amazing show!" Kip hollered, clapping me on the back as we jogged down the steps backstage. He was right – this feeling was like an addiction. The crowd, the atmosphere, the music… it's euphoric. Glorious. It makes you feel like a freaking god.

"Sure was!" I agreed, wiping the sweat from my forehead on the back of my forearm. We were swallowed by our security team as soon as we hit the bottom step. Jake and Neil flanked me either side, ushering me towards the exit.

"The car door is open and waiting for you," Jake told me, even though I was fully acquainted with the protocol. Nodding, I continued down the large corridor and to the exit. With one arm shielding me, Jake used his other to open the fire door where we were met with arena security who guarded the doors while we made it to our respective cars. Somehow, photographers had found a way into this private part of the arena grounds, they always do, and I looked to the ground, ignoring them as they yelled my name and tried to blind me with flashing lights.

"Amazing show," Jake whispered to me with what can only be described as a proud smile. He didn't need to touch me for me to feel him all over my body. Sliding into the back seat next to me, his warm breath swept over my face, his spicy aftershave teased my nose, making me want to bury my face in his neck so I could inhale the full scent of him, and his gaze brought prickly goosebumps to my skin wherever his eyes landed on me.

As soon as Neil slipped into the front passenger seat, Jake immediately shifted into 'professional' mode. It was like he had an inbuilt switch that turned him from lover to bodyguard in an instant. Diverting his gaze to the windows, flicking his eyes from one to the next as if looking for any signs of threat, he straightened his body, squared his shoulders and didn't look me in the eye again.

"We're heading straight for the tour bus. When we arrive, you need to get straight out of the car and straight onto the bus. Apparently there's already quite a crowd gathering, but with no barriers in place you can't afford to stop for them."

"Got it," I said, though really I hadn't heard a word. All I could think about was how tight his pants looked, and how my fingers were twitching to unzip them and release the pressure. That was shortly followed by thoughts along the line of 'What the fuck am I doing?'

"Is Elle travelling with us on the bus?" I asked, wondering why she didn't answer the text I sent her before the show.

"No. She's dealing with something at home so said she'll travel up by herself tonight. I-"

"I don't want her travelling by herself," I interrupted.

"If you'd let me finish," Jake began, "I was going to add that I told her I didn't want her traveling alone and so I've arranged for Jim to stay behind and accompany her."

"Oh," I muttered, feeling like a bit of a douche. I need to start remembering that Jake isn't just my ex-best friend from high school who I can't stop thinking about, he's also our head of security. He's the best in his field. He knows his job and I should start trusting him to do it.

"I know my job, Sawyer. While Elle is on the tour as your stylist, she is part of our team. I'm here to protect our team."

"I know. Sure. Sorry," I mumbled. Deciding keeping my mouth shut for the rest of the relatively short journey, I flopped my head back onto the padded headrest and closed my eyes. It eased the stinging caused by a mixture of smoke and sweat created on stage, and although fully conscious, I relaxed into my seat, slouching with my knees apart, and just...thought.

Turned out thinking is a dangerous pastime for me these days, given the raging hard-on taking over my pants. I sat up, shifting my position slightly in an attempt to inconspicuously relieve the pressure on my dick. Fuck these jeans were tight. Seconds later my phone buzzed in my pocket. I pulled it free, expecting it to be Elle replying to my earlier text.

Jake: Uncomfortable isn't it?

Huh?

Daring a sideways glance in his direction, I held my phone up and looked at him in utter confusion. Then my gaze followed the movement of his hand down to his crotch, where he traced the outline of his evidently swollen cock through the restrictive black material of his pants. I squirmed in my seat, forced out a cough to clear the lump forming in my throat and turned to the window. The effect Jake had on me completely baffled me. Sure I've been attracted to men before, but never to the point I had a constant erection in their presence, and most definitely never to the point where I couldn't seem to think of anything else but them.

When we reached the bus, it was a military operation to get us all out of our cars and straight on board without being ambushed by the awaiting crowd. I always felt a pang of guilt whenever we couldn't afford to stop and take a minute to chat with fans. We owe our whole career to them, and they deserve some attention when they've waited outside in the cold so late at night to see us. And Christ it was cold – not unusual for late March in England – and I zipped my leather jacket right up to my neck after stepping onto the bus. It hadn't had a chance to heat up yet.

"Ugh, this bus is a heap of shit," Matt grumbled, slinging his backpack onto the couches at the back end of the bus. Personally, I didn't see anything wrong with the bus. Granted, it's not as big or comfortably furnished as the bus we have in the States, but it'll do the job. "Why the fuck couldn't we just fly?"

"We've been over this," Gavin answered. "For the distance, it's less hassle to drive our kit up there."

"Doesn't mean *we* couldn't fly. Someone else could've travelled up with the kit."

"Shut your whiney ass up, Matt," I griped, before diving towards the bunks to claim the single bed space. The other guys could fight out between them who were getting the other bunks, but there was no way I was sharing a space with any of them – especially Matt.

"Oh come on, dude, you *always* get the single bunk!" Matt called after me. I sniggered to myself, ignoring him as I tossed my back onto the tiny bed. I was about to lie down on it, rest my weary body after belting it out on stage for the last four hours, when I heard Jake's voice below.

"Okay, guys, Neil and I will be travelling on the bus with you. Everyone else will be following behind."

Shit.

I didn't want Jake on the bus with us. The bus was too confined. He'd be too close. Sometimes it felt like I no longer had any control over my mind or my body when he was around – what if the guys picked up on something.

"There aren't enough bunks for everyone," I heard Kip say. "Neil could take the couch, and I guess you could bunk in with Saw. He has the biggest bed."

Oh fuck no.

Being Sawyer Knight

"I won't be sleeping," Jake assured. "I'll be fine right here."

Flooded with relief, I took the opportunity to climb down from my bunk and join them.

"Hey," I said as casually as I could manage, stuffing my hands in my pockets. "You riding with us?" Of course I knew the answer, but apart from discussing the fucking weather, all other options for 'casual' conversation eluded me.

"Yeah. Just waiting for Neil," he explained, shrugging out of his jacket and laying it neatly on the chair next to him. As if by magic, Neil hopped onto the bus in that very moment.

"It's fuckin' crazy out there," he said, shaking his head.

"We good to go?" Jake asked.

"Yeah. The roadies are still packing the gear into the truck but they'll be following on soon. Claire's already left, and Laurelin's riding up with Dave."

"Well I'm gonna crash for the night," I said to no one in particular, purposely avoiding eye-contact with Jake, knowing if I did my dick would automatically lurch towards him.

"Fuckin' pussy!" Matt piped up. "Stay up and drink with us!" He clinked his bottle of beer against Gavin's and Daz's, then he tried to do the same to Kip but all he got in return was the middle finger. "Not tonight, man. Got a fucker of a headache coming on. Night guys."

"You're turning into such a fuckin' loser in your old age, dude," were Matt's last words before I climbed up into my bunk and drew the curtain.

I stripped quickly down to my boxers, stuffing my dirty clothes into my overnight bag. Then I got into bed, bending my knees slightly so my feet didn't hit the wall as I lay down. Sighing heavily, I closed my eyes and tried not to think about Jake being just a couple of feet away. I failed miserably, and ended up drifting off with a hard-on so huge it literally fucking ached.

"Nearly over for another year, eh?" Elle asked, slumping back into the plush couch in my hotel suite. We were leaving for the show soon. We'd rehearsed this morning, and then I spent the afternoon sleeping. I'd not seen Jake all day, which was weird because he's supposed to be my personal bodyguard. His absence also made this strange ache appear in my chest.

"Yeah."

The tour was coming to a close. Before arriving in the UK we'd made our way around Europe and then toured all the major US states. After tonight and tomorrow's gigs in Manchester we were travelling back down south, finishing with two more dates back in London. We've got a three week break after that before we hit Australia and then it's back to LA to get started on the new album.

"So what are your plans for the break you guys have got coming up?"

"Dunno," I shrugged. "Probably head back to LA. Keep my head down for a couple of weeks."

"What's wrong with you? You're normally buzzing before a show."

"Nothing's wrong," I lied. I didn't want to admit it even to myself, but the truth was I was missing Jake. How ridiculous? It'd only been a few hours.

"Okay, muscle man. You keep on with the bullshit if it makes you feel better."

"Don't be like that, Elle. I'm just tired, that's all. We've been touring for months. It takes it out of you eventually."

"Whatever," she dismissed, rolling her eyes. "So anyway, I'm coming with you to Australia."

"What? Why?"

"Jesus, Saw… don't get too over excited, you might strain something."

"Fuck off. You know that'd make me fucking ecstatic. It's just… you never venture further than Europe. What about Kylie?"

"I'll make sure she's got enough money before I leave. She doesn't know it yet but I've opened a bank account for her. She's growing up, Saw. It amazes me how mature she is. I think she's responsible enough to have access to some money that our mum will know *nothing* about."

"But why the sudden change?"

"You're not doing such a good job of convincing me that you *want* me to come!"

"You *know* I do," I assured her. "So quit whining."

"I guess I just want to see more of the world," she shrugged. "And besides, I miss you when you're on the other side of the world for months on end."

"Aww, gorgeous girl," I cooed, playfully kicking her foot with my own. "That's about the sweetest thing I've ever heard."

"Dude! You in there?" Kip's voice on the other side of my suite door cut into our conversation, followed by a knock.

"I'll get it," Elle said, jumping to her feet. She sashayed over to the door, purposely wiggling her hips like a catwalk model. Then she winked at me, clearly proud of her little strut, and opened the door.

"Cars are ready, mate," Kip informed me. Instinctively I looked down at my watch. "Neil's waiting for you by the lift."

Neil? Why not Jake?

"Sure, man. Be down in two."

Kip disappeared as quickly as he came. Jumping to my feet, I picked up my phone, quickly glancing at the screen in case I'd missed any contact from Jake, then sighing when I saw that I hadn't. After stuffing it in my pocket, Elle approached me and fiddled with my hair, trying in vain to get my fringe to stay out of my eyes.

"Ugh," she groaned. My floppy hair has always been a pain in her ass. "We'll fix it when we get to the arena."

"Come on, gorgeous girl," I said, exhaling a small laugh. It amused me how frustrated she could get at a couple of strands of hair. "I've got songs to sing."

Chapter Eight

~Jake~

"*The* guys need to know about this," Laurelin said, standing tall with one hand on her hip as if that made her look intimidating or authoritative.

"I agree." She blinked in surprise, dropping her hand from her hip.

"May I suggest we get these last few UK dates out of the way first?" Claire spoke.

"Hmm," I pondered. "I think it's gone too far to keep this on the down low any longer."

I had been at the arena all day after getting a call from Claire saying on-site security had found a suspicious parcel in Sawyer's dressing room. Upon inspection, the inside of the box revealed a black and white cat with it's throat slit, lying in a pool of its own blood. On top of the animal was a note splattered with blood, the words formed from newspaper clippings. Very amateur.

Nicola Haken

The future only ever brings the end

It was a quote – taken from the lyrics of one of Souls of the Knight's biggest hits. The message was clear. Whoever sent this wanted our attention, and after this stunt they definitely had it.

"Well I trust whichever decision you make," Claire replied. *I should think so too.* That's why she employed me after all.

"Right," I clipped, looking at my watch. "We need to wrap this up, the guys are on their way."

Claire nodded and then headed out to the back of the building to wait for the guys to arrive. I issued the rest of my team with their orders for the night, answered any questions they had, then I straightened my black tie, secured my earpiece and went to join Claire.

The second I saw Sawyer's long, denim-clad legs swing from the car I became very aware of my pulse. It thudded in my ears, increasing in speed and pressure. Once he was out, standing by the car door, his eyes caught mine and they narrowed, causing my own to widen in surprise. He snatched his gaze away quickly when Neil came up behind him. Slowly, they walked towards Claire and me, and then he simply brushed past me without a word.

Tiny sparks of fear sparkled in my gut. Was he having second thoughts about us? Had he found out about the threats?

Fuck.

Being Sawyer Knight

I'd told myself a thousand times I could still do my job effectively despite the feelings I had for Sawyer, which is why I needed to talk to him immediately. Right now, I couldn't focus on scanning the perimeter, I couldn't remember what positions my men were supposed to be stationed in, which meant I couldn't do my fucking job. All I *could* think about was why Sawyer looked at me the way he did.

Arena security escorted the guys to their dressing rooms. Claire followed Matt and Isaac into their shared room, Gavin and Darren headed into theirs and I followed Sawyer to his. Elle was outside when I reached his door with her hand hovering over the handle.

"Mind if I just take a minute alone with him?" I asked. My words came out in a rush and by the look of confusion sweeping across her face I knew I'd appeared too eager. "I just need to run over the itinerary for after the show." I purposely forced calm into my voice this time, but I knew I hadn't fooled her.

"Um, sure," she said warily. "I'll start with the other guys," she added, giving me the once over with suspicious eyes before dragging her suitcase full of hair crap across the corridor.

I walked into Sawyer's dressing room without knocking. He was bending down to his guitar case, unclipping the latch when he heard me come in.

"One sec, gorgeous girl," he began to say, obviously expecting Elle. Then he straightened up and turned around. When he saw me his neck jerked back in surprise. He didn't speak and this worried me. It felt like something had shifted between us and I didn't like it.

So, needing to close the gap between us, I stepped forward, cautiously raising my hand to his face.

"You've been gone all day," he whispered, closing his eyes as he buried his cheek into my palm.

"Is that what's wrong with you."

"Kind of."

"Kind of?"

"I… *missed* you."

"And that's a *bad* thing?"

"It's an *unfamiliar* thing. I'm not sure how I feel about needing someone so badly."

"You *need* me?"

My heart thumped so fast and powerful in my chest I wondered if he would be able to hear it. Deciding he probably couldn't, I took hold of his hand and pressed it to my chest.

"Yes," he answered on a sigh. "Yes I think I *do*."

"Fucking hell, Sawyer," I breathed, my chest swelling with all kinds of emotion. Releasing his hand, I cupped his face, bringing his lips to mine. I wasn't sweet or gentle. I kissed him like I wanted to fucking devour him. I attacked his mouth, twisting my tongue around his, like I was starving. "You have no idea how long I've waited to hear those words coming from that delicious mouth of yours," I whispered, breaking our kiss and resting my forehead on his. "I'm going to fuck that mouth so hard tonight," I added, making him shiver in my arms.

"Jesus…" he groaned when I stroked his dick through his jeans. He was hard and ready for me. He always was. "You shouldn't feel this good." Briefly, I wondered if he'd ever overcome the doubts or shame that he felt, but I quickly dismissed it, choosing instead to revel in the gruff moans escaping his throat as I continued stroking his erection.

"Tonight, baby," I whispered, smiling into his strong neck as I pulled my hand away from his groin. "I want you to fuck me tonight." Sawyer drew in a sharp breath, his body stiffening slightly. "By the time I'm finished with you, I promise you'll want to."

"I… I mean what if… I might not do it right."

"You'll be *perfect*," I assured him. Uncertainty contorted his face as I pulled away from him. I wasn't worried. I would take care of him… relax him. I had no doubt I would provide him with the best fuck of his life. "I need to get back to work," I said reluctantly, adjusting first the uncomfortable bulge in my pants and then straightening my tie. "Have a great show, Sawyer," I tacked on, flashing him a wink that made one side of his mouth turn up into a half smile. Then I turned towards the door and left, feeling pretty damn amazing as I headed off to find Neil.

Just over an hour later the support act were finishing up their set and it was time to gather the guys. They should've all been waiting in Sawyer's dressing room as instructed, but I came to learn pretty quickly that Matt didn't handle instruction very well.

Nicola Haken

"Where the fuck is he?" Isaac blared, pacing across the dressing room floor. "Have you checked his dressing room?"

"Yeah," Darren replied. No sign of him."

"I'll go and look for him," I announced, shaking my head in frustration. I imagined dealing with Matt was what high-school teachers had to live through every damn day.

"I'll come with you," Sawyer said, getting up from his chair. I forced myself to look away from him, knowing the sight of him in those tight jeans and ripped shirt would have me hard and throbbing for him in a nanosecond.

We paced quickly down the corridor together. There was a good foot of space between us but I could almost feel the heat coming from his body. His spicy aftershave danced up my nose with every stride we took, making my cock twitch with every breath.

I paused when we reached a door marked 'Maintenance'. What could only be described as grunts were seeping from the gap beneath the door and by Sawyer's raised eyebrow, I was sure we'd found our missing band member.

"What the fuck are you playing at?" Sawyer blasted when he opened the door, revealing Matt with his pants around his ankles and a young blonde bouncing up and down on his lap. "We're on in two!"

"I'll be... ah fuck, baby... five minutes," he growled, keeping his hands firmly on the woman's waist and encouraging her up and down. My eyes flitted to the ceiling, but my ears couldn't escape the sound of flesh

114

slapping against flesh. They didn't stop for even a second – as if it was completely normal to have people walk in on you having sex and just carry on like you were chatting about the weather.

"Claire. Maintenance room, now!" I looked to Sawyer who was ending a call I didn't even see him make. Within seconds Claire was barging in behind us with a scowl on her face.

"Matthew!" she scolded. As if someone had just thrown a grenade at his feet, Matt rolled off his chair, practically tossing the blonde to the floor, and then tripping over his pants when he tried to stand. "You!" she barked, pointing to Blondie. "Out. Now!"

The moment confirmed the fact that Claire was the 'mother' of the band. Good to know for when the next situation like this arises – because I have no doubt it will. Picking up her knickers from the floor and then smoothing her skirt – or was it a belt – down, Blondie scurried from the maintenance closet like a red-faced teenager who'd just been busted by her parents.

"Sorry, Claire," Matt muttered guiltily, sweeping the floor with his eyes.

"Get your butt on that stage," she ordered. Nodding, Matt walked past her, still adjusting the zipper on his jeans. Claire rolled her eyes and followed behind him. Smiling at me, Sawyer cocked his head for me to follow him out of the room.

So I did, and I didn't take my eyes of his fine arse all the way to the stage.

As usual Sawyer was literally glowing after finishing the show. His dark hair was damp and swept back from his face, all traces of Elle's styling efforts completely gone. His cheeks were warm shade of red, visible beneath his heavy coating of stubble, and his skin was glistening with a light sheen of sweat. I imagined the other guys probably looked the same, but I didn't notice them. Only Sawyer. I've only ever noticed Sawyer since being fourteen years old.

Getting the boys to their cars and back to the hotel was a military operation – one that ran as smoothly and quickly as I expected. With the guys and the team we naturally took over the top floor of the Hilton. Claire is in charge of booking accommodation, and by happy coincidence, my room was situated next to Sawyer's. I didn't know whose room we would end up in tonight, but as we rode the lift to the top floor I knew regardless, he would be on top of me, buried balls deep inside my arse, at some point in the next few hours.

My dick twitched and my heart swelled at the thought.

"My room. Tequila. Hot girls. Come on!" Matt hollered, jogging down the long hallway towards his room. A collective 'Hell yeah' resounded in the narrow space, followed by several high fives.

"Nah, man, I'm gonna pass tonight," Sawyer interrupted. I bit down on the inside of my lip, refusing to let the smile tickling the edges of my lips show.

Being Sawyer Knight

"You pass every fuckin' night lately," Matt grumbled. "You're turning into an old fuckin' man, what the hell is wrong with you, dude?"

"I'm just beat, that's all," Sawyer said, pursing his eyebrows in frustration.

By this point Darren and Gavin were already in Matt's room, the rest of my team were dealing with hotel security downstairs and Claire was at Spur, an exclusive club in the city centre, confirming the after show party details for tomorrow night. I had no idea where Laurelin was and I didn't particularly care. She's just one of those people who grate on your nerves, even though you can't pinpoint why. She rubs me up the wrong way, and if I'm honest I don't really see the point of her. None of the other guys have a PA. I think Sawyer is just being a fucking diva.

"G'night, guys," I said, heading towards my room. This conversation didn't involve me. I was here to protect the guys, not party with them. Sawyer nodded, and I could tell by the position of his mouth that he was biting the inside of his lip. As I unlocked my door and stepped inside, the only thing on my mind was that I would be tasting that lip very soon.

I was still alone in my room at 2AM. I'd expected Sawyer to join me almost immediately, yet three hours had passed and there was still no sign of him. I'd showered, shaved, ordered up a bottle of chilled red wine – which was now almost empty – and stared at the TV, unable to concentrate on whatever was showing.

Giving up and sighing heavily, I knocked back the last mouthful of wine in my glass, set it down on the glass coffee table and decided to turn in for the night. My foot was hovering over the plush white bedroom carpet when it came – a knock on my door. Walking over to it, I purposely loosened the knot in my robe a little. I was certain I would find Sawyer on the side - no one else would stop by during the middle of the night.

"You came?" I stepped aside, holding the door open as he walked into my room. His shoulders were hunched and his head down as he took one last glance into the corridor before I closed the door.

"You doubted I would?"

"Maybe," I shrugged slightly. "I thought I'd scared you off by telling you I want you to fuck me."

The short distance between us made my chest ache, so I closed it – making small steps closer to him and fixing my hands to his hips. I briefly closed my eyes, inhaling his unique scent mingled with stale whiskey and body wash.

"You *did* scare me. But that's not why I'm so late. The guys have noticed a change in me apparently. I can't afford them to start poking their noses into my business so I went back to Matt's room for a few drinks. I need to make the effort. I can't seem to muster an interest to spend any time with anyone but you, and… they're starting to notice."

"So you want to spend time with me, huh?" I asked with a devilish smile, ignoring his comment about me scaring him. By the end of the night, he wouldn't feel any fear – only pure desperation to come deep inside me.

"So much," he whispered, cupping my face in his strong hands. His calloused thumbs, rough from years spent playing the guitar, smoothed along my freshly-shaved face, making me moan. "I've *never* wanted to be with anyone as much as I want to be with you," he admitted, making my heart dance to a hundred different melodies.

Sawyer instigated the following kiss. Dropping his hands to my waist, he undid the loose knot on my robe and slid his hands inside, grabbing my bare arse cheeks with his hands. Then his tongue darted out, tracing the edges of my lips before delving fully into my mouth. I pressed my erection up against him as I pulled him in by the hips. Breaking the kiss, he looked down at the throbbing head, nestled between us and peeking up at him, and he grinned.

"I can't wait to taste you again," he murmured, giving my arse one last squeeze before completely abandoning me and walking towards the bedroom

Holy fucking hell… Where were his nerves? His doubts? You know what, I didn't care. Sawyer Knight was making his way to my bed, tugging his ripped jeans down and exposing the top of his glorious arse along the way. Fuck, the thought of burying myself between those firm cheeks almost set my body on fire.

Discarding his clothes to the floor as he walked, Sawyer wasted no time in lying down on my bed, propping himself up on one elbow. Biting my lip in anticipation, I followed his lead - undressing quickly and throwing my robe behind me, dismissing my usual routine of folding it over a chair.

I climbed in next to him, on top of the bed sheets, and laid a flattened palm on his perfectly sculpted abs. Fuck, he's so beautiful. He always has been. My hand wandered down over his firm muscles until my fingers reached the patch of hair surrounding his cock. I drew tiny spheres on his pubic bone with the tip of my finger, making his cock twitch. Unable to wait a second longer, I wrapped my fingers around his erection, hugging it tight before stroking him up and down. Sawyer let out a throaty groan, tossing his head back and encouraging me to move faster.

Still gripping his cock, I shifted myself closer to him and buried my face in his neck. I licked and kissed my way up along his strong, stubbled jaw and settled on his lips. He parted them willingly and I dipped my tongue inside, kissing him passionately and moaning into his mouth.

"I need you to touch me, Sawyer," I gasped. I was so hard I could've bent steel and if my balls throbbed any harder I was sure they would explode. "And then I need you to fuck me."

"A-are you sure?" he stuttered nervously.

"God yes. I've wanted nothing else for so damn long," I assured him, loosening my grip on his cock and rolling onto my back. Drawing his lip into his mouth, he rolled with me, cupping my face in his hands and swiping his tongue across my lips.

"Can I go down on you first?"

Being Sawyer Knight

"Hell, Sawyer… the answer to that question will *always* be yes."

After the briefest of kisses, Sawyer nibbled and sucked his way down my body. I smoothed my hands across his broad shoulders, up his neck and then twisted his hair between my fingers, anchoring him to me. After shimmying down the bed, he hovered his mouth over my balls, looking up at me with that nervous, yet fucking stunning glint in his eyes. I gasped when I saw the tip of his tongue slide out of his mouth and he hadn't even touched me yet.

"*Jesus…*" I whispered hoarsely when he started licking small circles on my sac. I felt it all the way through my body, causing me to writhe on the mattress, desperate for more.

Lifting my head slightly, I watched him take me into his mouth. I couldn't take my eyes off him as I encouraged his head up and down with my hand wound into his thick, dark hair. It was an image I'd imagined countless times in my life, one I'd now actually seen a couple of times, and one I would *never* get tired of watching.

Unlike Sawyer, I'm not cut, and when he rolled down my foreskin and dotted slow, tender licks around the sensitive head, I almost exploded there and then in his mouth. Releasing my dick with a loud pop as if he sensed how close I was, I stared curiously as Sawyer licked his finger. When the said finger started travelling south I knew exactly what he was going to do and I couldn't fucking wait.

"Oh fuck…" I panted, bucking my hips as he pushed one finger slowly inside me. "Yes… fuck yes…"

"Does that feel good?" Sawyer asked. His voice was curious, like he was asking a genuine question.

"You have no idea."

With that, he inserted a second finger and I swear my eyes rolled into the back of my head. He scissored his slick fingers slightly, stretching me and making me want to scream from the pleasure. Then he crooked one finger, hitting my prostate gland... and it was too much.

"I'm ready, baby. I need you to fuck me now."

Slowly, Sawyer's fingers withdrew from my body. I missed the closeness already, so I sat up and started working his cock with my hand while I kissed him.

"Um... you should turn over," he mumbled apprehensively into my mouth.

"No," I said. "I want to be able to watch you. I need to look into your eyes as you fill me." A faint look of hesitation swept over his face, causing his eyebrows to knit together. "What's wrong?"

"Nothing. Well... it's just... I've never, um... *done* it that way before."

"You mean fucked up the arse or face to face?" I asked, putting it bluntly and finding the blush in his cheeks adorable.

"Both."

"You mean... you've always done it from behind?"

Seriously?

"I don't like having to look them in the eye. Makes it too personal I guess." He shrugged and looked away from me. I felt his dick begin to soften in my hand and I sure as hell refused to let that happen.

The Sawyer Knight kneeling naked and glorious in front of me wasn't the confident, notorious and gifted man the rest of the world thought they knew. The man I was looking at, the man whose cock I was holding, the man who I have loved since I was fourteen years old, was fragile and innocent. He was afraid of rejection and that made him ashamed of who he really was.

I vowed in that very moment to change that. I will show him that love is love, no matter what gender they may be, and I will prove to him that he deserves to love and be loved.

"Baby look at me," I demanded, stroking his dick, bringing it back to life while I turned his face to mine with my free hand. "I'm not '*them*', and you *will* look at me. I'm different, Sawyer. *We're* different. This isn't just about what you're feeling here," I said, gently squeezing his cock. "It's also about what's going on in here." I laid my palm over his heart. I could feel it throbbing in rhythm with my own and I knew he could feel it too.

"Okay," he breathed, his eyes locking onto mine. I brought him in for another kiss. Wrapping my arms around his waist, I caressed his back, smoothing my palms up and down and moaning into his mouth at just how good his skin felt against mine. When I broke away, I leaned across to the bedside table and plucked out a condom and some lube. Sawyer's eyes widened just a little, so I kissed him again while hugging him hard.

"I've got you, baby," I assured him. "Take it as slow as you need. Just enjoy it."

Dropping the condom and lube onto the mattress beside me, I laid down on my back with my legs apart. Never taking his melted caramel eyes off mine, Sawyer tore open the condom and rolled it down himself. He stroked his handiwork up and down a few times before smothering his impressive erection in lube, and I couldn't do anything but stare at him. He fascinated me. Everything about him.

I love him.

Sawyer nestled himself between my legs and I lifted them, supporting the weight with my hands behind my knees. His thick cock nudged at my hole while he rubbed his hands over my flat stomach. I was ready for him. It felt like I'd been ready for him forever.

"You're sure?" he asked.

"Just do it, baby. Fill me." Closing his eyes, Sawyer finally did what I'd been waiting a lifetime for. He pushed in slowly, stilling completely when he was met with the ring of resistance. "Keep going," I encouraged.

"I don't want to hurt you."

"You won't, I promise." Opening his eyes and staring down at what he was doing, he drove all the way, making me gasp. "Oh, God *yes*."

He didn't move for a few seconds, as if he instinctively knew my body needed time to adjust to him. My dick started to weep pre-cum when he started doing slow, shallow thrusts. I don't think I'd ever been so goddamn hard in my life and at this rate I was going to come without even touching myself.

"Fuck, you're so tight," he ground out, gritting his teeth. Hearing him as well as *feeling* him did insane things to my body and I could already feel the beginnings of an orgasm starting to tingle in my spine. He continued with torturously unhurried thrusts, making me moan in a mixture of pleasure and frustration.

"I need you deeper, baby. Faster. I won't break."

Sucking his bottom lip between his teeth to stifle his groans, Sawyer tucked his hands under my arse, dragging me closer to him and raising my hips. I hooked my legs over his shoulders and he tipped his head back, dragged in a deep breath and started pounding into me so hard my head bounced repeatedly off the headboard. Reaching down, I curled my fingers around my cock, not allowing myself to stroke because I knew I would come with just the slightest friction.

"Open your eyes, Sawyer." It took a few seconds but eventually he did. His eyes pierced mine and I could see the doubt swimming behind them as he drew his eyebrows together. "Stay with me, baby. Look at *me*. We're in this together."

"I... I'm gonna come, Jake," he stuttered, giving me all the ammunition I needed. I tightened the grip I had around my cock and started tugging. Sawyer's speed increased and he slammed into me hard and deep, his balls slapping against my arse with every thrust. My free hand reached out and I ran the pads of my fingers down the front of his taut body, massaging the mist of sweat dusting his skin into the deep grooves surrounding his inked muscles. "Oh fuck... I'm-I'm..."

"That's it, baby," I encouraged, my voice rough and eager as I continued to tug myself off. "Fuck yes! I'm coming, Sawyer. I'm gonna come so fucking hard." On the note of my last word, my orgasm began. Pleasure radiated from the base of my spine, spreading through my hips and down into my balls, drawing them up into my body as spurts of creamy white spunk shot out all over my stomach.

"Oh…my…*fuck!*" Sawyer rasped, digging his fingers into my arse cheeks as he crashed into me one last time.

His body juddered above me as his breath came in short, fast pants. He was fucking stunning. Angling his head down, his damp fringe concealed one of his eyes and instinctively I reached up with my fingers and brushed it aside. His cheeks were flushed, the skin on his body glistening. My waning erection started stirring again at the sight of him still inside me. The real thing was so much better than any one of the thousand dreams I'd had about this moment.

It was, and *he* was, perfect.

"That was… *amazing,*" I breathed, still a little breathless. "*You* were amazing."

"It was? I mean… I did ok?"

His nerves about pleasing me made me smile. Sure, he'd had sex before. Hell, if the papers were to be believed he'd bedded more women than he'd had hot meals. But this was a first for him in so many ways and it felt amazing to know he'd chosen *me* to take those first steps with.

"Are you fucking kidding me? Sawyer, that was the single most amazing moment of my life. Did you not feel it too?"

"Yeah," he agreed, sighing. "Yeah I did."

Smiling proudly, I ran my fingers down his arm.

"Come on. Let's get cleaned up. Then we can talk."

"Talk? About what?"

"Anything. Everything. I don't just want you for sex, Sawyer. I want you for who you are, and there's so much I've missed while I was away. It's time to start getting to know each other again."

Pinching the condom around the base of his softening cock, Sawyer eased out of me, immediately leaving me feeling like a piece of me was missing. He crawled off the bed and went to the bathroom to dispose of the condom and came back with a damp towel. His hand hovered over my stomach for a moment, as if wondering whether he should clean me up. Laughing softly, I took the towel from him and proceeded to wipe myself clean. Then, after tossing it onto the floor, I patted the mattress next to me for him to join me.

I didn't want the night to end.

Chapter Nine

~Sawyer~

"*How* do you feel?" Jake asked, rubbing his hand up and down my arm.

Hmm. How *did* I feel?

"Strange."

"Um, okaaaay. Good strange or bad strange?"

"Good. I think. It's difficult to explain."

"Try," he coaxed gently, curiosity lacing his smooth voice. His hand reached the top of my arm again but instead of going back down he stretched up and ran his fingers through my hair. I unconsciously nuzzled into his touch, like a cat rubbing against a leg. It didn't make sense to me how natural it felt to be with him this way. Naked, cuddling… touching.

"I feel…ugh how do I put this? It's like, ever since you left I've been surrounded by people. Friends, women, the guys, then fans, management, press… yet I've never felt so fucking alone. Now…" I trailed off, sucking in a shaky breath. "Now I don't feel lonely anymore."

"God, Sawyer, I've felt exactly the same for all these years."

I smiled lovingly at him. It was the type of smile that came naturally, the kind that take no effort, the type that make your heart swell in your chest.

"What about the sex?" he added with a devilish grin. "How did *that* make you feel?"

"Amazing," I sighed, my dick tingling at the memory. "I didn't know it would feel that good. But… does it feel good to, you know, be on the other end?"

"Are you asking me if it feels good to bottom?" he asked with a faint smirk.

"Yeah," I shrugged.

"Yes, it does," he answered without hesitation. "Takes a bit of getting used to, but I promise you when I get to fuck that tight arse of yours you'll never want me to come out."

My breath caught in my throat. The idea of being taken that way kind of terrified me, but at the same time my dick throbbed at the thought. Was it so appealing because it was a man suggesting he would do those things to me, or because it was Jake? My best friend. My…

Well, I'm not too sure what he is yet.

"Don't worry, baby, I'll take care of you," he added, snapping me back to the present. "You went a little white there for a second," he teased, stroking down the side of my face. I smiled, I think. I was still a little too paranoid about the nerves I was putting out to be sure. "What happened here?"

Using the tip of his forefinger, Jake traced the length of the scar above my left eyebrow. It's barely noticeable these days, unless you're as close up as Jake was.

"Jerry happened." Damn, I was hoping I'd never have to have this conversation again.

"Your stepdad?"

"Yeah."

Please don't ask me to elaborate.

"What the hell happened?"

"We got in a fight, that's all."

"About what?"

"Dammit, Jake, does it matter?"

"Whoa...I didn't mean to upset you."

Slowly stroking his way down from my face, along my neck and down to my chest, he laid gentle kisses along my shoulder.

"I'm sorry," I said, guilt making my voice gruff. "You didn't upset me. It's just... it wasn't a good time for me back then."

"Talk to me, Sawyer. I want to get to know you again. *All* of you."

The concern dulling his usually bright blue eyes made my chest ache, and in that moment I couldn't have refused him anything.

"The day at the bus station. The day when you... *kissed* me... someone saw us. One of Jerry's friends. When I got home he threw me against the wall and beat the living shit out of me."

130

I shrugged, aiming for nonchalance but failing miserably. Even after all these years the memory still managed to make my stomach roll and my eyes damp.

"How badly did he hurt you?" Jake asked, shifting closer to me on the bed and curving his hand around the back of my neck. His touch... I'd never felt anything like it. It made my skin tingle, my heart rate quicken... I was comfortable with him. I felt safe with him. When I was with Jake, I was no longer famous. I wasn't a star. I was just a man. A man who was possibly falling in love... and it was the most exhilarating, terrifying feeling in the world.

"Pretty bad. I was in the hospital for two weeks. He kicked me so hard he punctured one of my lungs."

I winced at the memory. It's as fresh and vivid in my mind as if it happened just this morning. 'Dirty fucking queer' he yelled at me, over and over again while he punched me. I fought back, of course I did. Landed a few bruises on him here and there but he was so much stronger than I was. I remember everything up until the point I heard my nose crack under the weight of his fist, then he must've knocked me out because my next memory is waking up in the hospital after being 'jumped for my wallet'.

I screamed at him until the point he'd knocked all the air from my lungs. I denied it, blamed Jake. I told him I wasn't queer and that the thought of it sickened me. I shouted it until my throat burned, said Jake forced himself on me and that I hated him for it. At the time, I did. At least I *wanted* to. I wasn't gay – a poof, bender, shirt lifter, shit stabber... that wasn't who I was. It's only now I'm starting to wonder if maybe I *was* that person, I just didn't *want* to be.

"Jesus Christ. I'm so sorry." Jake's arm was draped across my stomach and he snuck his hand under my back, squeezing me a little tighter. "I hope they locked that bastard up for long fucking time."

"I didn't report it," I admitted, avoiding eye-contact with him.

"Why the hell not?"

"Because I wanted to forget it!" I snapped unintentionally. I immediately felt guilty and softened my tone. "I didn't want anyone to know what he saw. I was so… ashamed I suppose. My mum would've disowned me, my friends would've ripped the ever living piss out of me. I couldn't talk to anyone. You were gone and I hated it. Then I hated that I hated it. I've never stopped thinking about you, Jake. Fuck knows I've tried, but since that day… I've just never felt 'right'. I've got a life most people can only dream of yet I've always felt like something was missing. I never knew what that something was, until now."

"Sawyer," he breathed, leaning up to nibble my neck.

"Mmmhmm?"

"I need you to fuck me again."

Without a second's doubt, I gripped Jake's shoulders and forced him onto his back. Rolling on top of his toned body, I brought my face to his, our noses touching.

"What the fuck are you doing to me?" I whispered hoarsely, then I crashed my lips to his, and made love to him until we were both numb.

When I started to stir, an arm draping over my hips startled me to full consciousness.

"Shit!" I exclaimed, making Jake jump to a sitting position. "It's 4AM! I need to stop falling to sleep with you."

I tried to throw a leg over the edge of the bed but Jake pulled me back.

"Calm down, Sawyer. When have you ever known any of the guys to be awake at this hour the morning of a show? I'm not saying it's not time for you to leave, but let's just take a moment, huh? Wake up together."

"Hmm," I sighed, pulling my leg back into the middle of the bed. "Ok. Just a few minutes though."

I lay down back down on my side so we were face to face. He was so close I could feel his breath on my face. For the first time, I looked at him, getting lost in his eyes, and I allowed myself to admit something both to him, and myself.

"You're really beautiful," I said, raising my hand and stroking my fingers through his short, black hair. To admit that out loud was terrifying, yet it rolled off my tongue as if it was the most natural thing in the world to be so attracted to him.

"You think so?" He was wearing a teasing smile, staring back at me with the most hypnotic eyes I'd ever seen. Honestly, they were crystal blue. Flawless. Completely mesmerising.

I never stood a chance.

"Tell me how you feel about me, Sawyer. I'm not asking you to say you love me, I just need to know where you're head's at. If we're heading towards the same goal."

Wow. Serious much?

"I don't know what my goal is," I said honestly. "I haven't let myself think that far ahead. Guess I'm still trying to get used to *this* first. To us."

"And how's that going?"

"I can't stop thinking about you. I can't stop wanting you, *needing* to touch you. You need to know I really care about you, Jake. I don't know if that's what love is, but I know I will never intentionally hurt you. I don't ever plan to push you away again, but I also can't promise I won't. You're the only person in the world who knows me absolutely. My whole life is an act, and I can be myself with you. You have no idea how liberating that feels."

"That'll do for now," he whispered, leaning into me and brushing my lips with his.

"Listen, I've been thinking."

"You sure that's a good idea?"

"Funny," I said, forcing sarcasm into my voice. "I own a house in the Lakes. It's really secluded, far away from everything and everyone. I thought maybe you'd come

134

and spend a week with me there before we need to head to LA. We'd have to think of an excuse. I don't want anyone knowing I'm there, or especially that you're there with me. And of course, if you don't want to then, you know, that's ok. It was just an idea. You know what, it was a stupid idea…"

"You finished rambling?" he teased, running his hand along my spine towards the base of my neck. "That sounds *perfect*. I can't think of anything I want more than to wake up with you every morning." I smiled, sighing with relief. "I kinda love how nervous I make you," he added, massaging the back of my neck as he encouraged my head forward until our noses were touching.

"I never knew you were such a sadist."

"There's a lot you don't know about me, baby. We need to change that."

I continued staring at him, studying his face, when a random thought popped into my mind.

"You know, you kinda look a bit like Justin Bieber."

"What the fuck?" Jake yanked his head back, screwing his face up in what could've been either confusion or disgust. I guessed probably both. "Justin Bieber is what? Twelve?"

"Ok, his dad then."

"Have you been smoking weed?"

"I'm serious! Obviously you're older and have darker hair, but if you squint your eyes a little, there's just something there that reminds me of him."

"So you think Justin Bieber's attractive?"

135

"Fuck no! You're hardly his fucking double. I just meant, some of the expressions you do kinda remind me of him. You're like his much sexier, much smarter, much older uncle."

"Jesus, I'm twenty-eight. You make me sound ancient."

"Sorry, Beebs. Didn't mean to make you feel old," I joked, playfully punching his arm.

"*Beebs*? Seriously? How the hell did we go from a deep and meaningful conversation to *this*?" He rolled his eyes at me, but then met me with a dazzling smile. "It feels like a dream, being here with you," he continued, his face smoothing into a serious expression.

"For what it's worth, I'm sorry about how I treated you that day. I've never forgotten it, and I've always regretted it."

"We were just kids, Sawyer. I was leaving anyway, no point in going over old ground."

"I'm still sorry."

"You can make it up to me," he whispered suggestively, raising an eyebrow.

"Oh yeah? And how could I do that?"

"Let me show you."

Pressing his lips to mine, he slipped his tongue into my mouth while gently tugging at my hair. My body automatically arched, pushing my cock against his. He was hard, like me, and I ground myself against him before slipping my hand between us and gripping both of our erections in one hand.

Being Sawyer Knight

Then, I made it up to him.

"Yo Sawyer! You in there, buddy?" Kip's voice bellowed through the door, accompanied by knocking.

I was back in my own suite after leaving Jake's around 5:30AM. I snuck back into my room, showered and changed for the day. I thought about going back to sleep, but every time I closed my eyes all I could see was the image of Jake writhing beneath me on his bed. Needless to say, that sparked an instant hard-on, but if my dick had any more friction in one night I probably would've gotten freakin' blisters. So I distracted myself by packing up my small case, then, draping a damp towel over my head I hovered my face over a bowl of hot water, breathing in the steam and loosening my vocal cords ready for tonight's show.

"One sec!" I hollered, making my way to the door.

"Claire rang you yet?"

"Um, no. Why?" Kip walked straight past me and plopped himself down on one of the couches.

"She wants us all downstairs in twenty. She had her serious voice on. My money's on Matt getting some chick up the duff."

"Fuck," I mumbled. "That doesn't sound good. It's bound to be something to do with him. Always is. Stupid fucker."

"Hey, grab us a bottle of water from the fridge will you?"

"Fuckin' warned you, dude. We've been in this game ten years and you've not learned not to get shitfaced the night before a show."

"Yeah, yeah. Just get us the damn water huh, Dad?"

After grabbing two bottles of water, I joined Kip on the couch. I relaxed into the soft leather and popped my feet up on the coffee table.

"Hey, mate… is everything okay with you lately?" In a nanosecond, the atmosphere turned so thick and serious I almost choked on it. "You've been kind of… *off.*"

"Sure. I'm fine," I shrugged, aiming for indifference.

"Come on, mate, we've been friends forever. I know when something's going on with you. I've been thinking it's a chick, but then I reckon I'd know. We live in each other's pockets. I'd have seen her."

"Kip, there's nothing wrong with me. Jesus!" I snapped, and then I became even more frustrated with myself. I should've just laughed it off, that's what I'd have done if there was in fact nothing wrong with me.

"Hey, chill the fuck out. I'm just worried about you, that's all. It's a woman isn't it? Just tell me. You know it won't go any further."

"Fine! It's a woman, okay? Now just fucking drop it."

I knew the second I'd said it I'd fucked up. But surely I could just spin the lie out for a couple of weeks and then 'break up' with 'her'.

"Who is it?"

"No one you know."

"Bullshit! We've been on the road for months. You couldn't have kept her hidden from us." Yeah, I'd definitely fucked up. "Holy shit, it's Laurelin isn't it?"

"*What?* Hell no!"

"Oh fuck me, please don't tell me it's *Claire?*" he pressed, wrinkling his nose in disgust. "Mate, she's practically our fucking mother!"

"Of course it's not Claire. Stop being such a dick."

"Then who the hell is it?"

"Elle!" *Shit.* "Happy now?"

It was the first name that came into my head, and now I had officially, wholeheartedly and irrevocably… fucked the hell up beyond repair. Or had I? Elle would go along with it. She's my best friend. If I just explained to her what'd been going on, she'd have my back. Actually, this might turn out to be a pretty good plan.

"Hey, where you going?" Kip jumped up suddenly, making his way to the door.

"We're wanted downstairs, remember?" And with that, he opened the door and left, slamming it behind him.

"Guess I'll see you down there," I said to the empty room. What the hell did I do to piss him off?

After chugging down my bottle of water in one, I dragged my shoes on and headed out. Neil was waiting for me by the lift and together we made our way downstairs to one of the smaller conference rooms where Claire was apparently waiting for us. We were the last to arrive and the first person I noticed when we entered the room was Jake. I allowed myself a quick glance up and down his body, admiring how fucking hot he looked in one of those black suits he always wears and trying not to imagine them lying on the floor next to him. The second person to catch my eye was our manager, Philip. If Phil was here, something was seriously wrong.

"Ok, now we're all here," Matt began, rubbing his hands together. "Let's get this party started."

Hmm, well Matt seemed to be his usual twat of a self. That ruled out this meeting being about him.

"Ok, guys, something potentially serious is going on," Claire said, followed by a heavy sigh. "We've been receiving some threats. Most likely some kind of stupid prank, but you need to be aware of what's going on."

"What kind of threats?" Gavin piped up.

"Death threats," Jake said firmly, taking over the conversation.

"Jake," Claire interrupted. By the way she shook her head I suspected she didn't want us to know the full extent of whatever the hell was going on.

"They need to know, Claire." Turning his attention to us, he continued. "It began a few months ago. At first it was a few letters. In my opinion the efforts of an amateur. They started out quite cryptic, but now they're making it pretty clear what they mean. Before the show yesterday we found a dead cat in Sawyer's room with a note attached to it."

"Holy fuck!" Daz said. "What do they want?"

"They've not said. It's likely nothing, you know things like this come with the territory," Jake tried to assure. I'm sure it worked for the rest of the group, but I knew his eyes, and the way they were drawn down slightly told me this was a real concern for him. "The police are aware of the situation and we're interviewing additional security recruits when we arrive in LA."

"Fuck 'em," I said. "It's probably just some stupid kid."

"I thought the same, until it became apparent they have access to your itinerary. They've been sending these letters to places you're scheduled to stay that only yourselves, appointed staff and security would know about. As yet, we haven't worked out how they know that information, and discovering that is my first priority."

"Look guys," Phil interjected, causally waving his hand. "We don't want you worrying about this. You should know what's going on, that's all. You have a great team behind you. Nothing's going to happen."

"I agree." And I really did. I trusted our security team undoubtedly. "I don't know about you guys but I'm not gonna give this shit another thought."

"So can we go back to bed now?" Matt groaned, stretching his arms above his head and yawning. "I'm fucking beat."

"Yes, I suppose so," Claire said. "What about you, Kip? Do you have anything to say?"

"No," he bit. He'd been silent with his arms folded across his chest the whole time. What was *with* him?

"I'm outta here." Matt was the first to get up from the table, closely followed by Pete. Eventually we all followed suit, Jake and I purposely keeping distance from each other, and then I headed back to my suite to get ready for tonight.

We'd been sitting backstage in the arena for almost an hour waiting for Elle to arrive. She was never late, and it worried me. I tried calling and got voicemail which only made it worse.

"Sorry sorry sorry!" she called, rushing into my dressing room where we were all waiting for her. A young guy trailed behind her, pulling a suitcase behind him. He was young, early twenties max, he had hand and neck tattoos and tapers in both ears. "I had to pick Ryder up from the station, take him to the hotel so he could sign the NDA Claire had drawn up and then my phone died. So guys, this is Ryder," she announced, gesturing her hand towards him. "He's my junior stylist and I'm bringing him along on the rest of the tour. I've cleared it with Phil and Claire."

We all greeted him with a mix of hey's, hi's and a 'wassup' from Matt. He came to each of us, briefly shaking each of our hands.

"It's great to meet all of you," he said with a wide smile. "Massive fan."

"Thanks," I replied, wondering why Elle hadn't mentioned him before.

"Guess we'd best get cracking," Elle said, bending down to the case Ryder had brought and pulling out her styling gear. "Ryder, you're with Sawyer and I'll get started on the other guys in another room." Great, so I was getting landed with the new kid. "There's no way you're ready to spend any time alone with Matt yet."

"Hey!" Matt piped up. "You know girls only diss guys when they secretly want to chow down on their man-meat."

"Maybe when I was fourteen, dickwad."

Soon enough, the room cleared, leaving me alone with Ryder.

"So," he began, standing behind me and making eye-contact in the large mirror I was sitting in front of. He had a deep, smooth voice. The judgemental side of me assumed he would talk like a prissy, what with him being a hairdresser. "How do you want it?"

"I don't care," I said. "Elle just tends to do whatever the hell she wants with it."

"Got it," he said, blowing out a short laugh, clearly understanding that you don't really say no to Elle.

"So how long have you worked for Elle?" I asked while he combed and tugged at bits of my hair.

"Coming up to three years. I trained with her. She's a cool boss to have and a pretty good friend too."

"She sure is. Don't know about the boss part though. I imagine she's quite the hardass."

"Ha! Let's just say you don't fuck with her," he said and I liked him instantly. "But seriously, mate, she's saved my arse so many times."

"How so?" I questioned and then quickly backtracked. "Hey, sorry, man. None of my business."

"No worries. I don't mind discussing stuff. I am who I am. If people don't like it, they can get fucked." Now I was really starting to like him. I admired his attitude to life. "Let's just say I was blessed with shit parents. They kicked me out last night. Had nowhere to go, so Elle arranged for me to come here with her."

"Shit. Sorry, dude."

"Don't be. I'll sort myself out. Always do."

"So what'd they kick you out for?"

"They found out about my second job." I looked up at him in the mirror and he drew his bottom lip, which was pierced on both sides, into his mouth as if to reign in his smile.

"*Second* job? You don't just work for Elle?"

"I'm also an actor and model," he said, cocking an eyebrow. Why would that warrant his parents kicking him out? "For a gay porn company." That would be why.

"You're fucking with me?"

"Nope," he grinned. "It's only a low budget company. But I enjoy it, you know. What's not to love? I get paid for doing the thing I love most in the world."

"You're a porn star? For real?"

"Also known as Kyle Kingston." Ryder winked at me and if he hadn't have been styling my hair I would've shaken my head.

"Wow. I'm actually pretty stunned here."

Being Sawyer Knight

I didn't know why I was so surprised. I'd met my fair share of female porn stars over the years. Maybe it's because those girls were at planned events – I knew they'd be there and what they did for a living. Or maybe... probably... it was because he's a guy.

"Don't worry, mate. I'm not gonna pounce on you," he joked. "Unless you want me to," he added with another wink.

"Nah, I'm good thanks," I assured him, laughing him off. "So does it not interfere with your job at the salon? I imagine there're some clients that would judge you for that?"

"The only kind of people who would find out would be those who use the adult entertainment industry. You wouldn't know unless you went looking for me, and out of those who do, most would be too embarrassed to admit it, and the others think I'm a fucking god or something. So no, it's all good on that front."

"And you're what they call a twink, right?" I'm pretty sure a twink is a young-looking gay guy, lean, slender... pretty boy I guess.

"You know your stuff! I'm impressed." Shit. Didn't think that one through. I decided to stay silent from then on before I really landed myself in it. "I fucking hate that term though. The stereotypical twink is thought to be dumb as pig shit. I like to think I've got a bit more going up here." Laughing, he tapped the side of his head with the end of his comb.

He'd finished doing his thing with my hair after about twenty minutes. I eyed myself up in the mirror and nodded in approval. He seemed to have managed to control my wayward fringe so it was a thumbs up from me. That damn bit of hair annoyed the fuck out of me when I was on stage. I should really just get Elle to cut it off.

"Cool. Thanks, man," I said, standing up from my chair while he started packing his things away.

"No problem. I'll go see if Elle needs any help in the other room."

"Oh and, twink?"

"Arsehole."

"Good to meet you, buddy."

"You too, mate." Smiling, he turned for the door.

When he left the room I slumped down onto the leather couch, exhaling a dumbfounded laugh. I sure as hell wasn't expecting that scenario today.

Chapter Ten

~Sawyer~

"*On* in ten!" one of the arena men called out before talking into his radio. Our support act, an up and coming band called The Mark, had finished up and the roadies were getting the stage ready for us. We all congregated in the long white corridor backstage, waiting for our cue.

"Hey," Elle whispered, sneaking up behind me and tapping me on the shoulder. "Can I talk to you for a sec?" she asked, cocking her head behind her.

"Sure," I agreed, following her lead towards the quieter end of the corridor, away from the guys. "What's up?"

"Just wondering if Kip has said anything to you? Something's off with him."

"No, not said anything to me." It wasn't technically a lie. Kip genuinely hadn't told me what'd been eating his ass all day. I *did* know something was wrong with him though. I also knew his weird behaviour started when I told him I was dating Elle. *That* was a conversation I didn't have time for just before we went on stage so I

147

pleaded ignorance instead. "I'll have a word with him after the show."

"Thanks. I love *all* you guys. It bothers me when something's wrong."

"Don't worry, gorgeous girl. I'll get to the bottom of it, I promise."

"Okay. Good," she nodded, not seeming convinced. "Knock 'em dead out there tonight, muscle man."

"Always do," I winked. I brought her in for a quick hug and told her I'd meet her at tonight's after party. Then I headed back over to the guys, pulling up the collar on my ripped white shirt, and waited for our stage call.

The sound of the screaming crowd was deafening before we'd even reached the stage. Popping my earpiece in, I stepped out last, following behind the guys. It is the most powerful feeling in the world looking out at the swarms of people shouting, cheering and screaming your name. They were here for *us*... five ordinary guys with a passion for music. I will never get used to, nor tire, of it.

"MANCHESTEEEEEER!" Matt called out into his microphone, making the crowd go crazy. Smiling, I hooked my guitar over my shoulder and familiarised my fingers with the strings. "WHO WANTS TO HEAR SOME FUCKIN' GOOD TUNES, HUH?"

I started into the song, strumming my thumb over the strings. 'Forgotten' was a number one hit for us in twelve different countries back in 2012. It was a guaranteed crowd pleaser, and as expected, they went wild when the first note rolled from my lips. Kip was on keyboard, and usually I would walk up to the rest of the guys as I sang, giving them a high five, sharing microphones, that kinda shit. But when I approached Kip half way into 'Chasing the Impossible' his eyes pierced into me like daggers – a silent warning to back the fuck off.

That was the very first time I'd ever not enjoyed a show. After that moment I sang with a fake smile, yelled to the crowd with false enthusiasm, and wished the set would be over already. Kip's my best friend and I'd obviously upset him somehow. It concerned me, nibbled away at my brain throughout the entire show.

"THANK YOU, MANCHESTER!" I addressed the fans before raising both hands above my head. "AND GOODNIGHT!"

"ROCK ON MOTHERFUCKERS!" Those were Matt's parting words at the end of every show. Fuck knows why but the fans love it. They love *him*. They see him as the rebel, the playboy... instead of just a giant twat who's a few peppers short of a pizza.

Lifting my guitar off my shoulders, I passed it straight to a waiting roadie off stage. We were all immediately ushered off the stage and towards the back exit of the building where our cars were waiting for us with open doors. Obviously Jake and Neil were assigned to me, and so they were waiting for me by the car. Neil nodded, acknowledging my approach and Jake waited until I was inside the car before climbing in beside me. We were driving away in seconds, all in a row like a funeral procession.

"Great show, Saw," Neil said. I think he always felt obliged to compliment us, but really, he must be sick of our songs by now. I've caught him listening to Cliff freakin' Richards before now, so I don't think we're exactly his taste.

"Cheers, Neil."

I dared a glance at Jake and my breath faltered when I noticed his tie was missing and he'd undone the top three buttons of his white shirt, exposing just a glimpse of his firm chest. I swallowed hard, clearing my throat, and he must've noticed because he looked away and turned one side of his lips up into a smile. I don't think I'd ever seen Jake do the casual look, not since we were teenagers anyway, he was always pristinely dressed in a fine black suit, or jog pants if he was alone in his room – and by alone, I mean with me.

Pulling out his phone, Jake started tapping numbers on his screen.

"Have you informed them we're on our way...yes...good...ok we can give them ten minutes I suppose... thanks, Pete." He clicked his phone off and then shifted slightly in his seat to face me. "We'll be going through the front doors to the club. There's a gathering outside, we can walk you through them. Stop for a few autographs and such."

"Sure," I answered. "No problem."

"Elle and Ryder are in the car behind with Kip and Dave. I added them onto the guest list this afternoon."

"Why didn't you tell me about Ryder?"

"That's Claire's job, not mine. My job is to keep you safe, not discuss your staffing requirements." His voice was sharp and to the point. Had I pissed him off too? What the hell was wrong with everyone today?

I turned to the window and stayed that way for the rest of our twenty minute journey. Suddenly, this night wasn't looking like it was going to be so much fun anymore.

When we arrived at the club, Sawyer and Neil vacated the car first. My driver, Frank, stayed behind with me until the rest of the guys had arrived too. Once they had, Jake opened my door for me and I stepped out onto the crowded street. Our security team had formed a protective circle either side of us as we made our way towards the entrance of Spur.

"Sawyer! Sawyer!" Girls chanted my name, reaching their arms out in front of them, trying to touch me.

"Oh my God, oh my God, Oh my God!" one girl squealed when I strode over to her. "I love you so much!"

"Love you right back, baby," I said, giving off the wink it seemed every woman adored. "Hey, Neil!" I called him over, took the girl's camera phone out of her hand and passed it to him. I draped my arm across her shoulders while Neil took our picture. She clung onto me so tightly, fisting her hand in my leather jacket. Neil nodded, and passed the camera back. "Thank you! Thank you so much! Oh my God I love you!"

"What's your name, sweetheart?" I asked, taking the pen she offered as she held out a poster of the band in her other hand.

"Jasmine!" she choked out. Her hands were literally shaking as she held out the poster. It seemed so bizarre that I could affect someone in that way. It almost makes me feel bad for them.

"Nice to meet you, Jasmine," I said, smiling as I handed her the pen back.

I repeated this process several times as I made my way down the line. I looked behind me a few times and saw the other guys doing the same thing, except for Matt, who of course was practically dry-humping a blonde. When we neared the doors, Jake and Pete put a stop to any more people approaching us and steered us inside the building. We were greeted by the club's manager and several members of his own security team, who led us up to the private floor.

The music was loud and energetic, and when we arrived upstairs people were already half-wasted and dancing. It was an exclusive party – invite only. On this occasion invites were sent out to everyone who had helped out with our UK leg of the tour and our friends too. By friends, I mean acquaintances – mainly other celebrities and musicians. Unless it's someone you've known since you were a kid, there's no such thing as a true friendship in this business. On top of those, there always seemed to be a scattering of girls wearing barely more than their underwear at these parties. I'm pretty sure most of them are Matt's 'friends'.

Drinks were flowing freely. One of the perks of this game, you don't have to do jack shit for yourself. I hadn't even made it over to the table in the corner before someone had plied me with two bottles of beer.

Personally, I'm a whiskey drinker, but beer would do just nicely as a starter.

"What are you sitting down for?" Matt hollered over the raucous music. "Have you not *seen* the amount of pussy out there? Come on, dude. Get your ass out here on the floor!"

"Count me in!" Daz sang.

Daz has been an on-off relationship with a girl called Dana for the past five years. By the excitement in his eyes over the word 'pussy' I assumed they were going through an 'off' period. Gavin's also got a girl, but he just likes the chase. He's happy to buy chicks drinks and chat them up with the others but he always goes home alone. Matt… well I doubt anyone will be able to tame him.

"Just waitin' on Elle. I'll catch up with you later."

"Whatever, man," he dismissed, waving me off with his hand. He was gone as quickly as he came, Daz and Gavin following behind, and then I spotted Elle in the distance. She waved, letting me know she'd spotted me, then she shimmied over to my table in one of the shortest black dresses I've ever seen.

"You forgot to put your skirt on," I teased. She slapped me on the arm and then gave me the middle finger. Smiling, I took a swig of my beer and saw Ryder, Jake and Dave approaching.

"Have you talked to Kip yet?"

"Sorry, gorgeous girl, not had a chance yet. But I will before the night's out."

"Fuck me, I think I just saw Parker fucking Emerson over there!" Ryder screeched, making himself comfortable beside me. "This place is fucking amazing!"

I let out a small laugh. Places like this didn't blip on my radar anymore. Sad really. I kinda miss 'normal'. I miss being able to blend into a crowd, enjoy time with my friends without being watched. Hell I even miss simple things like taking a twenty out of my wallet and handing it to a barman.

"How do you go about getting a drink around here?" Ryder asked.

"Just head up to the bar, tell 'em what you want. You don't need money."

"Sweet!"

"How come you've never mentioned him before?" I cocked my head in Ryder's direction while Elle scooted closer to me on the plush bench seat.

"We never really talk about the salon. It bores you, remember?"

"Sure, but it sounds like you've done a lot for him. That must mean he's important to you. I thought we shared shit like that." Wow. I sounded like a teenage fucking girl.

"He's a good lad. Hard worker. Crazy fun too. I knew you wouldn't mind me bringing him with me and he'll have sorted somewhere to stay by the time the tour is over."

"Course I don't mind. He's seems nice enough. Never had you down for someone who'd employ a porn star though," I joked, raising my bottle to her.

Being Sawyer Knight

"He told you?" She sounded surprised but then seemingly thought better of it. "Of course he told you," she tacked on, shaking her head and smiling. "You should check out some of his movies. They're hot enough to make me want to grow a dick of my very own."

"You know, I sort of admire him. Such a young guy yet he seems to know exactly what he wants out of life."

"He wants to be happy, that's all. Sure, that's what we all want, but too often we let what *other* people want for us hold us back." Ain't the damn truth. "But not Ryder. He doesn't take shit from anyone."

Jake and Dave, drinks in hand (sodas of course), came to sit with us then, and our conversation about Ryder ended.

"So, Dave," I started, "How's the divorce going?"

"She's a fucking psycho," he said, offering his usual answer. "Says she's entitled to seventy percent of the house because she did the interior fucking design. Stupid bitch."

Dave's divorce has been going on for months, and it often leaves me wondering how you could possibly feel such a way about someone you once loved. Unless it wasn't really love. How do people even know what love is? I sure as hell don't. It's not like you get a badge, or your nose turns blue or anything. There's no proof it even exists. It's just a word people toss around too often that usually ends up causing pain. Or, as in Dave's case, excessive debt.

Ryder came back over to our table and put his beer down before sitting on the plush red stool opposite to me.

"The people here are pompous fucking twats," he grumbled. "Seriously, does no one know how to use manners anymore?"

"You'll find most people in this business are like that," Elle said.

"But not *all*," I added, feigning offence.

"You're kidding right? Bloody hell, Sawyer, you are the *king* of all miserable shits!"

Hmm. Yeah, she was probably right. So I let it go.

"Why do you invite these kind of people? We should just go some place else," Ryder suggested.

"Not that simple I'm afraid. You saw the effort it took to get us in here right?"

"Yeah I guess," he agreed. "Shame though. I know an *awesome* club not too far from here. Spiral. I used to come up here a lot when my grandma was alive. I'd come stay with her when shit got too bad at home."

"Spiral?" Jake butted in. "I know that place." He did?

"Amazing, right?"

"We might have time to sort something out. I can arrange something with my team if you want to go, Sawyer?"

What the hell? Jake didn't do spontaneous. *Ever.* That was another thing I missed though – spur of the moment.

"Sure," I said. Taking another swig of my beer, I used my free hand to start texting the guys to tell them to come to our table. "What about Claire? She won't be happy."

"She never is," Jake said, rising to his feet. Every one of us, except Ryder who hadn't had the pleasure of getting to know Claire yet, laughed.

Ryder went to find a toilet and Elle and I talked while we waited for Jake and the guys to get back. She asked me if the flights to LA had been arranged and I felt like a giant dick because I'd forgotten she was coming with me. Problem was, I'm not going straight to LA anymore. I'm taking Jake to my house in the Lakes. *Fuck.* I decided I would tell her in the morning, but as yet hadn't decided if I was ready to tell her about Jake coming with me.

"What the fuck, dude?" was Matt's response to my text when he walked up to me. "I was two fucking minutes away from nailing the most perfect piece of ass you've ever seen."

"They're *always* the most perfect piece of ass you've ever seen. You'll find another when we hit this new club."

"I don't get what's wrong with this place? Why the fuck did you book it if you wanna go elsewhere?"

"Claire booked it, and it won't kill us to be spontaneous for once, Matt. Don't you miss being able to go wherever the fuck you want?"

"Not really." I should've known better than to try and drag something meaningful out of Matt. "So when are we going?"

"Going where?" Gavin asked, coming up behind Matt. Daz and Kip followed, but of course Kip stayed back from the table. I was starting to feel really guilty and I didn't even know what for.

"We're ditching this place and heading to a new club Ryder told us about."

"Yeah?" Daz said keenly. "Cool."

"As long as that's the last place," Gavin chipped in. "I'm out to get wasted and I can't do that if we're playing musical fucking clubs."

"Okay, guys. We're on," Jake announced proudly when he got back. "Spiral are expecting us in an hour. They wanted to bring in some additional staff so we'll have to hang back here for a while first." Something was going on with Jake, I was certain of it. He seemed altogether too happy for a man that was usually so focused and serious. The cars will be back here for us in forty-five minutes, so all make sure you're at this table by then and we'll head out."

"Cool," Gavin shrugged. "I'm gonna go grab another beer." Kip and Dave followed him, and Matt had already disappeared. My guess was he was already banging some chick senseless against a wall somewhere.

"Back in a few minutes. Dave, you stay here." You see? *That* was the Jake we all knew. Stern and bossing people around. Not only was I curious where he was going, I also wanted to grill him about his fluctuating mood tonight.

"Going for a slash," I mumbled to Elle, trying to keep a subtle eye on Jake's movements.

Being Sawyer Knight

I weaved through the sea of people dancing, past the bar and then down the steps that led to the bathrooms. Perfect. Jake was just going to the toilet. It would be quiet and hopefully private enough to grill him.

I was relieved to see they were private bathrooms and not communal stalls. He hadn't seen me behind him, but I followed him inside and locked the door behind me.

"Sawyer?" he asked in surprise, turning to face me when he caught my reflection in the mirror. "What are you doing in here?"

"I wanted to see you."

He stepped slowly towards me and reached out to cup my neck. His touch sent sparks coursing through my entire body and I leaned my forehead against his, breathing him in.

"You were off with me in the car. Have I upset you?"

"I was '*normal*' with you in the car, baby. I treated you like I treat everyone else. I thought that's what you wanted?"

"Oh. I mean yes. I *do* want that. Sorry."

"You're flustered," he noted, stroking down my cheek that I could feel heating up. "I wonder if I'll ever stop making you nervous," he teased, grinning. "You're sexy when you're nervous."

"I want you so bad right now," I moaned against his mouth before flicking his tongue with mine. I pressed my hips into him, reaching between us and stroking his erection through his slacks.

"Then take me," he said. "Right here. Right now."

"Oh *fuck*…" I breathed when he tucked his fingers down the front of my jeans and gripped my dick in his hand. "We…*can't*." It was too risky. Hell, I'd already broken all the rules I'd set in place in my head just by coming in here. I couldn't fuck him somewhere so publicly.

"You locked the door right?"

"Yes." Didn't I? What if I didn't? Shit, I couldn't remember. "Wait I don't kn-"

"I love how you're always so hard for me, baby." He started stroking me up and down as far as the restrictions of my pants would allow. With one hand he started unbuttoning me, and when the air hit my rigid dick, I tipped my head back and moaned. "There are condoms and lube in my wallet," he whispered into my neck before smothering it with hungry kisses.

Why did he carry condoms around with him? Was he always expecting my walls to drop despite everything I'd said? When he pushed my pants down to my ankles and started pumping me harder however, I decided I didn't actually care.

"Fuck, Jake…" Reaching into his back pocket, I plucked out his wallet. Inside, hidden between the credit cards were two foil packets and a sachet of lube. I plucked them out eagerly, bringing them to my mouth to rip the packets open. Jake worked his belt and zipper, wriggling free from his pants while I suited myself up.

"You need to be fast, Sawyer. Fast and hard."

"But… it'll hurt."

"I'll be fine. We only had sex this morning. I don't need stretching."

Being Sawyer Knight

"Turn around," was my reply, and so he did. Gripping onto the sink in front of him, Jake bent over, exposing that striking ass I loved to pound so much. I squeezed half the sachet of lube onto my dick, spreading it with my fingers, and applied the rest around Jake's hole. I wasted no time in nudging at his entrance. Then I slowly eased inside, making him hiss in pleasure.

"You feel so fucking good inside of me, Sawyer."

I stilled for a moment, knowing he needed to get used to the intrusion. Then I started with slow, steady thrusts, easing in and out of him slowly. He quivered and moaned in front of me, turning me on to an astronomical level. Gripping his shoulder with one hand and bending over his back, I started grinding into him, bucking my hips as fast as I could go.

"Take your dick, Jake. Make yourself come for me," I panted. "Be quick. I won't last long."

I steadied myself on the sink unit with my other hand and tightened my grip on his shoulder, digging my nails into his flesh. I could see his face in the mirror and I stared at him intently. The sight of him biting down on his bottom lip made my dick pulse inside his tight ass, forcing me to slam even faster.

"I…love…fucking…your…ass," I cried out between harsh, deep thrusts. "So…fucking…much."

Leaning down, I nipped the skin on his back with my teeth, making him tremble.

"Don't stop, baby. Fuck me." It was starting. The tingle, the heaviness in my balls that were slapping against his ass as I fucked him. "I'm coming, Sawyer! Oh…my…*fuck*."

I reached around his waist and palmed his cock. He cried out with his release, biting into the sleeve of his jacket to stifle the sound as he shot his load over both of our hands. That was all it took. Feeling his warmth coating my fingers and feeling him shudder beneath me sent me crashing over the edge.

"*Fuck yes,*" I growled. "Damn, Jake…fuck yes."

I came with a violent shudder and poured myself into him. I was sweaty and breathless as I wound my arms around his waist and braced myself on the sink. But then in an instant, the blood drained from my body, pooling at my feet when I heard the bathroom door creak open.

"Oh shit!" Elle said, covering her eyes with her hand. "Sorry, sorry, sorry," she kept mumbling as she shot straight back out and closed the door behind her.

"Fuck!" I blasted, pulling myself out of Jake. "Fuck fuck *fuck!*"

"Calm down, Sawyer," Jake attempted to soothe while he rinsed his hands under the tap. After pulling up my pants I did the same in the sink next to his. "She's your best friend. You know you can trust her."

"THAT'S NOT THE POINT!" I yelled. "I screwed up goddammit! I can't control myself around you! We're becoming too complacent. We should've been more careful! This isn't going to work," I said, growling in frustration and slamming my fist into the wall. "This has to stop, Jake. I can't… I can't stop wanting you. It has to end here."

"Because you *want* me?" He jerked his neck back as if my words had literally punched him in the face. "You want to end this because you want me too much? That doesn't make any fucking sense! Listen to yourself!"

"Of course it does! It's too risky. When I'm around you common sense seems to fly straight out the fucking window. Sure, it was Elle, but it could've been anybody! What if it was one of the guys? Or papa-fucking-razzi? I've gotta get outta here."

"Sawyer WAIT!" he called after me, but I was already gone. I'd barely touched the bottom stair when he grabbed my arm, pulling me back.

"What are you *doing*?" I scolded. "We're in fucking public!"

"You either come with me or I'll say what I have to say right here."

"Are you threatening me?"

"No, Sawyer. I'm just not letting you go. Please, come with me."

Closing my eyes, I nodded. Didn't exactly give me a choice, did he?

He led me past the toilets and out through a fire exit, bringing us outside at the back of the building. He closed in on me, backing me up against the wall.

"We'll be more careful," he said. "Don't give up on us, Sawyer. *Please*. We've waited too damn long for this."

"It's too dangerous."

"No! It isn't! Let's spend the week together like we planned. Alone. Just you and me. Then when we get to LA and add to the team I'll appoint you a different bodyguard. We'll hardly have to see each other during the day. We can work this out. You ride with Elle to Spiral. Put up the partition and just talk to her. She'll help you out with this, I know she will."

"Jake I…"

"You feel it, Sawyer. I know you don't know what it is yet, but you feel *something*. Don't let that go. Not yet. Look, I'm going to go back to the hotel. Spiral is smaller than here. You guys will be fine with one less guard."

"You don't have to do that."

"Yes I do. You need some time to get your shit together, and I suspect I'm only going to make that more difficult for you. I let you push me away once before, and I've told you I *won't* let you do it again. We're going to the Lakes tomorrow and we're going to spend this week exploring each other. Body and mind. Do you hear me?"

"Yes," I breathed, unable to deny his eyes as they penetrated mine with so much hurt, *need…*love.

"The cars will be here soon," he said after breathing a sigh of relief. "I'll go and make my excuses, you round up the guys and head outside."

"Okay."

"I won't ever give up on you, Sawyer Knight, so don't you *dare* give up on *me*."

Those were the last words he spoke before he jogged back to the emergency door. He held it open for me and once I was inside he disappeared into the crowd.

Now all I had to do was face Elle.

Fuck.

Being Sawyer Knight

"You can't tell anyone about what you saw," was the first thing I said to Elle, the very second the partition rolled up, separating us from our driver.

"I can't believe you think you even have to say that to me!" she scowled, clearly offended. "You're my best friend in the world, Sawyer. Of course I wouldn't."

"Fuck. I know. I'm sorry. I'm just... oh fuck, Elle I don't know what the hell I'm doing."

"You care about him don't you? You always have."

I sighed heavily, unsure what to say. I decided at this point honesty was probably the best policy.

"Yeah. I really do."

"But you think that's wrong don't you? It's written all over your face. You're ashamed."

"I don't *want* to be. But I can't help it. The thought of people knowing terrifies me. Talking to Ryder before in my dressing room, I admired him so much. You know, there aren't many people I respect in this world, but he's one of them. Crazy, huh? I don't even know him."

"I know we've had this conversation before, but what exactly is it that scares you? Imagine the world finds out tomorrow, what's the worst that's gonna happen?"

"People will... I dunno... laugh. Put me down, put *Jake* down. I know it sounds ridiculous but I'm a fucking rock star, Elle. A celebrity. We're all wired with this crazy need for attention. To be adored, accepted. I *need* that. I need to feel like people want me, that they need me."

"But those people don't matter. People *do* need you. *I* need you. *Jake* needs you. Maybe you should have a long hard think about putting the people who genuinely care about you first. And don't take that as me saying we need to throw a coming out party with rainbows and butterflies tomorrow. It's your life and you deserve to keep parts of it private. All I'm saying is, don't push the only person I've known you care about in that way aside for fear or what *might* happen in the future. I don't think this is even about being gay. I don't think you want to let anyone in because you're scared of getting hurt."

"*What?* That's ridiculous."

"No it's not. If there's anyone in the world who understands you it's *me*. We're the same. Cut from the same cloth. You've never met your father and the only thing your mother's ever loved is her pride. The only difference between us is my mum chooses to love the booze instead. I know what it feels like to want somebody to love you, Sawyer. We all want someone to accept us, take care of us. Most people get it from their parents… we didn't and it's fucked up and hard to deal with."

"Is that why you've never had a serious relationship? Are you scared of letting someone in?"

"Looking back, yes. It was only recently I was forced to look back on how I reacted to people wanting anything more than a quick shag. I want more, Sawyer. I deserve more. And so do you."

"Are you saying you've met someone?"

"That's another story for another day. We're here."

I hadn't even noticed the car slowing down but, looking out of the window, I saw she was right. The other guys had arrived first and were waiting for us on the pavement. Ryder seemed to be quite at home, chatting away with Gavin. He was going to fit right in with us, however long he was around.

"About fucking time!" Matt complained. "Now… take me to that pussy."

"Oh," Ryder said, contorting his face into an 'ooops' expression.

"What?" Matt asked.

"Um… nothing." Ryder turned his head away from Matt and I caught the silent laugh he had to himself. Was there some kind of surprise waiting for us I hadn't been made aware of? Along with our own team, club security accompanied us into the building and the 'surprise' immediately punched me in the face.

Ryder had brought us to a gay club.

"What the actual *fuck?*" Matt yelled. "Where the hell's all the pussy?"

"Um, you'll still find some if you look hard enough," Ryder shrugged. "Straight people come here too. But I'm afraid they don't get many groupies looking for famous rock stars to fuck." The amusement on Ryder's face was palpable, and I couldn't help but smile.

"Ugh. Never again will I go along with you guys."

"Shut the hell up, twat," Daz said. "We're here now. Go and get us some beers."

"Fuck beer. The only way I will survive this place is to get off my fucking face and fucking quickly. Don't know about you guys but I'm having vodka. Lots of it."

Spiral was definitely a new experience for me. I'm not quite sure how I felt, most likely because I felt such a wide range of things during my time there. At first I was uncomfortable, possibly even nervous that somehow the people in here would 'know' about me. Like maybe they had some kind of sixth sense for spotting other gay people. Soon enough though, my discomfort morphed into a form of envy. I watched people dancing, couples embracing each other, laughing, joking, drinking… It was all so 'normal'. No different to any other regular nightclub, bar the fact most of the people groping each other were the same sex.

I realise now the reason for that is because it *is* normal. But it's too late for me. I've dug myself a hole too big to ever climb out of. If I was honest about who I really was now, people would want to know why I'd lied for so long. They'd know I was too ashamed to admit it for so many years. These people dancing and living their lives in front of me didn't deserve anyone being ashamed of who they are and what they represent. If I was to come out, I'd be letting them down.

"How long have you known?" Ryder's voice pulled me out of my thoughts. I hadn't noticed him sit down next to me. The rest of the guys were wasted, dancing and making utter twats of themselves on the floor somewhere no doubt, so I was alone. Our guards were around somewhere, lurking in the corners watching us from afar.

"Known what?" I asked casually. Ryder scanned the area around us as if looking for anyone who might hear us.

"That you're gay?" he whispered, hovering his mouth next to me ear so I would hear him above the music.

I felt the heat crawl down my cheeks, past my neck and down my body as the blood began to drain from my face.

"What the fuck are you talking about?"

"It's okay, mate. I'm not gonna tell anyone."

"I'm *not*..." I cut myself off. I was fucking exhausted. All these lies, all this worry... I was so tired of it, and like I told Elle earlier, for some bizarre reason my instincts told me I could trust this guy. "How did you know?"

"Because all your mates are out there getting pissed and having a good time. Whereas you, you've been sat here staring at people like you wished you could switch places with them. So I'm guessing this is all pretty new to you, even though I'm also guessing you've known all your life."

"Yeah, you could say that. To be honest, Ryder-"

"Call me Ry. Most people do."

"Well, Ry, I'm starting to piss myself off. Why the fuck does this have to be so difficult? It's not difficult for any of those guys out there." I gestured my hand towards the dance floor. "It's not difficult for *you*. I just feel kinda pathetic."

"Wow. Who would've thought Sawyer Knight – king of the music world - is a giant pussy?"

"Yeah," I agreed, laughing. "Sounds about right."

"Those people out there are happy because they've already been through and dealt with the shit you're going through. Happens to the best of us, mate. The doubt, the shame. Not everyone obviously, but most. But those guys you see out there have accepted themselves, and you will too."

"Yeah, I'm not too sure about that."

"Trust me. Might take you a little longer because you're a late starter." He winked at me and I shook my head. The guy's a real charmer. "Plus there's the fact you're a global fucking superstar... but you'll get there. Now, the more important question is, who is he?"

"Who's who?"

"The guy that's turned your world upside down."

"Someone I've known since I was a kid. He was my best friend."

"*Was?*"

"He had to leave when we were seventeen. His dad relocated him and his family to Australia. The day before he left... he kissed me and I turned on him. Told him I never wanted to see or speak to him again. The fucked up part of that is, I pushed him away because I wanted him so damn much. I just wasn't ready to admit it."

"And you're ready now?"

"You know what, Ryder? I have no fucking idea."

"I think you're nearly there. You wouldn't have told me shit if you weren't," he shrugged. "You don't even know me and you've probably just told me more about who you are than any one of your band mates. Am I right?"

"How old are you?" I asked curiously.

"Twenty-two. Why?"

"I'm probably gonna sound like an old man here but you're pretty wise for such a young man."

"Yeah, that happens when you have to raise yourself. That's why I live each day to the fullest. I do what I want, when I want, because I've spent too much time dealing with shit when I was growing up. Could be dead tomorrow, why waste it pretending to be something you're not? This is your only shot, Sawyer. Once they turn the burners on you don't get to come back and relive it. Right now, you look fucking miserable. Yet I bet when you're with your mystery guy you've never felt so fucking happy. Don't you wanna feel like that all the time?"

"But what if it doesn't last? What if something fucks up and I've lost all this, everything I've worked for, for nothing."

"Now you're just talking bollocks. You're not gonna lose anything. Those guys over there… they're your *friends*. Friends support each other. If they don't, then you never meant anything to them in the first place. Look at who you are and what you've achieved. You don't get that far in life without balls and determination. You need to stop waiting for the 'right' time. Trust me, there isn't one. Take a leap, Sawyer. It'll be the best thing you ever do. And on that note, I'm going outside for a smoke. Coming?"

"Nah. Think I'm gonna head back to the hotel actually."

"I hope to be not too far behind you…" he trailed off, scanning the room. "With that fit piece of arse over there by the bar."

"Well good luck with that," I said. Ryder downed the last of his beer and stood up, pulling his smokes out of his pocket. "And thank you. I'm glad we met, twink." I flashed him a smirk, knowing he would call me out for that remark.

"I might look like a twink, babe, but I fuck like an *animal*."

Funnily enough, I didn't doubt that for a second. After watching Ryder disappear into the sea of dancing bodies, I pulled out my phone and swiped across the screen until I hit Neil's number.

"Hey, dude. Can you get a driver to take me back to the hotel? I'm not feeling too great."

"Sure, Saw. No problem. I'll send Pete over to escort you out."

"Thanks. Catch you later."

"Sure, man."

"Can I come in?"

Being Sawyer Knight

Jake answered the door to me dressed in only his jogging pants. He searched my eyes with a curious expression and I gave him a weak, apologetic smile.

"You already know the answer to that." He stepped aside and I brushed past him, already feeling comforted by the smell of him. I walked straight into his bedroom, stripped off my clothes and climbed into his bed.

"Sawyer?" he asked, a trace of doubt tainting his voice.

"I just want you to hold me. No talking. No questions. No sex. Just hold me."

Jake stepped out of his pants, folding them neatly over the dressing chair before crawling onto the mattress. He settled himself back and pulled the covers up to our waists. Holding his arm out for me to nestle into, he leaned down laid a gentle kiss on top of my head. I moved in close, resting my head on his bare chest and holding onto him with my arm over his hips.

"Goodnight, Sawyer."

"Goodnight, Jake."

Chapter Eleven

~Sawyer~

I was awoken by something nudging my shoulder. I tried to ignore it, wanting to head back into the deep sleep I was in just seconds ago.

"Sawyer. It's 5AM. You need to wake up and get back to your room."

Groggily, I prised open my eyes and turned my head to face him.

"Not yet," I told him. "I'm fine just where I am." Jake's eyebrows furrowed together, once again staring at me with eyes that were bursting with questions.

"What are you saying here, Sawyer?"

"I'm saying I want to stop putting so much pressure on myself. On *us*. I'm saying this is still brand new and I want us to enjoy time on our own before we announce it, so we still need to be careful. But I guess... I guess what I'm saying is that one day, I don't know when, I want to walk down the street with you on my arm. I want to show you off to the world and let them all know you're mine and I'm yours. I'm saying... I want us to give this a real shot. I'm saying that we've missed out on too many years already, and that I want today to be the start of many years to come. What I'm saying, Jake… is that I love you."

"Fucking hell, Sawyer," he choked out, rolling onto his side and wrapping me in his strong arms. "Thank you, baby. Thank you so fucking much for believing in us."

"Hey, Jake?"

"Yes?" he answered in between trailing firm kisses along my jaw.

"I want to suck your cock so badly right now."

"Too bad," he whispered, making his way down my body and nestling himself between my legs. "I'll be too busy sucking yours."

Fuck yes…

"Do you need anything before you go?" Laurelin asked as I packed my stuff into Jake's rented car. We'd given the excuse Jake was taking me to my house in the Lakes as he had family nearby who he was visiting. Everyone agreed it was for the best if Jake was reasonably close by given the situation with these threats.

"No thanks, Lin. Wait… actually could you have my calls redirected to my landline? There isn't great reception out there."

"Sure, hun. No problem. What exactly are you going for?"

"Just a break from all the madness. I plan to just chill. Write some songs. Play some music."

"Sounds good. Okay, well I guess I'll see you in LA. I'm heading out there on Wednesday. I'll go and sort your phone out right now."

"Thanks, Lin. You're a star." I leaned over and gave her a peck on the cheek. She did that bashful thing chicks do where they smile up at you and flutter their lashes.

"Ready to go?" Jake asked in that cool, professional and sexy as fuck voice he uses when we're in public.

"Almost. Just need to grab my guitar from upstairs."

Nodding, Jake followed me back up to my suite. Matt and Gavin had already left for the airport, Daz was catching a later flight and I don't know what the hell Kip was doing because he still wouldn't talk to me. The second the lift doors opened when we reached the top floor we were met with the sounds of Elle crying and Kip yelling.

"What the fuck?" I said, dashing out of the lift and running towards the sound. "What the hell is going on?" I demanded when I reached them. Elle tried but failed to compose herself as she wiped the tears from my eyes.

"Nothing," she barefaced lied. "We're fine."

"Fine are we? What's the matter, Elle? Don't want your fuck on the side finding out about us, huh?"

"*What?*" Elle gasped. "What the hell are you talking about?"

"YOU! And lover boy there."

Being Sawyer Knight

Oh shit.

"Kip... Ah, fuck. Dude... "

I didn't see it coming, probably because I never expected it. Kip is my best friend. We'd never fought over *anything*. So I didn't see his fist flying towards my face until it was only millimetres away from my nose.

"ENOUGH!" Jake roared about the same time spurts of blood started flying from my nose. "Isaac," he continued, standing between us and separating us with his arms. "Let us into your goddamn room where we can discuss whatever the fuck is going on here like adults!"

"I'm going nowhere with *him*," Kip spat. "I swear, mate, you need to get him the fuck away from me."

"I don't know what you think's going on here, Kip, but-" Elle tried to explain but Kip cut her off.

"Sawyer's filled me in about exactly what's been going on so I don't *'think'* anything, you lying bitch! You told me you fucking *loved* me!"

Elle looked at me with a confused look on her face, sweeping the strands of hair that were sticking to her tearstained cheeks out of the way.

"Please, I can explain. Kip there's nothing going on between me and Elle. I... I *lied* to you."

"You WHAT?" Elle blasted. "Why the fuck would you tell him that, Sawyer?"

"Please can we just go inside?" I nodded my head past Kip towards the open door of his suite.

"This better be fucking good," he agreed, seeming to have calmed down a little. Wiping the drips of blood off my nose with the back of my hand I followed Kip's lead into his room with Jake and Elle coming in behind me. Jake closed the door behind him and then once again resumed position between Kip and me. "Go on then. Give me a reason why I shouldn't break every one of your lying fucking teeth."

"She was the first name that came into my head. You were pushing me to tell you who I was seeing! I didn't want you to know so... so I lied about it. How the hell was I supposed to know there was something going on between you two?"

"Bullshit! Why wouldn't you want me to know? We've never kept anything from each other. Besides, like I said at the time, I'd fucking know. It *has* to be someone who works with us. We've been on the road together for months. What've you been doing, huh? Carrying her around in your fucking suitcase?"

"He's telling the truth, Isaac, I swear to you." Elle risked a step forward and reached her hand out to cup one side of his face. "You've no idea how difficult it was for me to tell you I love you. It took me so long because I was afraid. I was terrified something would go wrong and I didn't know if I was strong enough to cope with how much that'd hurt. But I risked it because it's true. I *do* love you. I know you know that. I also know deep down you know Sawyer would *never* do something like that to you."

Kip sighed, giving me hope we were getting somewhere. I couldn't wrap my head around him and Elle being together and I wondered how long they'd been keeping it a secret. I was also feeling disappointed that she didn't feel like she could tell me. I'm her best friend. I'm Kip's best friend too. If I'm honest, it really fucking hurt that they didn't tell me.

And that's what made me take the biggest fucking leap of my life.

"Jake," I said to Kip. "I've been seeing Jake."

"Now's not the time for taking the damn piss, Sawyer." Kip stared at me with a scolding expression. When my face didn't falter, he realised I was telling the truth. "Fuck me, you're serious?"

"Yes."

"You're... I mean...you're..."

"Gay. I'm gay." As soon as I'd said it the air rushed from my lungs and it felt like the first decent breath I'd taken in years. It was in that moment I realised it was the first time I'd ever admitted it out loud.

"Jesus..." he breathed, scratching his head. "But... you fuck women. I've fucking seen you! And we're not just talking the odd one either. You've fucked more chicks than I've had bottles of beer! How can you just *turn* gay all of a sudden?"

"It's not all of a sudden. I think I've known my whole life. I just didn't want to admit it."

"Why? What the fuck difference would it have made?"

I couldn't help exhale a small laugh. I've spent years feeling so damn ashamed of myself. Certain that others wouldn't be able to run away fast enough. And Kip didn't even care. I daren't look at Jake in case he was wearing an 'I told you so face'.

"I was scared, Kip. I still am. Look it's a really long story but it'll have to wait. We need to leave soon. But… I can't go leaving things like this between us. You're like a brother to me, man. I'm sorry. I'm sorry I didn't confide in you and sorry I lied about Elle. I just… hell, Kip, I'm still trying to get used to the idea myself."

"You were a fucking idiot for lying to me."

"I know."

"But you're right. You *are* my brother." I puffed out a relieved breath when I saw him take a stride towards me. He pulled me into a hug – not a usual guy hug, not a one-armed pat on the back kind of hug – but a full on hold with both arms wrapped right around me, crushing me to his chest. "You're a fucking prick, Sawyer," he said, never releasing his grip on me. "You can tell me anything, you stupid dick. You should've known that already."

"I'm sorry." What else could I say? Kip clapped my back, backing away from me. "And Elle…" I turned to her. "I owe you an apology too. If I'd known… It was a kneejerk reaction and I knew I'd fucked up the second I'd said it. But, in my defence, never in a million fucking years did I think you two would ever get together."

"I'm sorry too, babe," Kip apologised, taking hold of Elle's hand. "I should've talked to you first. I should've trusted you enough to let you explain. I saw red. I panicked. I'm scared of losing you too."

"Yeah, well," she said. "Maybe we should've been honest too. In some way, we're all partly to blame for this mess."

Being Sawyer Knight

"Just let me know when it's time to whip out the violin, guys." I turned to Jake, smiling at the sarcasm lacing his voice.

"So you're a fairy-boy too, eh?" Kip teased. "I mean, as much of a surprise as it was, Sawyer's a musician. Creative. He's got style. That's kind of an excuse right there. But you, man you're like *tough*, and if I'm honest, a controlling arsehole most of the time. Never would've guessed it with you."

"I'll take that as a compliment," Jake replied with a lopsided smirk. "But for the record, my sexuality isn't a secret. If anyone ever asks, I'll only ever be upfront."

"Maybe that douche over there can learn a thing or two from you then." Kip cocked his head in my direction

"No, Kip. This can't go public. You can't tell anyone about this."

"Umm, if that's what you want then sure." He drew his eyebrows together in confusion as he spoke. I didn't expect Kip to understand why I was more comfortable living a lie. How could I? I didn't even understand it myself. "So we're all good?"

"We're good," I assured, bumping my fist with his. "We really do need to get going now though."

"You're going together aren't you? To your place in the Lakes?"

"Yes," I answered after dragging in a deep breath. I still felt a sense of embarrassment when admitting out loud anything relating to my relationship with Jake. It was however, beginning to lessen. "Come here, gorgeous girl." I pulled Elle in for a squeeze, whispering 'sorry' into her ear. When she pulled back she smiled up at me and I knew she'd both forgiven me and understood my reasons, even if she didn't agree with them.

"We're leaving for the airport in an hour," Elle informed me. "LA was the plan anyway until you decided to dump me for a piece of ass." She winked at me and I heard Jake chuckle quietly behind me, trying but failing to keep his usually impeccable calm. "So I guess we'll see you when you get out there next week."

"Sure thing," I agreed, kissing her forehead. "What about Ryder?"

"He's coming too. If he ever drags his lazy arse out of bed."

Elle and Kip walked us out of their room, and as I crossed the large corridor to go and grab my guitar from my suite, a half naked Ryder stumbled out of his room, suctioned to a man twice his age, and *not* the same man from the club last night.

"Elle!" he called while still attached by the lips to the other man.

"Ryder we're leaving in an hour!"

"I know, I know," he said, releasing his prey. "I was just saying goodbye to, um… sorry what was your name again?"

"Dan," mystery man spat, shaking his head. Ryder's lips twisted into a pucker, the kind of expression that screamed 'oops', and before he could speak again 'Dan' was nowhere to be seen.

"Met him on Grindr. Cute huh?"

"I hope you're being careful, Ry," Elle chided as if she was his mother.

"Yes, Mum. Always wrap it before you tap it. Got it."

"Besides, you can't be bringing people up here without running it by security. Now go shower and get some bloody clothes on." Winking, Ryder saluted her, laughing as he made his way back into his room.

Finally, after an hour of shit I most definitely wasn't expecting, I got my guitar and Jake and I left for our week alone. I don't think I'd ever needed anything so badly as I needed this week with him. I was about to find out what being in a relationship really involved, and whether I was cut out to do it.

Jake had hired a car to get us to my house. No one would know who it belonged to that way. We didn't stop until we reached the house and I can't remember the last time I'd enjoyed being cooped in a car for so long. In fact, I don't think I ever had. I've always hated travelling. Ironic really, considering I spend most of my life doing just that.

Jake's eyes widened as he drove us down the long, private road, skirted with tall evergreen trees, that led to the house. I could see his gaze flitting in all different directions, taking in the lush scenery before we passed through the huge iron gates.

"This place is amazing."

"Yeah," I agreed, not realising just how much I'd missed it until we pulled up outside the grand house. It's an old-fashioned building, built in the late eighteenth century I believe. It's an old country cottage as opposed to a modern condo like my other places dotted around the world and I think that's quite possibly why it's my favourite. It's refreshing. Simple. Uncomplicated. Sometimes I need reminding what that's like.

When I climbed out of the car I stretched my arms above my body and started making my way to the front door.

"Wait," Jake ordered, bracing his arm in front of me to stop me moving forward. Instinctively I scanned the grounds, assuming he'd seen or heard something. "I need to check the place out first. Give me the passcode and your key."

"Jake, no one ever comes out here. No one knows this place belongs to me, remember?"

"You might be bringing me here as your lover, but I'm still your bodyguard." My dick twitched at the word 'lover' rolling off his tongue. "Go and wait in the car," he added, tossing me the keys. "And lock the doors."

"You're being ridicu-"

"Just do it, Sawyer."

I almost wanted to laugh at how serious and bossy he was being. But I knew he was only doing his job. His senses were on heightened alert since the dead cat incident and I couldn't blame him. Just thinking about what was inside that box sends a chill down my spine and I didn't even see it.

Being Sawyer Knight

Sitting in the car, I never took my eyes of Jake as he walked the perimeter of the house. When he disappeared inside, I got bored and after several minutes made the decision to follow him inside. He was in the kitchen when I found him, tampering with the alarm system.

"You lasted longer than I expected," Jake teased, keeping his eyes on the alarm. "This needs updating."

"It's an alarm, Jake. It makes a loud noise when someone comes in the house. What else do you need?"

"There are only sensors fitted on the ceilings. There needs to be activators on the windows, doors and at lower points on the walls. I'll arrange a new system this week."

By the time he'd finished speaking I was standing right behind him. I snuck my hands around his waist, pulling him into me. Nuzzling my face in his neck, I kissed along his stubble before giving his ear lobe a little nip with my teeth.

"No work this week," I whispered in between light kisses. "It's just you and me. No one else."

"You need to start taking this seriously, Sawyer. This is your *life* we're talking about."

"Oh come on, Beebs," I whispered through a smile into his ear. "You can't stay mad at me forever."

"Keep calling me Beebs and I can."

"Come on," I encouraged, taking his hand. "Let me give you a tour."

"I could actually use a shower first. I've been trapped inside a car for hours, I need to freshen up."

"I have a bath big enough for both of us." I gave him a suggestive smirk before drawing my bottom lip between my teeth.

"Is that so?"

"Come on, babe. Let's start getting to know each other."

Later in the evening Jake and I were curled up together on the couch in front of the log fire. This might sound stupid, but it was like we were a 'real' couple. Dressed in our robes, Jake had his legs sprawled along the cushions and I was nestled between them with my feet dangling over the edge. As he ran his fingers through my hair, I closed my eyes, enjoying the feel of him. I'd done so many things in my life – met so many people, travelled all over the world, achieved things most people can only dream of. I'm very privileged, I've got an amazing life that I am insanely grateful for. But right here, lying in the lap of a person I now had no doubts I was in love with, even though fear had stopped me telling him more than once, I had never felt more content. Jake has given me things no amount of fame or money has ever been able to. He accepts me. He makes me feel safe, cared for. He makes me feel like for the first time in my life I am just 'me' – Sawyer Knight - a regular guy from a shithole of a housing estate in London with nothing to prove to anyone.

Being Sawyer Knight

"I've been thinking," I began, twisting my neck so I could look up at him. "I'm ready. I want you to fuck me. Tonight."

"Baby you know there's no rush. If you're nervous we can wait."

I could feel his dick beginning to wake under my head, contradicting his words entirely.

"I'm always gonna be nervous about this, Jake. But I trust you. And I *want* you."

Feeling bold, I crawled onto my knees and straddled his lap. The way he looked at me, so intensely, like the sight of me mesmerised him, made me instantly hard. I leaned forward and kissed his lips. We were both unshaven, and the rough feel of him under my lips made me kiss him harder. I sucked on his bottom lip before swirling my tongue around his mouth. He tasted of whiskey and I lapped it up while sliding a hand down his chest and untying the knot on his robe. When his dick sprung free, standing proudly between our bodies, I flashed him a suggestive smirk before licking my lips.

Wordlessly, I made my way down his body, kissing and nibbling as I went. Knowing what I was about to do, Jake shuffled his ass to the edge of the couch, leaning back into the cushions. I started slowly, teasing him. I kissed his balls and inner thighs, making him squirm in front of me. Seeing him writhe and pant for *me* felt fucking amazing. It spurred me on, giving me the courage to take the lead.

"Lift your legs," I said, encouraging them upwards with my hands under his thighs. Jake looked at me suspiciously, even though he must've known what I was about to do. He bent his knees, holding them to his chest and exposing his ass to me. My heart was hammering nervously in my chest but I pushed past it, wanting nothing more than to please him.

Parting his firm cheeks with my hands, I took a moment just to stare. I fucking loved being inside him… but tonight it was *his* turn. I wanted it. I *needed* it. My tongue darted out of its own accord as I pushed my face forward. I swirled my tongue around his hole, making him gasp and moan. I continued to lick, and every so often I would dip my tongue inside just a little.

"Oh yeah," he rasped. "That feels so fucking good." Spreading him wide open with my fingers, I delved in deeper with my tongue. I pushed it in and out over and over again, forcing his hips to jerk. "Suck my dick, Sawyer. I want to feel those hot lips of yours around me."

I licked my way up to the base of his cock and he relaxed his legs, letting them fall either side of me. I kissed the moist tip lightly before surprising him and taking it straight to the back of my throat.

"Ah…*fuck*…"

"You like that, huh?" I asked after releasing his cock from my mouth with a pop. "You like me sucking your dick?"

"Fuck yeah I do."

My fingers curled around the base of his cock as I slid him repeatedly in and out of my mouth. With every withdraw I would pull down his foreskin and sweep my tongue around his swollen head. I looked up at him as I sucked him, locking my eyes onto his. Biting his bottom lip, his face screwed up into an expression of pure pleasure.

"Take me to bed, Jake," I said, raw desperation dripping from my voice. I stood up, untied my gown and shrugged it from my shoulders, letting it drop to the floor. Jake took the hand I was offering and I pulled him up, yanking him closer to me. Sliding my hands up his chest, I smoothed my palms up towards his shoulders, rolling his open gown off his body and enjoying the sensation of his skin against mine. Our dicks were pretty level with each other's and, pressing his body firmly into mine, he took them both in his hand, stroking us off at the same time.

"*Please*, Jake," I whimpered into his neck, softly thrusting my hips and loving the friction both his hand and his cock offered my dick. "Let's go upstairs."

He brought me in for one last kiss – a kiss full of passion, need and madness. He attacked my mouth roughly, tugging fiercely on strands of my hair and holding my face to his. Then he released me, tenderly stroking the back of his hand down my cheek.

"I want to be inside you so badly, Sawyer. I want to claim that fine arse of yours as my own, knowing no one else has been there before and no one but me will again."

"Then take me. I'm yours, Jake. I always have been, I just didn't know it."

Taking my hand, Jake led me up the stairs and into my bedroom. He pushed me backwards onto the mattress, spreading my legs with his knee so he could climb between them. He kissed me again, but only briefly, before roughly pushing my legs up so my knees were pressed against my chest.

He paid my ass the same attention I paid his downstairs and with every lick I could feel myself relaxing a little more.

"Relax, baby," he whispered. I knew why he'd said that when I felt the pressure of a finger pushing inside me. "You're really tight. Let me loosen you."

I didn't know how I was supposed to 'let' him loosen me, so I took the option of watching what he was doing to me and enjoying every damn second of it. I saw his finger slide in and out and my hand involuntarily wandered to my dick, gripping it tightly. My eyes never left Jake as he sucked on another finger before pushing them both in this time.

I felt his fingers scissoring inside me, opening me up for him. I was so close to coming just from the sight of him that I knew he had to take me and he had to do it *now*.

"I'm ready," I said, the crack in my voice betraying the confidence I was trying to portray. He never replied, but didn't take his eyes off me either, as he reached into the drawer beside the bed and pulled out the condom and lube. He suited up slowly, allowing me the pleasure of watching him. I can't lie, when he positioned himself between my legs my heart skipped a beat or three. He tucked his hands under my ass, pulling me closer to him.

"I need your legs higher, baby." I raised my legs as instructed, and Jake held them in position by using the back of my thighs to support his weight. He gazed down at me, his eyes bursting with a thousand different expressions that I couldn't even begin to decipher, and then he hooked one of my legs over his shoulder, using his now free hand to guide his cock towards my ass. "Relax."

I winced when I felt him push inside just a little. It stung as my body fought to reject the intrusion, but once through he slipped the rest of the way in easily.

"Don't... don't move yet."

"Are you okay?"

"Yes." But I wasn't actually sure yet. Slowly, *very* slowly, Jake started to slide out of my ass, only to push right back in again. It took maybe two or three gentle thrusts for the discomfort to subside and then...

"Oh hell yes," I gasped. "Oh fuck, Jake, that feels so fucking good."

He took that as his cue to move a little faster and the fact he was looking down at my ass, watching his dick pump in and out of me, turned me the hell on. His speed increased pretty quickly from that point and he grabbed hold of my ankles, using them as leverage as his gentle thrusts turned into hard, fast slams.

"Oh, hooooooly fuuuuuuuuuuuck!" I growled, fisting the sheets beside me.

"This arse is mine, you hear me, Sawyer?"

"Yes! God yes!"

"I've waited so damn long to fuck this arse. You feel amazing. You're so tight around my cock." Pre-cum leaked from the tip of my dick and I rubbed it in with my thumb before taking hold of my shaft and working my hand up and down. "Fuck yes. Come for me, Sawyer. Come all over that fine fucking body of yours."

"I'm close," I panted. "I'm gonna come all over myself."

Gripping my ankles tighter, Jake started fucking me like a man on a mission. He pounded my head into the headboard and I cried out when my dick started to throb in my hand. It surprised me how quickly my ass adjusted to him. The pain only lasted a couple of minutes before it was overtaken by pleasure so intense it resonated through my entire body.

"Fuck yeah! Fuck, fuck, oh my...fuck..."

"Oh yeah. That's it, baby..."

He fucked me impossibly faster, his hips practically as blur as my load shot out into the air, landing all over my stomach.

"I'm right there with you," he ground out. "I'm...I'm coming. Oh god, I'm coming so fucking hard. FUCK!" he cried on his final thrust. He lowered my ankles onto the bed and draped his body over mine. His cock pulsed and twitched in my ass as he took possession of my mouth with his. I gripped his broad back, holding him to me while we kissed, and then I rolled my head to the side to take in some much-needed air. "You good?"

"Never been better." And I meant every word.

Chapter Twelve

~Jake~

"*How* do you feel?" I asked Sawyer. We were lying on our sides, facing each other after I'd just taken his virginity, in a sense, making him mine.

"Like I'm scared to move in case I shit the bed."

"It'll wear off," I assured him, laughing at his honesty. "Did you enjoy it?"

"After the first minute or so… yeah. Yeah I did. I'm actually surprised just how much."

"Sooo, are you officially a bottom now?" I teased, waiting for his face to pale.

"No way. Not exclusively. I enjoy fucking you too much." Well Christ if that didn't make my cock hard again.

"Babe if I ask you something do you promise not to shut down on me?"

"Umm… I don't know. Depends what it is I guess."

"Do you still stand by what you said about keeping us secret?"

"Jake I…" he trailed off, sighing deeply.

"Hey," I said, wrapping my fingers around the back of his neck. "I'm not saying I want us to tell the world tomorrow. It's just… well what happened back at the hotel, I'd be lying if I said it didn't give me some hope."

"Jake this is still so new. Please don't rush me."

"I'm not rushing you. Believe me when I say I will wait *forever* if that's what it takes. Forget I mentioned it. It's too soon. I'm sorry."

"I want it, Jake. I swear I do. I just…" He shook his head sorrowfully. "I just don't know if I can."

"Honestly, forget it. Let's not ruin tonight by getting so serious. You're here with me, I don't need anything else from you."

Leaning forward, Sawyer touched my lips with his. He didn't kiss me, just lingered his soft lips over mine, not moving, and barely breathing.

"I don't want to be anywhere else, Jake," he whispered just inches away from my face. "We should get some sleep. I have plans for you tomorrow."

"You do, huh?" I questioned, wiggling my eyebrows suggestively.

"Not those kind of plans. I'm gonna take you hiking."

"*Hiking?*"

"Yeah, you know, *walking?*"

"I know what hiking is, Sawyer. You just don't strike me as a hiking kind of man."

"Well there's one new thing you've learned about me already. I *love* getting out there, up the hills and into the fresh air. It takes me away from all the madness. Reminds me that I'm still *me*."

"If you love it so much, then I'm sure I will love it too." Rolling onto my back, I opened my arm so Sawyer could nestle against my chest. Whenever we've slept together we've done it this way. I love having him wrapped in my arms, knowing he's mine and isn't going anywhere. "Come here." Pressing his naked and deliciously ripped body to mine, Sawyer draped his tattooed arm over my hips, laying his head on my chest. "I love you, Sawyer Knight."

"I love you too, Jake."

I don't care how much of a pussy this makes me sound, but hearing those words roll from his tongue made my heart swell inside my chest, and when I closed my eyes a single tear dripped from my lashes. It was difficult not to resent Sawyer's fame at times. I couldn't help thinking if no one knew who he was, this would be what life would be like always. Him in my arms, telling me he loved me, not having to worry about what the rest of the world would think.

But Sawyer *is* famous, and so I'll just have to take him anyway I can get him.

True to his word, the next day Sawyer took me on a hike. Not having any boots with me I had to nip out in the morning to get some before we set off, then once I was equipped for a day of walking up muddy hills he drove us a few miles out to what I had to admit was one of the most stunning places I've ever been. When he pulled up down a secluded dirt track we were surrounded by the most luscious green hills, trees and valleys. Although beautiful, they all looked the same to me – like a giant green maze – but Sawyer seemed to know his way around effortlessly.

Hooking his rucksack over his shoulders, he led me through a network of trees, along a hidden trail that wound around a shallow stream. I followed behind him, keeping my eyes on the ground to avoid rogue branches and rocks.

"This isn't part of the tourist trail. No one ever comes this way. That's why I love it so much."

Sawyer navigated the rough terrain like a pro. Me? I stumbled more than once and at one point fell flat on my face, much to Sawyer's amusement. There was something so tender in the way he held his hand out and helped me up from the ground. Concern creased his strong features first and I felt... *loved*.

"Where the hell are you taking us?" I grumbled. We'd been hiking for almost three hours. I'm a fit guy, I have to be for my job... but this walk was fucking *killing* me.

"Stop being a pussy. It's just up here."

"What is?"

"My favourite place in the world."

It's sod's law that his favourite place in the world would be up the steepest hill we'd climbed yet. But when we got there, the view punched the air clean from my lungs.

Being Sawyer Knight

"Wow..."

"Nice, huh?"

Nice? No. Fucking spectacular, yes.

I sat down on the damp grass, still a little breathless from the physical exertion it took to get up here. Sawyer joined me, tossing his rucksack onto the floor and pulling out two bottles of water. As I screwed the cap off, he moved closer to me, placing a hand on my knee. The touch momentarily paralysed me, making my breath hitch. To be 'out' with him, for him to be so open with me... it felt like a tremendous leap forward.

"How'd you find this place?" I asked curiously, curling my fingers around his hand on my lap. I stared out at the view. We were incredibly high up and the scene below us was breath taking. Lakes, trees, tiny roads...

"Just exploring," he shrugged. "I like the peace out here. Sitting here reminds me how small I am. Down there," he said, nodding his head down the hill. "People think I'm so fucking important. They all want a piece of me and it's easy to forget who I am. Up here, up here I can just...be."

We must've stayed, sitting on the top of the hill, for an hour or so. We barely spoke. We didn't need to. He sang to me – his version of Chasing Cars by Snow Patrol. The lyrics fitted the scene perfectly. We were lying there, forgetting the world. I only wished it could last forever. His voice on stage, live, was glorious. Husky, commanding, yet somehow impossibly smooth. But A Cappella, just inches away from my ears... it dove straight into my soul.

I draped my arm over Sawyer's shoulders, holding him close to me, and just enjoyed the fact we could be together like this. Out in the open, no hiding, no looking over our shoulders. A few times I nibbled and kissed along his neck, whispering what I planned to do to him tonight in his ear. He attempted to play it cool, but the noticeable strain his zipper was under gave me everything I needed to know.

"I'm so glad you brought me up here," I said, wrapping my arms right around his body.

"Me too. You know, I've always thought of you whenever I came up here. I don't know why. Maybe because I'm a nobody up here, like before. It reminds me of life before all the music and craziness."

"Sawyer, you have never been and never will be a nobody."

"Sometimes I think life would be easier if I was."

"Do you regret it? Signing to a label, hitting it big? Are you happy?"

"I could never regret something that's given me so many amazing opportunities."

"But are you *happy*?"

"I'm getting there." He smiled at me and it literally lit up his face. God, he's perfect. "I've always loved the music. It's the only thing I ever wanted to do. But… well I never could've prepared myself for the fame side of things. It feels like the day we got our first number one is the day my life stopped. I'm not saying I've been miserable. We've had a lot of fun over the years. I've met so many different people, travelled all over the world… but I just miss being able to take a shit without it being front page news."

"I was so proud of you the first time I saw you on TV. You were the supporting act for Blood Kings and you were all interviewed backstage."

"Fucking hell, I remember that! Matt was high as kite and spewed all over the cameraman the second he'd finished filming."

"Why doesn't that surprise me? Anyway, I taped it, watched it over and over. I was always pleased you were front page news. Somehow, it was like you were still in my life."

"I need to kiss you," he whispered, shifting his position so he was kneeling in front of me.

"There's always a chance someone could come out here, babe."

"I don't care."

Gripping the back of my neck with one hand, Sawyer brought me in for a kiss. He kissed the stubble on my jaw and then ran his tongue over my lips before dipping inside to taste me. I groaned into his mouth and he cupped my crotch with his other hand. I felt him smile against my lips when he felt my erection through my pants and it made me feel so fucking awesome that I grabbed his shoulders, pushing him to the ground. I straddled his body, running my fingers under his shirt and grasping his taut muscles while I kissed the hell out of him.

"I need to get you home," I panted. "We're going to get in the shower and you're going to suck my dick until

I explode in this hot mouth of yours," I said, tracing his lips with my thumb. "Then you're going to fuck me."

And so, that's exactly what we did with the rest of our day.

It was late afternoon and I decided to head out to buy supplies to make us dinner, leaving Sawyer alone with a notepad as he scribbled down lyrics which had apparently just burst into his mind. The nearest supermarket was a thirty minute drive away. I hadn't realised just how far out Sawyer's house was, although it made perfect sense. I made sure to be quick in case anyone recognised and subsequently followed me. So, armed with bags containing steak, potatoes, various vegetables and a chocolate gateau, I kept my head down and walked briskly back to the car.

Thanks to heavy traffic, the journey back took even longer and it was fifty minutes before I turned onto the long country road that led to Sawyer's house. I was about half a mile away when I saw soft plumes of smoke in the distance. It's not an usual sight in the countryside, with limited access to waste disposal people often burn things, yet still I found my foot pressing harder on the accelerator. Something didn't sit well in my gut and I cursed myself as I drove for leaving Sawyer alone.

My fears were confirmed when I wound onto the road leading to the huge gates guarding the property. Skidding to an abrupt halt outside the gates, not having enough time to wait for them to open, I leapt from the car and darted towards the house. Flames licked the windows, causing them to crack. I'm trained to handle dangerous situations. I stay cool, calm, collected. I have the ability to process the risk, solution and desired outcome within seconds.

Usually.

This time however, knowing Sawyer was in the house, logic eluded me. I was tackling this situation with my heart instead of my head and that went against *everything* I've ever been taught.

"SAWYER!" I yelled, running around the perimeter of the burning house, trying to find a safe place to enter. "SAWYER!"

I tried to enter via the back door but it was locked. Racing around to the side of the house, I tried the door there and that refused to open too.

"SAWYER!" I took a step back, raising my leg before kicking the door repeatedly. "SAWYER!" The door didn't shift so much as a millimetre but I continued kicking it out of pure desperation. I spotted a window to the side of the door that didn't have flames in view yet. Without hesitation I climbed up onto the rubbish bin and ripped my shirt off so I could wrap it around my fist. Then, after pulling my arm back, I punched straight into the glass, shattering it in one attempt. "Baby where are you?" I whispered into the smoky air.

Draping my shirt over the jagged glass jutting from the window frame, I hitched my leg up and climbed inside. The heavy smoke attacked my lungs the second I dropped onto the floor. I reached behind me, pulling my shirt from the frame and ripping it in the process, then I pressed the light fabric to my mouth as I hurried through the house.

My vision was compromised by the clouds of black smoke, making it harder to see the direction of the flames. I dodged falling plaster and stumbled over burning debris as I searched for Sawyer, but when I hit the hallway, I'd reached a dead end. Fire billowed through the air, blocking every turn off into the rest of the house.

"SAWYEEEEEEEEER!" The fire was spreading fast, heading towards me at the same speed I was heading for it. I had no choice but to back up and turn around. I would have to get back out through the window in the kitchen and try and find another way in on the other side. I wouldn't give up. I would *not* leave this building without him.

"*FUCK!*" As I jumped down from the window I caught my leg on the serrated glass. I fell onto my knees, the gravel cutting into my palms. Pain registered for the briefest second but immediately the task in hand took back over. Scrambling to my feet, I doubled over for a moment, wheezing and spluttering as I struggled to fill my lungs with air.

"JAKE!" *Oh thank God...* "Jake!" I could see a hazy vision of Sawyer running towards me. "What the fuck were you doing in there? Come on, we need to get away from the house."

He tugged on my hand, pulling me into a sprint. We slowed to a stop when we reached the iron gates and my arms instinctively reached out to wrap around him. He was here. He was safe.

He pulled away.

"The fire brigade and police are on their way," he said. "I thought you were still out. Then I saw your car and I couldn't find you. Why the hell did you go inside?"

"To find you! I thought you were in there!"

"Wait… you risked your life… for *me*? When you didn't even know I was in there?"

"It's my job," I said coolly. I was feeling offended, no fuck offended, I was downright hurt, that after I'd just ran headfirst into a blazing building to find him, scared out of my mind that he could be hurt or worse, he pushed me away.

"How are we going to explain you being here?" he flustered, scratching his head.

"Seriously? Is that all you're fucking bothered about? Either one of us could've died in there!"

"I know, I know. I'm sorry. I just… you're not supposed to be here."

"Then I'll leave," I spat acidly, reaching into my pocket for the car keys. For a moment, it seemed like he was going to let me. But when I reached the car, he grabbed my hand before I could reach the door handle.

"Don't go. I'm sorry. I just…panicked. I'll say I called you when the fire started. We'll go from there."

"I thought I could do this, Sawyer."

"Wait… what are you saying?" he interrupted.

"I'm saying… all this is fucking with my head! I just ran into a burning building for fuck's sake! I didn't check out the area, I didn't call for help, I didn't do anything I *should've* done because all I could think about was *YOU!* Then I get out here… I see that you're okay and my heart literally fucking *aches* to hold you, and you push me away in case someone sees us. Well DAMMIT Sawyer! I fucking LOVE you and I just don't think I can keep hiding it!"

"Shit," he mumbled. The sirens were getting louder, meaning people would be swarming around us soon. "Jake please… We'll talk about this later. But stop thinking like that. I'll give you everything you want. I promise you. Just…later."

I couldn't do anything but nod in agreement. Several firefighters jumped from their vehicle, shouting orders at one another as they ran towards the building. Another window blew, causing us both to duck instinctively. We were a good distance away from the house but the crackles of fire and the cracks of the house falling apart flooded the air. Looking behind me, I noticed two paramedics and a police officer approaching, so we started walking forwards, closing the distance.

"Officer," I greeted.

"Can you tell us what happened here?"

Sawyer gave his version first. He was in the bathroom when he smelled burning and so went downstairs to check it out. Flames engulfed the main living room, quickly spreading to the dining room and into the hallway. Sawyer fled through the front door, immediately calling for help. He waited down at the bottom of the garden, only coming near the house again when he saw my car. Our paths must've crossed by mere seconds and I mentally scolded myself for not following a procedure that should've been fucking obvious and scanned the grounds before running inside.

After telling my side of the story, the version laced with mistruths, the officers agreed it was best we bring forward our travel plans and head out to LA sooner rather than later. The fire was still blazing when I was led to the back of an ambulance to have my leg checked out, and it wasn't until then I remembered I'd been hurt. Thankfully, the wound was shallow and so when the paramedic recommended I get checked out at A&E, I refused. Getting Sawyer to safety was my immediate priority. We hadn't heard from the fire officers yet but everything about this screamed arson to me.

"Come on," I said to Sawyer. The flames were calming and it looked like the fire crew were finally gaining some control. "We need to check into a hotel, phone Claire and arrange a flight."

"You don't think this was an accident do you?" Sawyer's face was pale. If this was a targeted attack, his life was in danger, and the severity of that was evident in his anxious expression.

"No. I don't. But you're safe, Sawyer. I will *not* leave you again."

Chapter Thirteen

~Sawyer~

"*Holy* fuck, dude," Matt said before taking a long drag of his cigarette. We were at Matt's condo in LA. Everyone was here to discuss the fire and where we go from here. Jake's suspicions were right. The police got in touch after the fire department had finished their investigations and they found traces of accelerant throughout the downstairs of the house. Whoever was making these threats was no longer considered to be an amateur. They were getting serious. It was still unclear what they wanted, but until we found out we were all on high alert.

"We've cancelled the dates for Australia," Claire said. "We need to keep you guys on the down low until we find out who's doing this."

"Sooo… we're staying here?"

"Yes. We'd like you all to stay here. It's best if you're all in one place until we've hired extra security."

"No fucking way!" Kip piped up. "I'm not living with *Matt.*"

"Hey, dude! Come on, I get a shit ton of pussy passing through here. I'll share!"

Kip rolled his eyes, clearly not happy. Neither was I, but after what happened back at The Lakes, I was willing to suffer Matt's bullshit. I just hoped it wasn't for too long.

"Claire's right," Jake interceded. "This is for your protection guys. It's not ideal, I know, but it's best to stick together right now."

"And what about us?" Laurelin asked.

"It's not you they're targeting. We'll arrange a rota for there to be members of security here at all times, but as for the rest of the staff, we have no reason to believe you're in any danger."

"And what if you're wrong?"

"I'm not," he said confidently. I love that side of Jake – when he's all firm and masterful. Turns me the fuck on. "You'll be in a hotel with the rest of us, and of course there'll be security there too. We have everything under control here. The LAPD are working closely with us, so between us and them, you're all in safe hands. A repeat of what happened to Sawyer's home in the UK will *not* happen again."

"So," Daz began. "I assume we can leave? This isn't a fuckin' prison scenario right?"

"Of course you can leave," Claire assured. "But *not* alone and *not* without informing Jake, or whichever guard you're with where you're going."

"Fuck. I can't believe this shit is happening," Gavin sighed.

"It won't be for long. I promise you guys we *will* get whichever arsehole is doing this," Jake replied. "Ok, guys, I have some calls to make. My family were expecting me back in Sydney so I need to go and update them. Any questions before I go?"

"Yeah, how will I get laid if I'm not allowed out by myself?"

"God gave you two hands, Matt. Use them."

Matt mumbled something under his breath, which of course Jake ignored. Then he disappeared from the room while Claire went over what was expected of us. I was looking forward to seeing Jake's family again after all these years and I felt a stab of sorrow in my chest that we weren't heading out to Australia anymore, not to mention the guilt I felt for cancelling on the fans. Still, it's not forever. Once this shit is sorted we will no doubt reschedule the dates.

"It's back to the studio as normal in the morning. We can't afford not to get stuff done while we're here. Cars will be here to pick you up at 7AM, but until then... do whatever it is you guys do best."

"Well I don't know about you guys," I said. "But I'm hitting the sack."

"It's 5PM!" Gavin noted.

"And I've been travelling for fucking hours. I'm beat."

As I stood up to make my way to one of the guest bedrooms I plucked my phone from my pocket. I called Elle soon after the fire and filled her in but I told her I'd ring again when we got to LA so we could meet up. Turned out I didn't need my phone, and it was also looking like I wouldn't be getting an early night after all.

"Sawyer!" I turned around at the sound of Elle's voice and saw she was running towards me. She flung herself into my arms and squeezed me as hard as her tiny arms would let her. "You're alright."

"You *know* I am. You spoke to me on the phone!"

"I know but seeing you in one piece is different. This whole thing is scaring the shit out of me."

"Hey," I soothed, pushing her away from my body so I could see her face. "Don't you worry yourself, gorgeous girl. We've got a good team looking into this."

"I know," she sighed. "I just can't stop thinking about you being trapped inside that house. What if you hadn't got out? What if-"

"Stop it, Elle. I *did* get out. I'm fine."

"Sorry. I just love you. You're my muscle man." The snort bursting from Matt's throat didn't go unnoticed and I turned my head, giving him the harshest death glare I could manage. "I'm kinda gutted we're not going to Australia anymore."

"We will, just not yet."

I cocked my head towards the stairs in the middle of the open plan living space, signalling Elle to follow me to someplace private - i.e. somewhere away from Matt.

"I'll have to get back home soon and make sure Kylie's okay though," she continued when we entered one of the nine spare rooms. "I might not be able to join you guys depending on when it is. I've got Paris fashion week coming up."

"We'll worry about all that when the time comes. As it stands we've no idea how long it will be yet." Hopefully not *too* long. "Where's Ry?" I asked curiously, plopping down onto the four-poster bed. Holy shit – the dude has mirrored fucking ceilings.

"He's got an audition," she said solemnly. I raised my eyebrow, silently asking her to elaborate. "Some porno company," she explained, rolling her eyes. "Apparently it's one of the biggest in the industry and their headquarters are here in LA. He never dreamed he'd ever get to come here and he says he'd always regret it if he didn't give it a shot while he had the chance."

"You don't look pleased. I didn't think you minded him doing the porn stuff?"

"I don't. But… what if he gets it? From the way he bangs on about this company they could make him famous in the sex world. He's worked so hard to become the stylist he is today. I'd be sad to see him give that up."

"You're not his mother, Elle. You can't stop him doing what he wants to do. It's not like you to think otherwise, either. So come, cut the shit and tell me the real reason you're pissed with him."

"I'm not pissed with him," she said sincerely. "I'll just fucking miss him if he moves out here. It's bad enough you spend the best part of your life here. I know he's young, but apart from you, he's the only real friend I've got."

"Elle… things are changing for *all* of us. There's no point trying to guess the future because it's impossible and you'll just drive yourself crazy. Besides, you have Kip now."

"Yeah and I have *no* idea how that's going to work. I can't just drop everything to be with him. I have a sister, a business, responsibilities. I have to face the fact that with my work commitments and you guys touring and recording out here, we're going to apart a lot."

"It's going to work because you guys are gonna talk about this shit before you head home."

"Oh we are, are we? Since when did you become my personal agony uncle?" she teased.

"Um, since the day you were guiding me through our maths project and you cried about the fact Eric Walsh called you a heifer."

"Oh, God! I'd totally forgotten that! He was a twat."

"Yeah he was. To this day I wish you'd have let me deck the fucker."

"His parents were on the PTA. You'd have been expelled."

"Hey, it might've done wonders for my rock star image."

We both laughed, remembering the fond memories. We've both accomplished so much in the last ten years and it makes school seems like a whole lifetime ago.

"I love him, Sawyer."

"From the way he reacted the other day, I'm pretty sure he loves you too."

"Scary shit though, eh? This love business."

"Fuck yeah it is."

"So you love Jake?"

"Yeah," I breathed, smiling just from the thought of him. "Yeah I really do."

"I'm so happy for you, Sawyer. He's a good guy. He must be if he's managed to extract that permanent scowl from your face."

"Fuck off. I'm not *that* bad."

"Actually, yeah you kinda are," she said playfully, fist-bumping my shoulder. "It's like we're finally grown ups."

"Whoa, let's not push it."

"Are you going to tell the guys about Jake?"

"No," I answered automatically. "I mean yes. But… not yet. What about you and Kip?"

"Gavin already knows. Kip told him when he thought I was cheating on him."

"He told *Gavin*?"

"Well he couldn't exactly come to *you* now could he?"

"Yeah, I guess not."

"But we're going to tell everyone before I head back home. I think you should too," she added, wiggling her eyebrows at me.

"I'm not ready, Elle."

"Will you ever be?"

"I…I don't know," was the honest answer.

"Don't make him wait forever, Sawyer. It's not fair to him. Everyone deserves to hang the person they love off their arm. He loves you and he deserves to be proud of you, to show you off. And you know what? *You* deserve that too."

"I know." I sighed heavily, knowing I was being unfair but not being able to summon enough courage to change it.

"How are things going to work while you're staying here?"

"No idea. Guess I'm just hoping all this shit will be over soon."

"Claire said the police are working with them. And the police over here have guns and stuff so that makes me feel better. They can shoot the shit out of anyone who tries to get near you."

"This isn't Sons of Anarchy, Elle. No one's gonna be 'shooting the shit' out of anyone."

"Still makes me feel better knowing they *can*." Shaking my head, I laughed at her dramatics. "I'm gonna get my head down now. What are you doing with the rest of your night?"

"Kip and I have planned it," she said excitedly, rubbing her hands together like a teenage girl going on her first date. "I'm going to stay downstairs for a while, have a few drinks with the guys. Then before I know it, it will be really late so I'll just crash here. When all the others are passed out, I'll sneak up to Kip's room."

"How old are you again? Fourteen?"

"Shut up! It's exciting."

"You look really happy, gorgeous girl. And Kip's like a brother to me, I know he'll treat you right."

"I really-"

"ELLE!" Daz's voice boomed up the stairs, interrupting her. "YO, ELLE? YOU UP THERE?" His voice grew louder as he climbed the stairs.

"I'm in Sawyer's room!" she called back. "The one with the mirrored ceiling!" she added, giggling.

"They've all got mirrored fucking ceilings," Daz grumbled when he found the room we were in. "You coming down? We're gonna play strip poker!"

"I'm coming down, but I'm not playing strip poker."

"What's the matter? Know you're gonna lose?"

"Bullshit! I could play you guys under the table any day!"

"Prove it," Daz goaded with a wicked glint in his eye.

"You're on."

Elle practically jumped off the bed. Her face was eager and determined. Tonight sounded like it was going to be fun. I missed fun. I missed the guys. My mind has been so consumed with Jake lately I've neglected my best friends. The band bears my name and in that moment I realised I was letting them down.

"Wait up, guys!" I hollered. "I'll join you."

Being Sawyer Knight

By 4AM I think it's safe to say everyone was wasted. Elle never did make it up to Kip's room, instead passing out in just her bra and knickers on one of the sectional couches. Kip was close by, snoring with his feet right in Elle's face. Matt was well and truly stoned, sprawled across the coffee table completely naked. I'm sure he was losing on purpose – the dickwad was naked within the first five minutes of the game. Daz and Gavin gave up and went to bed a few hours ago and Pete and Neil were doing the nightshift, keeping an eye on the security cameras. That just left me and Jake.

I'd had a few beers, but of course Jake stuck to sparkling water. There was no way he would let his guard down even for a second right now. He spent the whole night on high alert – back straight, eyes flitting from one window to the next.

"I was looking forward to seeing your family again," I told Jake, nursing a half empty bottle of beer in my hand. He was sitting so close to me, yet at the same time so far away. A few times my hand reached out to touch him and then I remembered where we were and pulled back.

"I shouldn't be telling you this," he began, making my ears prick up. "There's a flight scheduled to Sydney next Tuesday. Together we decided getting you guys out of the country might be best right now. We needed to keep it off the books so to speak. Only essential people know right now and it needs to stay that way."

"So when were you guys planning to tell us?" I sounded pissed off, probably because I was. "You don't think we're essential? That this doesn't concern us?"

"Come on, Sawyer. You really think Matt would be able to keep this to himself? This is for your protection."

"I don't get what difference another country is going to make. They got to me in the UK. How do you know they won't touch us over there?"

"I don't," he said simply, shrugging. "But right now, the whole world knows you're here. We're going to try and make the trip as confidential as we possibly can. Plus, we're talking the other side of the world. We're hoping whoever's doing this hasn't got the time, inclination or resources to follow us out there."

"So who's coming?"

"As it stands, you and the guys obviously. Pete, Neil and I will travel with you and David and Sayid are hanging back here to continue working with the police. Claire isn't sure which option she's taking yet."

"What about new security? You're still hiring right?"

"Yes. Interviews are being held later today, but there won't be time to vet them thoroughly enough before we leave. I've told Claire she should stay behind and do that, then she can send some out to join us at a later date."

"When will you be telling the other guys? I don't like keeping shit from them."

"And I don't like keeping stuff from you, which is why I told you. But I also know you realise deep down how important this is, so I trust you to keep it to yourself."

"You know I will. So when?"

"Tuesday morning. You'll have just enough time to gather essentials before we leave for the airport. Anything else you guys need can be provided when we get there."

"Will everyone else be told Tuesday too? Elle, Laurelin…"

"Ideally we don't want to tell anyone else at all."

"I can't not tell Elle, Jake."

"I thought you'd say that."

"And Lin's my PA. She goes everywhere with me."

"You don't need a fucking PA, Sawyer," he grumbled. I never knew it bothered him so much. Did he not like Laurelin or something? "You have enough people running around after you. Stop being such a damn Queen."

"I didn't realise you had such a problem with her? What's she done to piss you off?"

"It's not Laurelin, it's the principle. And… well she seems to have a stick up her arse beneath that pretentious, saccharine smile. I think she's into you."

"Well of course she is. I'm Sawyer freakin' Knight," I teased, bumping my shoulder with his. It was the most contact we'd had all night and my dick started to stir from the closeness. "You're not jealous are you?" I whispered. Even thought it appeared everyone around us was comatose, you can never guarantee there are no hidden ears listening in.

"Completely. You've been straight for a *long* time, Sawyer. Of course it worries me you'll start to miss it."

Wow. The air around us turned dark and serious instantaneously.

"I wasn't *straight*, Jake. You know that. No one has ever made me feel like you do."

Jake's mobile started vibrating in his pocket and I was silently glad for the intrusion. The way he looked at me, so intense and wanting… I needed to take him to bed and I needed to do it *now*. My arms literally ached to take hold of his body and hold it to mine while I kissed him. That would've been a mistake, here in this house filled with so many other people, and if we'd have carried on talking, I don't think I would've been strong enough not to risk it.

"On my way," he spoke firmly into his phone. After tapping the 'End' icon he turned back to me. "Neil's reporting suspicious activity out by the entrance gates. It's probably nothing, but I have to go and check it out."

"Be careful." The words tumbled automatically from my mouth. I hated the danger this job put him in…and all because of me. It was never a concern really for anyone in my team in the past. We've had the odd crazy fan trying to climb the walls for an autograph but never have we experienced *anything* on this scale before.

"Always am," he assured. "Get to bed. I'll see you in the morning."

Sighing, I nodded. I didn't want to sleep without him tonight. It's like a piece of my heart is attached to him by an invisible wire, and every time we're apart he rips it out, taking it with him. I feel a sense of emptiness when he's not by my side and I struggle to find my purpose. Sounds dramatic, I know, but Jake is the only person who really knows me. The only person I can share anything and everything with. He's the other half of my soul. Now I just need to man the fuck up and tell the world that he's mine.

Chapter Fourteen

~Jake~

I breathed a contented sigh as I pulled up on to my parents' drive. We are a close family, always have been, and I missed them.

"Jake!" my baby sister Lily squealed, bounding out of the house and running towards my car. I still think of her as a baby, despite the fact she's fifteen. "You're here!" I climbed out of the car and gave her a hug before I'd even shut the door behind me. "Where are they? Are they coming here?"

She was talking about the band of course.

"They're settling into their hotel. Don't worry, sis, you'll get to meet them I promise."

"What are they like? Are they as cool as they are on TV? What about Kip? Is he as hot as he looks on the pictures?"

Lily has had a crush on Isaac for the past three years. Although he and Elle told the rest of the band about their relationship a couple of days ago, it wasn't public knowledge yet. Lily will be gutted I'm sure.

"How about we go inside first, huh?"

Not wasting a second, Lily ran back into the house. I locked up the car and followed her inside, smiling when I found my mum waiting for me in the living room.

"I'm so glad to have you home," Mum cooed, wrapping her arms around me.

"Glad to be here," I agreed, pulling out of her hug. "Where's Dad?"

"Working. But he'll be home this evening. We were hoping you could join us for dinner?"

"I'll try," was the best I could offer. "We're having some security issues with the guys right now. That's kind of why we're here."

"So go on!" Lily interrupted. "What's Kip like? Is he hot?"

"I think I can safely say they're all pretty hot, Lils."

I've always called her Lils. She hates it, and I suspect that's why I still do it. It's a big brother's prerogative to wind up his younger sister.

"You're so lucky," she sighed. "Do you have fans fighting to get to them all the time? And what about photographers? I saw your picture in Star Style magazine last week! I took it to school and showed you off to all my friends! They couldn't believe it."

"It's pretty crazy," I told her. "But I have a job to do. It's not all about the fun and parties for me."

"Ugh, you're always so serious about everything. At least tell me you ogle them when they're not looking."

"Be hard not to," I teased, winking at her. "I tell you what, I'll give the guys a call in a little while and you can speak to them."

"OH MY GOD you're kidding? I'm gonna call Katie and tell her to come round. Can she speak to them too?"

"Sure," I said, laughing at her excitement. Squealing, Lily ran out of the room, leaving me alone with my mum.

"I've missed you, sweetheart," she said, gently clapping my shoulder. "Let me go and put the kettle on."

"Actually I'll have something from the fridge. The heat out there is intense today."

"I'll turn the air conditioning up," she said, walking out towards the kitchen. I followed her, leaning against the countertop while she grabbed me a can of Pepsi from the fridge. Next she opened the cupboard housing the air conditioning controls, pressed the relevant buttons and then turned to me with a serious expression. "Something's troubling you."

"What? I'm fine. Tired from the flight, but fine."

"I'm your mother, Jake. I know when something isn't right with you."

I wondered if all mothers had an inbuilt problem radar or if it was just mine.

"I'm in love with Sawyer." There. I'd blurted it out. Christ it felt good.

"Sweetheart, you've been in love with that boy since you met him. I know it must hurt, but you can't make someone love you back. I knew this was going to happen when you left."

"That's just it. He *does* love me. We're sort of together."

"Sort of?"

"He's not ready to come out. He says he will, but God knows how long that will take. I love him so much, Mum. I just want everyone to know it."

"Oh, sweetheart. I hate to see you hurting like this."

"I'm not hurting. Not really. I've got Sawyer, that's all I've ever wanted. It's just so hard having to watch what I'm saying, having to remember I can't touch him, or even smile at him when people are around. I never thought I'd have to run back into the closet after all these years."

"And… you're sure he feels the same?" she questioned carefully. "He's not exactly famous for being the committed type. You've seen the papers, he has a different woman in his bed every other night."

"*Had*," I corrected. "I know what it looks like from the outside, but you don't know him. No one does, really. The women were just a distraction for him. I actually think he was using them to prove to himself that he wasn't gay. He's scared. Afraid he'll lose everything and everyone around him if he comes out. I have no doubt his mum would disown him, but he has so many other people who love him. His best friend, his band mates… they'd all stick by him I know they would."

"I never did like that mother of his," she chipped in. "Spouting all her religious crap. I remember her going into the school one day to demand they expel a young girl who'd gotten pregnant."

"Oh, I think I remember that," I said, nodding. "He loves her. I can't understand how she could ever turn her back on him, but still I know she would."

"Bring him here. Tonight. He can have dinner with us. It might help him to see what a *real* family is like. One that loves and supports each other no matter what."

"I know he's looking forward to seeing you all again, he still can't believe Lily is so grown up, but once he finds out I've told you, I'm not sure he'll be up for it."

"Of course he will. If he loves you like you say he does, he'll be here."

"I'm getting the impression you're not too sure about him."

"He's not good enough for you until he proves otherwise to me. I will make my decision when I've spent some time with him. I've not seen him since he was, what, sixteen? Seventeen? He was a nice boy, but he wasn't holding my son's heart in his hands back then."

"We'll be here," I decided in that moment. "I don't know what the plans for the rest of the day are yet so I can't give you a time, but I'll call you later."

"Perfect," she smiled. "Now, are you staying for some lunch?"

"Best not. I should really go and tell Sawyer about tonight – give him a few hours to get used to the idea." Downing the last of my can, I started walking out of the kitchen. That's when I spotted Lily hiding behind the doorframe. "How long have you been there?"

"Umm, kinda the whole time."

"Lily, this can't go any further," I said sternly. "Do you understand?"

"I'm not a kid, Jake, even though you think I am. I won't screw this up for you."

"I mean it, Lily. Not even Katie is allowed to know about this."

"I get it! I promise, I won't say anything to anyone. I know famous people have to do things different to the rest of us. I've not seen you smile so wide in forever as when you told Mum he loved you. I wouldn't mess that up."

"Wow. You really have grown up without me noticing haven't you?"

"But while it's just us, can I just say… Oh. My. God. My *brother* is boning *thee* Sawyer Knight!

"Lily!" Mum scolded. "Language!"

"Sorry, Mum. But seriously, this is *huuuuuuge*. Okay, I've got it out of my system. Lips are sealed." She pulled an imaginary zipper across her lips, making me smile. My family are amazing. The fact I was gay didn't even blip on their radar. They've never had any expectations of me – well my dad sure knew how to crack the whip when I worked for him, but that was business. Overall, they just want me to be happy. I can't wait for Sawyer to feel part of that tonight.

"Okay, I'll call you this afternoon," I said to my mum, giving her a kiss on the cheek. "And, Lils, I'll put the guys on the phone when I ring."

"Eeeeeek! I'm so excited!"

"Wait," Mum called when I reached the door. "He's not a vegetarian is he? I know a lot of these celebrities are into stupid fad diets."

"No, Mum. He eats pretty much anything," I assured her. "Just stick some steaks on the grill. No need to go to too much trouble."

"Okay, sweetheart. I'll see you later."

Closing the door behind me, I smiled up at the crystal blue sky. Tonight Sawyer would be with me and my family, and I would be free to just love him, out in the open surrounded by people who wouldn't judge us.

"Fuck am I glad to be outta there," Sawyer said as he slipped in the passenger seat of my rented car. We were setting off to my parents for dinner. Matt and Gavin had been making plans to go out tonight, which naturally involved lots of talk about tits and pussy. Originally, our plan was to keep the guys as hidden as we could, but when we landed at Sydney airport we were met with a mob of press. I always knew the chance of getting them here unnoticed was slim, but still we all worked hard on keeping it all clandestine. So now we're here, there really is no point in stopping them going out and enjoying themselves.

"Um, Sawyer?" We were driving over Sydney Harbour Bridge and Sawyer was admiring the scenery from his window. When I said his name, my voice nervous and uneven, he turned to look at me. "I told my mum about us."

"You did what?" He looked surprised, but not angry. I could work with surprised. "Why'd you do that?"

"Because she's my mum. Because she knew something was wrong with me. Because I love you and I've been so desperate to share that with someone."

"And why are you only telling me this now? When we're on our way to see them!"

"Because I knew you'd either worry about it all afternoon or make up an excuse so you didn't have to come. But my family isn't like yours, Sawyer. I want us to go in there and just be ourselves. The fact you're a guy doesn't mean shit to them. It'll be no different than if I were bringing a girl home. They accepted me from the start, and they'll accept you too. You don't need to pretend for them."

"So this is like a real meet the parents situation. Fuck, you know how to make me nervous."

"Sawyer, you've met my parents hundreds of times before."

"That was before I was fucking their son. Or before the whole world knew who I was. What if they hate me? I'm damn sure I wouldn't want my kid dating someone who had a new scandal in the papers every other week."

"They're not the type to believe everything they read in the press. Besides, no story lasts more than a week. Look at all those guys coming out saying they'd slept with you. That's all disappeared and we didn't even have to do anything."

If those stories would've continued, we had the paperwork in place ready to sue them for slander. But as I suspected, it all blew over in a couple of days.

Sawyer was quiet for the rest of the drive. Occasionally I would pull my eyes from the road just long enough to glance at him, and more often than not he was fiddling with the same strand of loose thread on his jeans. The man sitting next to me could dominate an entire arena filled with thousands of people, yet here he was, squirming in his seat from sheer nerves. I've come to learn though that the Sawyer on stage is an act, a persona. The *real* Sawyer is quite timid. He's shy, romantic, and terrified of exposing his true self to the world. I feel proud and privileged to know the man behind the fame, to hold him in my arms, to kiss him and make love to him.

"Here we are," I announced, cutting the engine after parking next to my father's car.

"Wow," he breathed, clicking off his seatbelt. "Seeing this place… it makes me feel so many regrets."

"Why?" I asked, confusion making my voice a notch higher.

"I should've been a part of this," he started to explain, gesturing around him with his hands. "You were my best friend. I should've been coming out here during the holidays. We would've hung out, played music, talked about random shit. I screwed it up."

"Everything happens for a reason, Sawyer. You weren't ready to accept who you were back then, and to be honest, I'm not sure how long I could've carried on pretending I was happy just being your friend. I think we would've eventually clashed either way. *Now* is our time, and I really believe it was always meant to be this way."

"Oh my God!" We both turned at the sound of Lily's voice. I was starting to wonder if she'd taken something – she'd been high as a kite all day over speaking to the guys on the phone earlier. "Wow," she sighed, eyeing Sawyer up and down. "You're even hotter in real life."

"Hey, Lils, I think you've got a bit of drool there," I teased, dabbing the corner of her mouth with my finger.

"Stuff off, Jake. Can I touch your hair?" she asked Sawyer.

"His *hair?*"

"I want to see if that bit of fringe that always falls across his eyes is as soft as it looks in the magazines."

"Um, sure you can," Sawyer agreed, bending down a little. I rolled my eyes, laughing in amusement as Lily fingered my lover's hair.

"God my brother is so lucky." Sawyer noticeably tensed at my sister's statement. His back straightened and he tugged down his tight-fitting white t-shirt, clearing his throat. "Don't worry. I've been sworn to secrecy. Though you really shouldn't worry, you know. Your fans adore you. They won't care. Trust me."

I was so proud of Lily in that moment. Her words instantly brought a smile to Sawyer's face, erasing the lines of worry that had been etched onto his face since I told him my family knew about us.

"Come on," I said. "Let's head inside."

Chapter Fifteen

~Sawyer~

As soon as we were in the hallway with the door closed behind us and out of public view, Jake took hold of my hand. I looked up at him apprehensively, but after he gave me an encouraging nod my fingers tightened around his. He led me out into the back garden where his dad was busy prodding the coals on the barbecue.

"Jake," his dad said, putting his tongs down as he approached us. "How are you, son?" He gave him a one armed hug, patting his back.

"I'm great. Dad, this is Sawyer."

"I know who he is, Jake," his dad said, tutting at him. "Good to see you again, buddy," he added, offering a hand for me to shake.

"You too, Mr Reed."

"Please, call me Martin."

"Oh you're here!" Jake's mum, Emma, said, walking through the patio doors carrying a crate of beer. "I didn't hear you arrive."

"Hey, Emma," I said warmly, taking the cans from her. I was comfortable calling her by her first name. I

231

always did when we were kids. She was like the mother I always secretly wanted. When I'd lowered the beers onto the garden table I brought her in for a hug. "It's been way too long."

"Aw, sweetheart. You're exactly the same boy I used to know."

"Did you think I wouldn't be?" I asked curiously, releasing her from my arms.

"Honestly? Yes. You're a completely different person on TV. I suppose I assumed fame as great as yours was bound to change someone."

"A lot of it's an act," I admitted. "You give the fans what you know they want. No one out there gives a shit about the real you. It's a very fickle industry."

"And you're okay with that? Doesn't sound like much fun."

"I do it for the music," I shrugged. "Sometimes it's been the only thing to keep me going."

Wow. Did I really just say that out loud? Talk about bringing the mood down.

"I can't help finding that really sad," she said, her face melting into a frown.

"I can't complain. I've experienced so many amazing things in my life. Sure, the industry has its drawbacks, but I'm still a very lucky man."

When I said that, Jake snaked his arm around my waist, pulling me a little closer to him. My instinctive reaction was to pull away and scowl at him, but I fought it. I took a deep breath, remembered how much I loved him and how much everyone here loved him too, and I relaxed into his hold. He smiled up at me proudly, and I even caught Emma smiling subtly as she turned towards the cans of beer. She plucked two from the tray, handing one to me and then one to Jake.

"Can I get one of those too?" Lily asked, biting her lip in anticipation of her mum's answer.

"You can have *half*," she said firmly. Lily grinned, taking a can from Emma and then pouring half into one of the tall glasses laid out on the table.

I was nervous as hell when I first walked into their house, but after just half an hour of being with these wonderful people I was completely at ease. We talked about the past, memories from our childhood, we discussed my career – most of which left Lily's mouth wide open in awe – and I even found myself touching and smiling at Jake without a second thought. It was little things like resting my hand on his knee while we talked, bumping my shoulder with his while we laughed, and when he offered me a forkful of his steak that had a different marinade than mine, I didn't hesitate to taste it as he popped it in my mouth, grinning at me like he…well like he loved me.

After finishing up the barbecue we all headed inside. We spent the evening pretty much the same way – chatting, laughing, swapping stories. After a few hours Emma excused herself to go and clean up the dishes left over from dinner. Giving Jake's knee a tender squeeze, I followed his mum out into the kitchen.

"You wash, I'll dry," I offered, taking the tea-towel off the counter.

"Don't be silly, Sawyer. You're our guest."

"Don't give me that, Emma. You didn't used to mind when we were kids. In fact, I think I remember you threatening to confiscate Jake's Nintendo once if we *didn't* help."

She laughed at the memory and then handed me the first clean plate. I dried it off with the towel, placed it on the counter and held my hand out for the next one.

"Sawyer," she said my name with such seriousness and concern in her sweet voice that I knew exactly what was coming. "I need to know, do you love my boy?"

I drew in a deep breath, feeling caught off guard. This wasn't the kind of thing I'd ever discussed with anyone but Jake and naturally my heart sped up with nerves.

"Yes," I replied with certainty. "I promise you, Emma, he means the world to me. When I'm with him, I'm so happy. I can be myself. He's changed me irrevocably. He makes me want to be better. He makes me believe I *can* be better."

"I just don't want him to get hurt. I hope you understand where I'm coming from."

"I would never hurt him."

"You already are." Her words winded me as if she'd just punched me in the gut. I raised my eyebrows, astounded. I'd hurt him? How? "Jake is a romantic man by nature. He wants to *love* you, Sawyer. He wants to take you out, wine and dine you, steal kisses from you in the middle of the day. Will you ever be ready to give that to him?"

"I want to so badly. Believe me I do."

"But you can't?"

"No. Not right now," I admitted and I felt like the asshole I really was. She was right. I'm stringing Jake along. I've told him I will come out, tell the world about us… but right now, I don't have any intention of doing that. I just…can't.

"Don't string him along, Sawyer. I ask as his mother. I love him and I've watched him hurt over you for too long. Please, don't hurt my boy."

"Wow." Jake's voice came out of nowhere and I turned around, startled, and saw him standing in the doorway. "I didn't know you were a such a domestic god," he teased, winking at me. *Shit.* How long had he been standing there? His expression was oblivious so I hoped that meant he hadn't overheard our conversation.

"I have many hidden talents," I replied with a smile.

"I have no doubt. Hey, Mum, we really need to get going now."

Emma removed her hands from the soapy water, drying them off on a towel. She walked over to Jake and wrapped her arms around him.

"Okay, sweetheart," she said, squeezing him a little tighter before letting him go. "Make sure you come back here before you leave."

"Of course I will. We're here for another week yet. Possibly longer. I'll go and say goodbye to Dad."

Jake left the kitchen to find his father, leaving me and Emma alone, drowning in a pool of awkward silence. My heart stuttered when Emma approached me, putting her hands on my shoulders.

"For what it's worth, I believe you. I've seen the way you look at him. You love him. I don't doubt it. Just...*try*, Sawyer. Be brave. Be honest. Be proud of who you are. You deserve that as much as Jake does."

"I will," I sighed. "Believe me when I say I just want to make him as happy as he makes me."

"Then you know what you need to do."

"Thank you, Emma. I really have missed you."

"Let's not leave it too long again, hmm?"

"No. Definitely not." Without even thinking, I hugged her. I squeezed all the love, respect and gratefulness I held onto her and then I let her go, kissing her cheek. "Thank you," I whispered. In those two simple words I was thanking her for *everything*. Thanking her for being a mother to me when I was young, thanking her for forgiving me for the way I treated Jake all those years ago, for accepting me, for letting me back into her life, for creating Jake... for making me feel like I might just have the courage I need so badly right now if I look deep inside myself.

In that moment Jake and Martin walked into the kitchen.

"You ready?"

"Yeah," I said, giving Emma one last grateful smile. "Goodbye, Martin." I proffered my hand, which he accepted.

"Come back soon, boys," he said, and something inside me began to warm. The way he referred to us as 'boys', something in his tone made it sound so endearing. I'd never really felt like part of a family until tonight and as Jake and I left his parents home, I spent the entire time praying for the strength not to let them down.

"Where are you going?" I asked, puzzled when I noticed Jake driving in the wrong direction for the hotel.

"I booked us into a different hotel for the night. Told everyone we were staying at my parents."

Wow.

"And don't worry, babe. They all know we grew up together, so wanting to catch up with my family doesn't look suspicious."

"I-I wasn't going to say that."

"But you were thinking it. I know you, remember? Better than anyone."

He was right of course. The second the surprise registered my first thought was what would the guys thinking of us spending the night away together. How am I supposed to do this?

"I'm sorry, Jake. I'm sorry I'm putting you through all this shit."

"You're not putting me through anything," he assured, keeping his eyes on the road as he took hold of my hand on top of my knee. "I've told you, I'll wait forever if that's what it takes."

"I just want to be what you deserve."

And right now, I'm not.

"You already are."

I didn't reply because I couldn't agree with him. Instead, I leaned my head against the cool glass window of the car and stared out of the window, absorbing the beautiful Australian scenery with my eyes. When we reached the hotel I shrugged on my jacket, despite already sweating from the heat. The leather would hide any tattoos that might make me recognisable. Slipping my sunglasses on, I kept my head down as we walked into the hotel. Jake dealt with check-in and then we made our way up to our room alone, with no one giving us a second glance.

There were champagne and strawberries waiting for us in the room, sitting proudly in a silver ice bucket on the walnut table next to the king sized bed.

"Did you arrange these?" I asked, swirling my finger around the rim of one of the champagne flutes.

"Yes," he confirmed. Closing the space between us, he wrapped his arms around my waist, resting his forehead against mine. "I've missed you. You've been by my side for days but you couldn't have been further away. I *need* you, Sawyer. I need to hold you, feel you, *love* you."

"God, I've missed you too," I moaned into his mouth. I teased his lips with my tongue, our chins grazing each other's as I angled my head to the side. "So fucking much."

As my dick started to swell all traces of tenderness disappeared, replaced by some kind of pure animalistic urge. I didn't want savouring or teasing. I wanted fucking. Hard. Now. Popping open the buttons down Jake's crisp white shirt, I pushed him back until he fell onto the mattress. He smiled up at me with pure hunger in his eyes and I bit my lip, working his zipper. Jake arched his ass off the bed while I tugged his pants down and the second his hard cock sprung free I leaned down to kiss the swollen head.

"Oh fuck, Sawyer," he groaned, fisting the sheets. I drew him into my mouth, moving my lips up and down along his shaft and tracing his thick veins with my tongue. I released him just long enough to pull my t-shirt over my head, then I sucked him again while I shuffled out of my jeans, throwing them to the floor. "Climb on top of me, baby," Jake said. "And turn around."

I did as he asked, straddling his glorious body, my greedy mouth hovering just above his dick and my ass right up in his face. Propping myself up on one arm, I moistened my lips and went back for more, massaging his balls with my free hand. Jake grabbed at my ass cheeks, separating them and exposing my hole.

"You have the most perfect arse." Jake slapped my ass cheeks, causing a throaty groan to leave my mouth, vibrating against his dick. Then he ran his lips over the tender flesh, making his way between my cheeks and rimming me to the point I wanted to scream. "Tastes good too."

He dipped his tongue in and out a couple of times before replacing it with two fingers. His cock never left my mouth as he pushed inside, my hips bucking to meet his gentle thrusts.

"Holy shit, Jake." I freed my mouth of his hard dick so I could take a deep breath. His fingers started to pump in and out of me deeper and faster and I met his rhythm with my hand around his thick cock. "Oh, *yeah...yeah...fuck*."

"Sit on me, Sawyer. Lower yourself down onto my dick."

Feeling slightly apprehensive about trying a new position, unsure if I'd be able to do it 'right', I gave the tip of his cock one last kiss before turning around to face him. I noticed a bottle of lube and a condom ready and waiting in his hand and I couldn't help grin at the devilish wink he gave me. He went to open the packet but I ticked my finger from side to side.

"Let me do it." I was straddling him, staring into his eyes – the eyes that took me away from everything, made me think of nothing but him. Pinching the tip of the condom, I rolled it over his throbbing erection. Holding onto my thighs, he tipped his head back, moaning into the air. Next I took the lube, squeezing a generous amount into my palm before massaging it over his dick. I used my fingers to wipe the excess over my ass hole and then I leaned forward, chest to chest, and kissed along his neck.

"I need you so badly right now," I murmured into his ear before gently nipping his lobe with my teeth.

"Then take me."

I reached behind myself, taking hold of his thick cock and guiding it into my ass. A hiss of pleasure burst from my throat as I lowered myself down, closing my eyes as I adjusted to the fullness. The mixture of pleasure and pain when he entered me was intoxicating and I opened my eyes, locking them onto his.

"Take your time, baby. Nice and slow." Gripping Jake's shoulders for support, I moved myself up and down slowly, enjoying the feel of him stretching me. His hands reached forwards, smoothing over my abs and he sighed in appreciation. "You're so beautiful, Sawyer."

A light mist of sweat coated his firm chest as his breath began to come in short, fast pants. I leaned down, licking the contours of his muscles and smattering kisses along his damp chest. My ass started to ache, pulsate around him, silently begging me to take him deeper. So I did. I tucked one hand behind his neck and started moving faster, higher and lower.

"Oh fuck, yes," he ground out through gritted teeth. He took the hand that was pressing onto my chest and moved it towards my cock. It was wet, glistening, and he started pumping it up and down, making me writhe. "Jesus, baby…"

"Holy…*fuck*," I hissed as he worked his hand on my cock in time with the rhythm I was riding him. "You feel so good in my ass, Jake. So. Fucking. Good."

The air was filled with breathy pants and moans. Fuck this was a good position to be in. I could take him as hard and deep as I wanted, and man did I make the most of it. I slammed down on him hard, my ass cheeks hitting his thighs. His fingers tightened their grip around my cock and he bucked his hips, thrusting himself deeper into me.

"I'm almost there, baby," he whimpered. "Don't fucking stop."

"I'm right behind you," I said breathlessly, feeling my balls tighten. "You're fucking amazing."

My orgasm was building quickly and my legs stated to tremble. Sensing my release, Jake took over, thrusting into my ass from beneath me. I held tightly onto his neck, bringing him up to me while he jacked me off with his hand. My dick pulsated against his fingers and I cried out his name as he pounded me harder.

"Oh, FUCK, Jake!" Powerful spurts of cum came shooting from my cock, hitting the base of his throat. It seemed to tip him over the edge, and he juddered below me, before milking himself completely with three more smooth, deep thrusts.

I collapsed onto his chest, his dick still inside me, and he tenderly stroked up and down my back with his fingers.

"You're getting good at taking it," he complemented with a wicked smile.

"Maybe because you're so good at giving it."

"Let's get cleaned up and drink this champagne before it gets warm," he suggested, sweeping my rogue fringe from my eyes.

"Sounds like a plan," I agreed, gripping the base of his cock while I pulled myself off him, rolling onto my side. "And *then*, it's my turn to fuck *you*."

"Deal."

Chapter Sixteen

~Jake~

Neil and I had gathered the guys in Darren's hotel room. Claire arrived late last night, complete with a plan I wasn't at all happy with. Laurelin was apparently following on her own and was due here this morning.

"Okay, guys, we have a gig tonight." And there it was. What a stupid and irresponsible idea given what was going on right now. I sighed and crossed my arms.

"Thought they were cancelled," Gavin said.

"We've reinstated tonight's show at the ANZ Stadium. We've heard nothing back from whoever was sending the threats, the police have come up with nothing and we have no reason to believe they would be out here in Australia. I think they've finally got bored and moved on."

"Arsonists aren't the type to get *bored*, Claire," I repeated for what must've been the thousandth time.

"Well we can't cancel again. Have you any idea how much effort it took, how many strings I had to pull to get this all back in place? Not to mention how pissed the fans would be if we cancelled again. It's happening. Rehearsals and sound check start in two hours."

"I want it noting that I am *not* happy about this."

"Yes, I think we've established that, Jake," Claire muttered acerbically. "But you don't need to be happy, you just need to do your job and keep the guys safe. We've managed to vet three of the new additions to your team. They flew in with me last night. You'll be meeting them after breakfast. That should give you enough time to get a plan together." I was seething, the blood simmering so hot in my veins my neck began to burn. "Right, guys, if you don't have any questions I'm going to pick Laurelin up from the airport."

Sawyer dismissed her with his hand, seeming as flabbergasted with the idea as I was. Although, he seemed to accept it better than me. I planned to go and see my parents today, seeing as I didn't know how long we'd be here and wanted to make the most of being close to them. Guess I would have to rearrange now.

"Hey, Daz, you okay?" Sawyer asked, turning to Darren who had been slumped backwards in the leather recliner with his hand over his face since we got here. "You've been lookin' kinda green this morning, dude."

"Dana's pregnant," he revealed, his voice literally shaking.

"Holy fuck, man. What the hell are you gonna do?" Matt asked.

"She wants to keep it. But seriously, guys, how the fuck am I gonna raise a baby on the road all the damn time? The whole thing is a fucking mess."

"See, Saw," Matt began, cutting himself off by laughing. "Ha! See what I did there? See, Saw – seesaw. Fuck I'm funny."

"Christ," Sawyer mumbled under his breath, clearly as un-amused as the rest of us.

"Anyway, this is why you and I got the right idea. Never get tied down. There are too many different flavours of pussy to stick to just one. Right, Saw?"

"Be serious, Matt. The guy's fucking struggling."

"I *was* being serious," Matt muttered to himself, shrugging.

"It'll be okay, man. You're not the first rocker to have a baby. There's always a way around stuff. We're here for you, dude. Does Claire know?"

"Oh fuck," Darren groaned. "Haven't even thought about what she's gonna make of this. Not to mention Phil."

"You're allowed a personal life, dude. They can't have a problem with it."

I gave Sawyer a sideways glance when no one was looking, wishing he could take his own advice as easily.

"Sawyer's right," I said. "You're entitled to a life outside this band. They'll just have to work around you."

"Thanks, guys. It's just a shock, I guess."

"Right, it seems I've got plans to put in place so I'll be off," I announced. "I'll probably head on straight to the stadium after meeting the new recruits. I'll send Neil and Pete to fetch you later."

"Sure, mate," Isaac said first. The other's nodded and offered a series of 'see ya's' and 'byes'.

The new members of my team seemed like decent enough men. They were experienced, professional and took orders well. But they didn't know the guys or how we worked things and that didn't sit well with me. Having no other choice however, I sucked it up, issuing them with a floor plan for the stadium marked with their positions for the night. I placed myself backstage, guarding the back exits. I couldn't risk the stage being in view, Sawyer would inevitably distract me.

My new team and I carried out my usual pre-show procedures, scouring the perimeter and inside of the buildings housing the conference and event rooms, and going through the schedule with the staff. The fact this was an outdoor venue made the whole idea even worse. I had less control in an environment such as this one than I would have in an enclosed building, and even then it was relatively limited. I called my parents, not mentioning that I originally planned to visit today. My mum would only be disappointed or concerned about the reason for the sudden change in plans.

The heat was intense today, so I removed my black tie and unpopped the two top buttons on my shirt on the way to meet the guy's stylists. They were the usual team we used when in Sydney apparently, but of course I hadn't met them yet and I needed to know everyone who would have access to the band tonight.

Mal, one of the new security members, met me outside when the guys were on their way. To my surprise, Laurelin arrived first, carrying a pizza.

"Sawyer asked me to meet him here with lunch," she explained, strolling past me and into the building behind us. See? Glorified servant.

The guys arrived seconds later, accompanied by Neil and Claire. Claire's arms were weighed down with various files and folders. I didn't know what they were, and the gentlemanly thing would've been to relieve her of some of the weight, but I was too pissed off with her so I let her struggle.

"Hey, Jake," Sawyer called, letting the other guys head on inside in front of us. I stopped in my tracks, turning to look at him. "You're positioned by the stage tonight right?"

"No. I'll be guarding the exits."

"I need you out front."

"That's not a good idea, Sawyer. I can't do my job effectively if I can't stop staring at you."

"Please," he said, his caramel eyes smouldering and making it increasingly difficult for me to resist.

"Why?"

"Just… be there. At the end of the show at least."

"I'll see what I can do," I agreed reluctantly, unable to refuse him. Damn those eyes of his.

I stayed out of sight and earshot while the guys rehearsed. I needed to keep myself in check and that was impossible with Sawyer around. I fixed it with Mal that we would swap positions for the last half an hour of the show. I didn't give him a reason because I didn't technically have one. One of the perks of being in charge however, is that they do whatever I say, no questions.

Neil and I, supplemented with additional stadium security controlled the crowd as they made their way through the gates and to their seats. I'd made a conscious effort to stay out of Sawyer's way, but still my mind kept wandering to what he might be wearing. I imagined, as usual when he's on stage, he'd be donning ripped jeans and a tight-fitting t-shirt that clung to his tattooed biceps. The thought alone was sending my body haywire and it only confirmed the fact I was better off keeping to the back of the stage. It was going to be hard enough being able to hear that delicious and compelling voice of his through the speakers.

The show appeared to be going by without a hitch, but I wouldn't relax until all five guys were back at the hotel. As rearranged, Mal and I swapped positions for the last three songs of the set. I stood in front of the stage, just off to the left in front of the barriers. The Australian heat mixed with the floodlights coming from above made me uncomfortable and I mopped my brow with a tissue from my suit pocket, looking forward to getting in the car and being able to shrug out of my jacket.

The set came to a close, and when the encore did too I started to wonder why Sawyer wanted me to stand here. Until he spoke…

"Okay, guys," he called to the crowd. "I have something new I want to play for you all. I only wrote it last week so you guys are the first to hear it." The crowd

Being Sawyer Knight

went crazy – screaming, cheering and stamping their feet. "Hope you enjoy it."

The rest of the guys, apart from Isaac, looked at each other with a confused look on their faces. Then Sawyer nodded in Isaac's direction and when he hovered his fingers over the keyboard, ready to play, I knew he was a part of whatever was about to happen. Closing his eyes, Sawyer started strumming his long fingers against the strings of his guitar. The intro was slow, seductive almost, and then came the most precious sound in the world.

He started singing.

I pushed you aside so I could live my life,

But without you isn't living, I have been so blind

I'm trying to find the words I know you want to hear,

But the truth is, I'm still drowning in a giant pool of fear

It's taken so long and I'm still not strong,

I can't tell you how I feel, so I put it in a song,

You saved me, you loved me, showed me who I am,

So forever if you'll let me, I will be your man

You are everything I wanted but I couldn't admit,

You brought me back to life with just one kiss,

I wish I'd known it sooner, hadn't been so weak,

Nicola Haken

But know I've always loved you,

You make me complete

I remember the feel of your body against mine,

But I pushed you away, refused to give it time

I was young, I was scared, didn't know who I was,

I should've looked for answers but instead, I gave up

You are everything I wanted but I couldn't admit,

You brought me back to life with just one kiss,

I wish I'd known it sooner, hadn't been so weak,

But know I've always loved you,

You make me complete

My heart felt swollen and I pressed a hand to my chest, trying to alleviate the sudden ache. He'd never been able to truly express how he felt, not in words, but this song... this song he'd written just for me, told me everything I *needed* so desperately to know. The guys disbanded from the stage and I had to pull myself together as I jogged around the back to meet them.

When I got there, the scene unfolding instantaneously put me on high alert.

"What the hell is going on?" I barked at Claire, watching in utter disbelief as Laurelin was handcuffed and escorted to a police car by two uniformed officers.

"I don't have time to explain. We need to get the guys out of here. *Now*."

"What the fuck?" I grumbled to myself, rushing to the back of the stage where the guys were making their way down the steel steps. Within seconds the area surrounding us was flooded with police cars. "Guys hurry the fuck up. We have to leave."

"What's going on?" Sawyer asked, his face paling in panic.

"I don't know," I was forced to admit. How was I supposed to protect them when I didn't have a clue what was happening? "The cops have taken Laurelin away."

"*Laurelin?*"

I didn't have time to elaborate, not that I even could. Neil and Damien, another new recruit, escorted the guys to their cars. Sawyer and I sprinted behind them, until I saw a shadow in the distance that I recognised immediately. It was a silhouette of a man with what appeared to be a 9mm pointing in Sawyer's direction. Without a second's hesitation I jumped in front of Sawyer's body, everything slowing down the moment the gun sounded.

People screamed, I think. Somehow I'd fallen to the floor without conscious memory of how it happened. I felt pressure in my chest, but no pain, despite the blood I could see starting to soak through my white shirt when I looked down. I searched for Sawyer's eyes, but something black blocked my view. It blocked everything – there was nothing but heavy darkness no matter which direction I looked. As my lungs began to burn, as if I were inhaling shards of glass, the sounds started fading too. People stopped screaming, police stopped yelling.

There was nothing.

Chapter Seventeen

~Sawyer~

"*No* no no! Oh please, God, no!" I cried, dropping to my knees beside Jake. "Jake, please, baby, wake up. Oh fuck, please wake up!"

"Don't move him!" one of the police men called out. "You need to get out of the area. Now!" they ordered from afar. There were tens of them now. I don't know what they were doing, I didn't care. I also didn't listen to them.

"Come, on, Saw!" Kip yelled.

"I'm not leaving him!" Tears clouded my vision and my hands were covered in Jake's blood. I took hold of his hand, clutching it to my heaving chest. "I love you, Jake. Oh, God, I love you so much. Please don't leave me. Please don't leave me."

I heard the cops barking orders, the sound of tyres screeching, sirens of incoming ambulances... but nothing would keep me away from Jake. I'd been such a fucking idiot, refusing to admit how much he meant to me. Now I was losing him and I would *never* forgive myself.

"SOMEBODY FUCKING *HELP* HIM!" Why was nobody coming? Jake was unconscious, bleeding out onto the concrete.

"All clear!" I heard someone shout.

"Oh thank, God," I breathed as four paramedics came rushing over to us. "They're gonna help you, Jake. You're gonna be okay. You *have* to be okay."

"Please, sir, you need to move."

"I'm not leaving him!"

"Come on, mate." Kip's hand tugged on my arm, pulling me to a standing position. "Let them help him."

"Why are you here?" I asked, my voice weak, noticing the other cars were gone. Only Neil remained, along with the swarm of police and ambulance crew.

"You're my best fucking friend. I'm not leaving you."

My gaze fell back to Jake's lifeless body. If I stared intently enough I could see his chest rising and falling... barely.

"I can't lose him, Kip. I can't fucking lose him."

"You won't. They'll take care of him. He's too much of a stubborn sod to give up on you that easily."

Yes. Yes he was. Jake is a fighter. He's always in control, so he'll control this. He'll fight for me. He has to.

"Sir?" A paramedic emerged in front of me, startling me and forcing my eyes from Jake. "Sir, are you hurt?"

I shook my head, unable to speak past the tears lodged in my throat. I stepped to the side, looking past the paramedic and over to Jake. They were lifting him onto a board. Instinctively I raised my leg to run to him, but Kip pulled me back.

"Where are they taking him?" I asked, flustered and terrified.

"Westmead Hospital. You can travel with him if you like."

"Yes," I said immediately, not needing a second to process his question. I started running towards the back of the ambulance where they were taking Jake, who was now strapped to a gurney.

"We'll follow in the car!" Neil hollered.

"I need to accompany him," one of the guys who I recognised as part of our new security team said. I didn't remember, nor really care for, his name. One of the crew nodded in silent understanding. Obviously he knew who I was and what being me entailed.

I let the crew get Jake into the back of the ambulance, mainly because Kip was holding me back. When they gave the all clear I hopped in after them, noticing Kip run over to Neil as I sat down in the drop-down chair. One of the male paramedics closed the door while the other started attaching all kinds of wires and tubes to Jake's body.

"He's gonna be okay, right?"

"He's lost a lot of blood," he explained with a sympathetic expression that told me to prepare for the worst. Well I wouldn't. Jake wasn't going to die on me. We'd spent too many years getting to where we are now.

"And there doesn't appear to be an exit wound, which means the bullet is still inside him somewhere."

"Well where is it? Can't you get it out?"

"That's the plan. Your friend will be going straight through to surgery when we arrive."

"He's not my *friend*," I spat. "I love him."

See how easy that was? Why the fuck I didn't have the courage to say that out loud before to anyone was beyond me. There was no one more important to me than the man lay fighting for his life in front of me, and from now on I would make sure the whole damn world knew it.

"How is he?" Kip asked when he reached me. The police wanted to speak to him and all the other guys so he had to go back to the hotel while I came here.

"He's in surgery," I shrugged, not knowing what else to do. I'd been pacing up and down the corridor with the new guard watching me from a row of waiting chairs for the past hour, and as yet, not one person had walked out of the double doors that I knew led to Jake.

"Come here, man," Kip said, holding his arms out and cocking his head. I willingly fell into his arms, crying onto his shoulder as he patted my back. "They've got the guy that did this. It's over, Saw."

"Who the fuck is it?" I growled, yanking myself away from Kip.

"The police are coming to talk to you soon."

"You're keeping something from me," I said, eyeing him up suspiciously.

"Jesus, Sawyer...I don't know how the fuck to tell you this."

"Tell me what? Spit it out, Kip!"

"It's Jerry."

"*Jerry?* My old stepdad Jerry?" What the fuck? "That doesn't make any sense."

"Hey, man, I can't give you specifics. All I know is the cops caught him running from the scene... and that Laurelin has been the one giving him the inside info. They've been working together."

"*Laurelin?*"

"I'm sorry, mate."

I didn't even hear Kip's last few words because I saw a doctor emerge from the heavy double doors, removing his elasticated mask from his face. I jogged towards him immediately, stopping right in front of him.

"How is he?" My voice was rushed and desperate.

"We've sourced and removed the bullet and stopped the bleeding. Luckily it barely skimmed his heart."

"That's good right?" I interrupted, clasping my hands together in the praying position.

"Most definitely. We're taking him through to recovery now, and I'm pleased to tell you we have every reason to believe he'll be just fine."

"Thank you. Oh, Christ, thank you so much." In that moment it felt like I released a breath I'd been holding in for the last two hours. "Can I see him?"

"Soon. We need to get him settled upstairs first and wait for him to come around from the anaesthesia. Someone will come and let you know as soon as you can see him."

"Thank you," I said, genuine adoration, for the amazing man who saved Jake's life, saturating my voice. "Thank you so much," I repeated, shaking his hand.

The doctor, whose name I didn't even think to get, made his excuses and disappeared. When I got back to Kip, Claire was now with him. Her expression was a mixture of shock, concern, fear… everything I felt just minutes ago.

"He's gonna be okay," I breathed, smiling in relief.

"Thank God," she said, pressing a hand to her chest. "Jake's parents are on their way. This will be all over the news any time now. I had to tell them."

"Shit! No, of course. Thank you." How did I forget to call his parents? They're his parents dammit!

"Sawyer, why the hell didn't you tell us there was something going on between you two? I mean… *you*…and…*him?*"

"Let's give him a break, huh, Claire?" Kip interrupted, completely saving my ass. No way could I be bothered dealing with a mass of questions from her right now. "What does it even matter?"

"Of course it matters," she snapped. "But you're right. We'll discuss it later. The police are outside, they want to talk to you."

"Now? Can't it wait until I've seen Jake?"

"No, sir, I'm afraid it can't," an official-looking man waving a badge in the air, interjected, seemingly coming from nowhere.

"There's a family room over there," I said, nodding across the corridor. "We can go in there."

The officer nodded, following my lead to the empty room. Closing the door behind him, he introduced himself and his colleague before motioning for me to take a seat with his hand.

"Mr Knight," he began. "We have reason to believe the man we have in custody is your stepfather."

"Kip, sorry I mean Isaac, told me."

"We're still trying to get to the bottom of why he holds such a vendetta against you. Do you know what that reason might be?"

"Why the hell would I? I've not seen the guy in over eight years. And what's Laurelin got to do with this?"

"It appears your PA has been in a relationship with Jerry for the last six years. We believe the sole reason she sought employment from you was to aid your stepfather in his plan to…" he trailed off, as if his words might shock me.

"Kill me?"

"Yes. We're planning to charge them both with attempted murder."

"But… *Laurelin*? There's no… I mean I just… what the hell did they want from us?"

"He keeps asking to talk to you."

"He *what!*"

"Of course you're under no obligation to do so, and if you *do* decide to speak with him there will be an officer present with you at all times."

"I…I…" My mind was starting to shut down. I couldn't process this amount of information. Jerry? Laurelin? Nothing made sense. "I need to think about it."

"Of course. We will need to take a full statement from you as soon as possible. I understand you wish to get back to your friend right now, but if it's okay with you we would like to come and see you at your hotel first thing in the morning."

"I'll still be here," I said firmly. I wouldn't be leaving Jake. Not ever.

"That's fine. Just call us if that changes," he said, handing me a card from his wallet. "Thank you for your time, Mr Knight. We'll see you tomorrow."

Nodding, I followed him, and the one that never spoke, back out into the corridor.

"Everything okay?" Kip questioned, weighing me up and down as if I were about to break.

"My head is fucked, man. I just want to see Jake. Everything else can wait."

Being Sawyer Knight

"Mr Knight?"

"Yeah?" I spun around immediately to face the blonde nurse.

"I can take you up to see Mr Reed now."

"Thank you," I breathed, sighing in relief. "Hey, Kip?" I called over my shoulder. "Will you wait around and fill his parents in?"

"Sure, mate. No problem."

I followed the young nurse to the stairs at the far end of the corridor. I ran up them, two at a time, eager to get to Jake. We stopped by a set of blue swing doors and, hovering her hand in front of them, she paused.

"He's still very groggy," she advised. "Don't be surprised if he isn't talking much sense, and don't push him too far about what happened. It's imperative he stays relaxed right now."

"Got it," I said, nodding. "Thank you."

Stepping inside the white and clinical room, my eyes darted straight to Jake. He was lying on the bed, the sheet folded just above his waist. There was a large dressing on his chest, just off centre, and he was hooked up to various bleeping machines. I walked cautiously over him, trying not to make any noise. Pulling up a chair, I sat down beside him, cradling his hand in mine.

My touch caused him to stir, and I watched intently, impatiently, as his eyes started to flicker. When they opened, they locked onto mine and the faintest smile pulled on the corners of his lips.

"Thank God you're okay," he whispered hoarsely.

"*Me?* Jesus, Jake... Thank God *you're* okay. You scared the shit out of me."

"Sorry," he said, smiling softly. "I'll try not to get shot in future, huh?"

"Jake..." I breathed, unsure of what to say but knowing it was important. "I'm so sorry for how I've been behaving." He cocked an eyebrow, confused. "I'm sorry for being so fucking afraid. For hiding you. For not showing you how fucking *proud* I am of you. Because I am, Jake. I'm so fucking proud of you. I love you. I *need* you. And thinking I was going to lose you? Fuck, Jake... it almost killed me. Right there beside you, I felt my heart slowing down. You belong to me, Jake. Always have, always will. I'm just so sorry I didn't realise that before it was almost too late."

"What are you saying, Sawyer?"

"I'm saying I'm ready. I'm ready to love you in front of the whole damn world."

"Don't say things you don't mean just because I'm in here. Take your time. Think about it."

"I'm done thinking about it. I'm ready. I love you."

"So, you're going to release an official statement?"

"I kinda think that ship's already sailed," I admitted, not feeling an ounce of shame or regret. "I meant it when I said the thought of losing you almost killed me, Jake. After my reaction at the scene, there's no way the entire world doesn't know by now."

"And you're okay with that?"

"Yeah. I really am."

"Come here," he said, gingerly raising his arm. Smiling, I crawled up onto the bed next to him, squeezing myself into the tiny portion of free space.

"I don't want you to be my bodyguard anymore," I confessed, draping my arm over his hips, careful not to apply too much pressure.

"That's not an option, Sawyer."

"And this isn't your choice. I'm serious. You're not going to protect me anymore. I can't risk this happening again. Ever."

"And what am I supposed to do with my life? This is what I'm trained to do. It's all I know. Besides, as soon as we catch this bastard-"

"They've got him," I interrupted, cursing myself for not telling him sooner. "They caught him running from the scene."

"Thank *fuck*..." he breathed, sighing against my head.

"It was Jerry."

"*Jerry?*"

"My stepfather."

"You're fucking kidding me?" he snapped, jerking his body back and then wincing from the pain.

"Hey, don't move. I need you better."

"I just...it doesn't...*why?*"

"I don't know," I shrugged. "He wants to meet with me apparently."

"You're not going to though," he said firmly. "Sawyer, you're not going to, right?" he repeated, sensing the uncertainty in my expression. "He tried to *kill* you!"

"I don't know. Maybe. I just feel l need an explanation."

"And Laurelin? Why were they carting her away before it happened?"

"She's been sleeping with him. Apparently only took this job to get closer to me, get inside info on where I'd be. Really, I think that hurts the most. I mean, it's *Laurelin*. She's been a good friend to me for so long. At least, I *thought* she was."

"It doesn't make any sense," Jake said, looking as confused as I felt.

"That's why I need to talk to him. I *need* to know why."

"I'm not happy about it."

"He can't hurt me, Jake. There will be an officer with me."

"Well don't rush into it. Promise me you'll really think about this first."

"I will. I promise." I leaned up, brushing my lips against his while tracing his soft stubble with my thumb.

"Have you spoken to Elle?"

"No. Not spoke to anybody yet. Claire said she'd call her though."

"You should go back to the hotel. Call her. She'll be worried sick."

"I don't want to leave you."

"Baby, I love you, but you stink. Your clothes are covered in blood and dirt and that after-show glow you get has morphed into full on mouldy sweat. Go back, take a shower. Come back when it's daylight."

A light knock on the door interrupted us and I jumped quickly off the mattress, assuming I wasn't technically allowed to hop in bed with a patient.

"Hey, Kip," I said, breathing a slight sigh of relief.

"How you feeling, mate?" he asked Jake after nodding at me in silent greeting.

"Like I've been shot."

"Your parents are here. Nurse said they can only visit for a few minutes, then they're booting us all out."

"Thanks, Isaac. You can send them in." When Kip left the room, Jake turned his gaze back to me. "*Go*, Sawyer. I'll see you in the morning."

"I'll be back first thing," I reluctantly agreed, sighing despondently. I bent down, kissing the top of his forehead and breathing him in. "I love you."

"I love you, too," he answered. "Always will."

Claire was still at the hospital, waiting for me when I left Jake's room. I rolled my eyes, facing away so she couldn't see. On my way over to her I passed Jake's parents, giving his mum a brief hug and assuring her that Jake was okay. Claire was up in my face the second they disappeared down the corridor.

"I hope you're prepared for what's out there," she said, nodding towards the automatic glass doors.

"Press?"

"More than you've ever seen in your life."

"Fine," I said, drawing in a deep breath. "Let's just get this over with." I started walking forwards but she pulled me back by my sleeve.

"Say *nothing*. Don't respond to them. Look down, don't acknowledge them and Neil will get you to a car."

"I know the drill, Claire," I muttered, exasperated. I noticed Mal sitting in the corner of the waiting area with Kip in that moment. Claire summoned them both with her finger and they headed over to join us.

"You ready?" Neil asked, patting my back.

No.

"Sure."

I had no idea what time it was, likely almost morning. Standing tall and dragging in a deep gulp of air, I stepped up to the automatic doors, looking straight ahead.

"SAWYER! ARE YOU REALLY GAY?"

"DO YOU LOVE HIM?"

"SO THE RUMOURS WERE TRUE?"

"SAWYER! SAWYER!"

"ARE YOU PLANNING TO MARRY HIM?"

"IS IT SERIOUS?"

"DOES HE LOVE YOU?"

Being Sawyer Knight

Head down. Walk. Head down. Walk. I repeated the mantra in my head, trying to block out the incessant questions and flashes of light. When I reached the car Neil stretched his arms out, keeping a wedge between the press and myself. He closed the door behind me once I was inside and I noticed Kip was already sitting to the right of me.

"Fucking crazy out there, mate," he said, weighing up the crowd through the blacked-out windows.

"Tell me about it."

"It'll pass. You're doing the right thing you know. You shouldn't have to hide who you are."

"Don't exactly have much of a choice, do I? Not after the way I fell apart outside the stadium."

"And if you had a choice? Would it be different?"

"No," I answered determinedly. "It's time."

Neil hurried around to the front passenger seat, slamming the door behind him. Once inside he announced that Mal was following behind with Claire, and also that we had *more* press waiting for us outside the hotel.

The fact that I was prepared for it didn't make bustling our way through the sea of reporters and photographers any easier. The same inane questions were being yelled at me from every angle, lights blinded me, people pushed into me. When I reached the hotel lobby I immediately backed up against a wall and sighed, rubbing my hands down my face.

"What did you expect, Sawyer?" Claire asked, placing her hand on my shoulder. Her words were harsh, but

267

her tone was laced with sympathy. "You should've told us. We could've done this properly. Now… it's all such a mess."

"I'm sorry." What else could I say?

"We'll sort it. We always do, right? If we can get past Matt stumbling into a church, stoned and with his pants around his ankles, we can get past pretty much anything." I laughed at the memory. Sometimes I really don't know how the fuck we've put up with him all these years. "Neil will escort you upstairs. Shower and sleep. We'll organise a meeting in the morning – plan where we go from here."

"Thanks, Claire," I said, sincerity oozing from my every pore. I pulled her into an impromptu hug, forgetting the fact I was covered in blood and smelt like shit.

"You boys are like sons to me," she whispered before pulling away. My jaw dropped a little, stunned by her honesty. I always knew we meant a lot to her, to most of us she's like the mum we never had…but she's never really been one for sappy shit, so to hear the words on her lips made my heart swell. "Neil!" she called with authority. "Take Sawyer to his room."

"You okay, bud?" Neil asked as we made our way to the lift.

"Yeah," I replied casually. I wasn't really okay, a lot of shit would be coming my way, but for the first time in years, if not ever, I *knew* I was going to be.

Chapter Eighteen

~Sawyer~

Eight days later…

"*Fuck*, dude…" Matt groaned, falling backwards onto the large leather couch in my hotel room. We're still in Sydney, waiting for Jake to be discharged from hospital. "I'm in so much fucking trouble."

"Ah, Jesus, Matt, what the hell have you done now?"

"It's what I *haven't* done."

"Care to elaborate?"

"I've been fucking the *same* pussy for over a week. Fuck, dude, I can't even *think* about any other pussy. She's…I mean…I can't get her out of my damn mind."

Oh fuck. Matt was falling in love. God help the poor bitch.

"So what? You love her?"

"FUCK NO! Whoa, dude, don't say shit like that to me."

"But you *like* her?"

"I *really* fucking like her. She does this thing with her tongue where-"

"Yeah you can spare me the details."

"Oh yeah, forgot you're a ring raider these days."

I think I found Matt's acceptance the most surprising. He was always the first to poke fun at the 'faggots', the 'fudge packers' and the 'back door bandits' of the world. What I should've realised long ago however, is that he spouts derogatory shit about *everyone*. It doesn't mean he doesn't like them, it's just his way - you know, given the fact he's a natural born asshole. Asshole or not, he's a fucking good friend.

"Well what are you gonna do when we leave here? Australia's a pretty long way away from LA."

I knew exactly what he was going to do of course – move onto the next one.

"I don't know, Saw. I feel like I'm not ready to leave her. How fucked up is that?"

"She got a name?"

"Belle," he said dreamily, closing his eyes. Jesus, I think he really *is* in trouble. "You know, like Elle, but with a B."

"Yeah, Matt. I get it." Man, he's hard work sometimes. "Speaking of Elle, she'll be here soon, so piss off back to your own room."

"Is my raw sexual magnetism making you uncomfortable?"

"Yeah, that's totally it. Now fuck off."

"Whatever, dude. Give Elle a lick from me."

Being Sawyer Knight

"Over Belle already?"

"No, but I *have* to flirt with Elle. It's practically the fucking law."

Once Matt had left I checked the time, noting I had about twenty minutes before Elle was due to get here. After catching up with her I planned to visit Jake, then I had an interview booked with Gold Magazine. The media circus surrounding my sexuality still hasn't calmed down, although the press have given up camping outside the hotel. Claire has arranged a guest appearance on The Levi Davidson Show in three weeks time which I'm nervous as shit about, but also looking forward to getting my views across without fear of them being skewed like is often the case with the written word.

The most nerve-wracking part of today though, was that I had a visiting order to see Jerry at 4PM this afternoon. I was awake most of the night trying to decide what I would say to him, only to decide I'd just have to figure it out when I get there.

The day after Jake was shot I gathered his things from his room and brought them into my own. I was packing him a bag, tossing in some clean underwear, when I heard the door to my suite open. I didn't even have chance to turn around before Elle's squeals pierced my ears.

"I'm so sorry I couldn't come sooner!" she wailed, throwing herself into my arms.

"Need... to... breathe, gorgeous girl," I teased, purposely rasping because she was clinging to me so tightly.

"Sorry," she muttered, smiling. "I just can't believe what's happened. You could've died, Sawyer. Jake could've died. God, just thinking about it…"

"*Don't* think about it. It's over now."

"Are you still planning to see *him* today?"

"Yes. I am. I have to, Elle. I know nobody seems to understand but I *need* to know why he did it."

"Um, because he's fucking crazy! Sawyer, there's never an acceptable reason for stalking and plotting to *murder* someone!"

"I *know* that. And maybe you're all right, maybe I won't achieve anything by going. If I don't however, I'm always gonna wonder what the bastard had to say."

"I'm sorry, Sawyer. I'm sorry you're having to go through *any* of this."

"Let's change the subject," I suggested. "I've been drowning in serious shit for weeks… I need to talk about something 'normal'."

I headed towards the couch and plopped myself down. Elle grabbed us two bottles of water from the fridge and then followed suit.

"Well," she began. "I'm not sure this could be classed as 'normal' but Ry landed that deal he was after."

"No shit!"

"Yeah. He's been in LA ever since, although he'll have to come home at some point to sort out a more permanent visa."

"So what's he gotta do? You know, apart from fuck people?"

"He's signed exclusively with Back Door Studios. Apparently they're like the very top of their game. He'll shoot, model, travel with them…"

"You're still not happy about it are you?"

"I just miss him. He's like my little brother, you know? But he's happy, he's safe, and from what I can tell the guys who run this company treat their boys really well. Like family, almost."

"You should go out there, check it out, see what kind of place he's working at."

"Oh I plan to. I'm here for a couple of days and then I need to head back for the Hairdresser of the Year Awards in two weeks. Then, providing no VIP clients book in, I should be able to head out there after that."

"That'll probably coincide with when we're back too. But if we're not, you know you can stay at my place."

"Thanks. Hey, you mind if I tag along to see Jake today?"

"Are you for real? He's expecting you!"

"Great," she smiled. "But first, can you order up some room service. I'm *starving*."

"Sure, gorgeous girl. What d'ya fancy?"

"*Everything.*"

"One of everything coming right up."

Mal accompanied Elle and I to the hospital, and when we got to Jake's room he was standing by the window, looking out onto the grounds. He was dressed in blue jog pants and a white t-shirt that hugged the perfect ridges of muscle and I took a moment just to stare at him with my top lip drawn between my teeth.

"Hey, baby," he said, turning around at the sound of us entering. He walked over to me, curled his arms around my waist and kissed the tip of my nose.

"You guys are too adorable," Elle piped up. "How are you doing?"

"I'm doing great. Doctor said I can be discharged this afternoon."

"He did?" I urged, grinning like a lovesick fool. "That's great news."

"So I'm coming to see Jerry with you."

"No you're not," I said resolutely. "You'll be going back to the hotel and climbing straight into bed. You've been *shot*, Jake. You need to rest."

"I've been in bed for over a week. I'm coming with you. I've already cleared it with Claire."

"So I don't even get a say in this?"

"No."

"Ugh, you can be such an arrogant asshole!"

"Hey, guys…" Elle said in a singing voice, waving her small, manicured hands in the air. "I've come to visit. You're not being very hospitable."

"That's settled then. By the time you get back from your interview I'll be back at the hotel, then you can pick me up on the way to see him."

"Well you're not coming in. I mean it, Jake. I want to do this on my own."

"I'll stay right outside," he agreed. "Scouts honour. So, Elle... what've you been up to?"

Elle stayed purposely silent, looking around the room and twiddling her hair around her finger.

"Oh *me?* You guys ready to actually talk to me now?" she teased.

"Stop being a princess, gorgeous girl. It doesn't suit you."

"Well I'm going to get a coffee from the machine while you two kiss and make up. Want one?"

"Please," I said while Jake shook his head. "I'm so glad you're coming home," I whispered into Jake's neck once Elle had left the room. I kissed my way along his jaw, stopping at his lips. "I can't wait to sleep next to you."

"You'll have to be gentle with me," he murmured into my mouth before dipping his tongue inside and tasting me. Our lips crashed together and I wound my fingers into his short hair, pressing him to me. My hips urged forwards, pressing my erection against his body, making him groan in response.

"I love you so fucking much," I ground out, breaking the kiss. "I won't *ever* spend another night away from you."

"I'll hold you to that."

275

"I need to kiss you again."

"Then do it."

"You can turn around at any time," Jake said, gently gripping my knee in the back of the car.

We were on route to see my stepfather, straight from leaving the head offices of Gold Magazine. As with *all* interviews, it was pretty pointless. There was no Dictaphone, just a pen and paper. I studied the way her fingers flexed while she wrote and decided she was just writing whatever the hell she wanted down rather than what I was actually saying.

"I know," I appeased, looking down at his hand on mine. Sometimes I still instinctively flinch a little when Jake touches me in public, even at something as insignificant as accidently brushing his arm against mine. It's habit I guess, and one I hope to break very soon.

The journey to the prison where they were holding Jerry seemed to go on for hours. By the time we arrived my palms were clammy, my heart thudded and my mouth was dry. As agreed, Jake only came as far as the visitor reception area, letting Neil take me the rest of the way accompanied by two wardens and the detective in charge of the case. People turned as I walked by, clearly recognising who I was. Some whispered, some pointed, but I was too busy scanning every face in search of Jerry's to pay much attention.

Being Sawyer Knight

"He's in the interview room," the tallest warden informed me. I sucked in a deep breath, unsure when I would be able to take another. He led us down a long, clinical looking corridor with windows guarded by steel mesh, keeping us out of contact with other inmates. "I'm sorry, I can't allow you to come in any further," the guard said, talking to Neil. He raised his palms, accepting their rules. I had two wardens and an officer of the law with me after all.

His face was the first thing I saw when the guard opened the door. He was sitting at a plain, grey table with the same twisted look in his eyes I saw the day he beat seven shades of shit out of me. He'd aged significantly since I last saw him. His hair had greyed, his cheeks sunk. We must've stared each other out for a whole minute before I broke the silence in temper.

"*Why*, Jerry?" I demanded, my voice so forceful it burned the back of my throat. "What the *fuck* did you want from me?"

"I wanted you to have *nothing*. Just like I have for all these years, because of *you*."

"What the hell are you talking about? How am *I* responsible for your fuck up of a life?"

"This fucking lifestyle you're leading? That should've been *mine*. I was your manager, and a fucking good one. You think you'd have gotten noticed by the big guys if I hadn't set you up with all those gigs? I was on course to have *everything*. I did so fucking much for you. Set you up with your equipment, rented rehearsal space from my own fucking pocket, not to mention the fact I had to put up with your whiney bitch of a mother for all those years."

277

"You know what, screw this," I said, standing from my chair. I was stupid and naïve to believe I would leave here with some sense of understanding or reason. Elle was right, there is no rational reason behind what he did. "*You* ruined your own future, Jerry, when you laid your hands on my mother!"

"She'd been asking for it for years. You know that as well as I do."

"I hope you fucking rot in here," I spat, scraping my chair legs against the floor as I pushed away from the table.

"It won't last, Sawyer," he called as I made my way to the door. "One day you'll wake up and it'll all be gone."

I laughed at the poignancy of his words. Part of me wishes it *would* all be gone when I wake up tomorrow. This life - the fame, the money, the constant intrusion… I'm starting to think I just don't want it anymore.

"What's going to happen to him?" I asked the detective whose name I couldn't remember. "Will he be extradited?"

"I doubt it. I'm sorry I can't give you much information right now, but I assure you you'll be kept fully involved throughout his case."

"What about Laurelin?"

"My guess is she's probably going to get off lightly, but again, I will tell you more as the case goes on."

"But are we free to leave here? Head back to the States?"

"Yes, of course. We'll be liaising with the LAPD and Cumbria Constabulary in the UK so providing the details we hold for you are up to date, we'll be able to contact you when needed."

"I have no idea." Hell, I don't even know my own phone number. "I'll get our PR manager to call you."

"This isn't over, Sawyer!" I stiffened at the sound of Jerry's voice. He growled my name with such malevolence as two wardens dragged him past me, kicking and yelling, towards the floor to ceiling bars that led to the next part of the building.

"I need to get out of here," I muttered under my breath, wiping the sweat off my forehead with the back of my hand.

"Wait up, Saw!" Neil called after me as I charged towards the exit. I didn't stop. I *couldn't*. I needed out of this hellhole. I needed air, I couldn't breathe.

The second fresh air hit my face I filled my lungs, sucking deep as I doubled over, bracing my hands on my knees.

"What happened?" Jake's voice startled me. I'd forgotten he was waiting for me in reception and I realised I must've sped straight past him. "Sawyer, look at me," he encouraged, gently pulling on my arm. I straightened my back and looked him in the eye, instantly feeling calmer. "You okay, babe?"

"Yeah," I sighed. "Yeah I just… hell, I don't know. It was weird seeing him again I guess. But you were right, the whole thing was pointless."

"But you've been, and it's over. You don't have to wonder 'what if' anymore. No regrets?"

"I'm not sure yet. I just want to go home, Jake. I'll think about it later."

Cocking his head, Jake led me back to the car. We climbed inside, and as soon as he closed the door behind him, he leaned across the back seat, taking me in his arms.

"I'm so proud of you," he whispered in my ear, cradling my body against his.

"Proud of me?" I questioned, pulling back so I could see his face but keeping hold of his arms. "For what? Letting you get shot for me?"

"I'm not talking about that, babe. I mean *this*," he said, motioning his hand over us. "We're in a car, in *public*, and you're letting me hold you. I know you weren't ready for this yet, it was thrust upon you, but still you're *doing* it. You're embracing it, and for that, I'm proud of you."

For a few minutes we did nothing but hold each other. We didn't talk, or kiss, we just...*were*. It didn't last nearly as long as I'd have liked however. Neil came strolling back to the car, pausing outside while he talked on his phone.

"Hey, Jake?" I asked quietly.

"Um hmm?"

"Did the hospital say how long it would be until you could, you know, *do* stuff?"

"What kind of 'stuff', Sawyer?" he probed mischievously, grinning devilishly at me.

"I think you know what kind of *stuff*."

"Are you saying you want to *fuck* me, baby?"

"God yes," I breathed, my dick bulging just from the thought. "That's *exactly* what I'm saying."

"I'm sure if you're gentle with me, we'll be just fine." He winked and my heart pounded in my chest, working hard to pump the blood that was rushing straight to my cock.

"You guys ready?" Neil opened the door, slipping inside the car and snapping me back into the real world.

"Sure," I said, wondering if my face gave away how flustered I was. "Tell Claire I'll catch up with her in the morning. I don't want to be disturbed tonight."

"Too much fucking info, man."

"No I didn't mean… I mean… oh fuck it, yeah that's just what I meant."

Jake laughed, such a sweet sound and one I hadn't heard nearly enough, but then pressed a palm to his chest.

"Shit, laughing hurts."

Good job everything I had in store for him tonight didn't involve any laughing whatsoever.

When we got back to the hotel I called Elle and filled her in about my pretty uneventful visit to the prison. She was staying in our hotel too, sharing with Kip, but honestly I really didn't feel up to seeing anyone.

Except Jake of course.

We showered together, taking our time, washing and caressing each other's bodies. The hospital gave him some waterproof patches to apply over his dressing, but I was still careful to try and avoid that area. I turned him so his back was against my chest, tilting his head back while I washed his hair. After rinsing the shampoo off, I dotted tiny kisses along his neck, pressing my erection up against his ass.

"I think we're clean enough," I whispered, taking hold of his hand. We stepped out of the shower together, only letting our hands fall apart to dry ourselves off with towels. When we'd finished, I tossed mine to the floor, but of course Jake folded his and tucked it neatly over the heated rail.

Naked and still slightly damp, we made our way into the bedroom, and I kept a foot behind so I could admire the way his ass flexes when he walks. Jake lay down on the bed, gingerly rolling onto his back. I crawled up beside him, positioning one of my knees between his parted legs.

"Fuck I've missed you," I told him, bending down and kissing around the edges of his dressing. "Does it hurt?" I asked, immediately feeling like a moron. "Of course it does," I muttered, smiling up at him.

"It's actually not too bad. I actually thought getting shot would hurt a hell of a lot more."

"What about… when it happened?" I pressed nervously, unsure whether bringing it back to the forefront of his mind was a good idea.

"Honestly, I didn't feel it. I felt pressure… *intense* pressure, but before I could feel any pain my senses started shutting down. The only thing I really remember is searching for you."

"I was right there," I assured him. My chest ached, throbbing with hurt, and also pride for him. "I was right by your side the whole time."

I kissed my way up along his chest, softly licking the grooves between his muscles. I paused at his neck, taking a little extra time kissing him there, knowing his head would angle to the side and soft moans would escape his throat. When I reached his lips, I dipped my tongue into his mouth and curled my fingers around his cock. He was always so hard for me, so ready. It twitched from my touch, begging me to explore.

I moved my fist up and down, smearing the pre-cum over his sensitive tip with my thumb. His hips bucked, thrusting himself further into my hand. I lowered my body, brushing my dick up against his torso, needing the friction.

"I won't fuck you yet, Jake." His eyes widened, weighing me up sceptically. "I'm going to make *love* to you. I need this slow, and gentle. I need to *feel* you, savour you."

"Then do it, Sawyer. Make love to me."

I moved myself further down the bed, crawling between his legs. He widened them instinctively, giving me access to his perfect ass. Burying my fingers between

Nicola Haken

the crevice of his cheeks, I parted them, lowering my head and teasing his hole with my tongue.

"Fuck, that feels good," he groaned, arching his hips. Encouraged, I kept swirling my tongue around the puckered rim before entering him. The noises coming from his mouth turned me the hell on as I fucked him with my tongue, reaching up to caress his balls with my fingers. "Fuck, yes," he hissed, as this time I inserted one, then two fingers into his ass. I pumped them in and out, pleasuring him, *stretching* him.

"I *love* fucking you with my fingers."

Slowly, I licked my way up to his balls, drawing them into my mouth and releasing them with a pop before tracing the veins on his dick with my tongue. His whole body jerked when I took his rigid length to the back of my throat. Keeping my mouth moist, I worked my lips up and down his shaft, twirling my tongue over the broad head, moaning at the delicious, salty taste of him.

"I want to suck you, baby," he said, fisting his hands in my hair.

"No," I said softly. "You need to take it easy."

"I won't break, Sawyer. I need to taste you."

"Later," I said simply, crawling up onto my knees. Reaching across to the nightstand I opened the drawer, only to want to punch myself in the fucking head when I did so. "Shit. We're out of condoms."

"I'm clean, baby. I swear to you I've never been with *anyone* without protection," Jake assured.

"Neither have I," I confirmed. "And I get tested regularly." I regretted that comment the second it spilled

284

from my mouth. I might as well have just said, 'yeah I used to fuck around a lot with random groupies so I always made sure I was clean'.

"Lose the guilt, Sawyer." I looked up at him, confused. "I can see it in you, *feel* it in here," he added, holding his palm to his chest. "I know about your past. Shit, most of the damn world knows about it. But I don't care. I don't care who you've been with, only who you're going to be with in the future."

"You," I breathed. "Only *ever* you." I'd never spoken truer words in my life. There is no one else for me. Ever. There never has been, I was just too much of a pussy to confront it.

"Then grab the lube and make love to me. I *need* to feel you, baby. Skin to skin."

Fuck, if those words didn't make me harder than steel. I took my time, squeezing a generous amount of lube onto my palm and smoothing it up and down my cock. Dipping my fingers into his ass, I massaged him with the lube, working it in and around his tight hole, driving him crazy.

"*Now*, Sawyer. I need you inside me."

I shuffled onto my knees, spreading my legs slightly apart to steady myself. Positioning my cock at his entrance, I folded myself over onto his body, careful not to apply too much pressure to his wounded chest.

"Kiss me," I whimpered. "I want to taste your mouth when I enter you."

Crashing his lips to mine and pulling my head closer to him with his hand at the back of my neck, he kissed me hard. The way our tongues tangoed together was like a dance of pure passion and need. Reaching between us, I gripped my cock, guiding it into his ass. Oh mother of fuck… being so bare, so *close* to him… I had never experienced something so intense, so powerful.

"Oooooh, *fuuuuuck*," he choked out.

"You like that?" I teased against his lips, sliding back and forth torturously slowly. "You like my dick in your ass?"

"*Yes*," he groaned. "Move faster, baby."

I wound my arm around the back of his neck, using his strength to support my weight as I thrust in and out of his body. A light sheen of sweat dusted my skin as I picked up my pace. We continued to kiss, moaning and whispering into each other's mouths as I made love to him. I was slow and gentle as promised, only gradually increasing my speed.

"*Please*, Sawyer," he begged. "Harder."

"Not yet."

I wasn't ready for this to be over yet. I was enjoying it, enjoying *him*, too much. Jake's legs wrapped around my waist, hooking together by his ankles as I continued to slide into him. I went deeper with each thrust, the pleasure radiating up my spine and making my heart beat faster.

I kissed him once more before straightening myself up, resting back on my heels so I could admire his weeping cock. Reaching out, I took it in my hand, sliding my fingers up and down. Pre-cum wept from the tip, seeping down his impressive erection and making it glisten under the ceiling lights.

"*Now,* Jake. *Now* I'm going to fuck you."

I didn't give him a chance to respond before I started pounding his ass fast and hard. Keeping a firm grip on his cock, I jacked him off, keeping my eyes on his the entire time.

"I'm gonna, holy shit, baby, I'm… I'm coming already!" he said through gritted teeth. His ass clenched around my dick as he shot his load all over his stomach. I continued to milk him while my own orgasm took hold. Feeling his ass contract around me made my head spin and my balls tighten.

"Fuck, fuck…ah, fuuuuuck!" My dick jerked as I poured myself inside him, giving him *all* of me, and I collapsed onto him, falling off centre to avoid his bandage. "That was…"

"Incredible."

"*Intense.*"

"Thank you, Sawyer."

"For fucking you?"

"For completing me."

God, I love this man, and in that moment I silently vowed to spend the rest of my life making up for all the years we missed out on.

"You complete me too. You're my best friend, my lover, and the person who saved my life in every way imaginable. I *love* you, Jake. And just like the night you were shot, I will *always* be right by your side."

Epilogue

~Sawyer~

Three weeks later…

I woke up at 5AM with the motherfucker of all headaches, most likely due to the fact I'd been lying awake all night fretting about my appearance on the Levi Davidson show later today. Ryder's shadow startled me when I entered the kitchen, dressed in only my boxers. He's been staying at my place, given it's close to the Back Door studio, and because he doesn't have anywhere else yet. I don't mind him staying with us. He's a good kid who has quickly become one of my best friends. Plus, I only spend part of the year in LA anyway so for the most part, he'll have the place to himself.

"Sorry, mate," he mumbled, rubbing at his eyes when I flipped the ceiling lights on. "Didn't mean to wake you."

"You didn't. Couldn't sleep."

"Nervous about the show today?"

"Yeah, I guess." I reached up to the cabinet, opening the glossy black cupboard and grabbing a glass from inside. I popped in two dissolvable aspirin that I picked up from the bathroom on way in here before topping the glass up with water. "So how was the party?"

Gavin finally proposed to his girlfriend last week. They've been solid for years, he's talked about marriage before but when it came to doing anything about it he chickened out. It's kinda weird really, what with Matt *still* being in love after a *whole* month, Daz having a kid, Gavin getting hitched, Kip getting serious with Elle, and me ready to pledge the rest of my life to Jake, it's like we're all finally growing up.

Last night the guys went out to celebrate all of our recent announcements. They understood me passing up, knowing I wanted to get my head in the game for today's interview, and also that Jake was still having to take it easy. He's kind of still my unofficial bodyguard, seeing as he accompanies me everywhere. But I won't allow him to let it become his *job* again. We've not decided where we go from here regarding his career, but he's coming around to the idea of working for some other side of the business.

"Fuckin' mental," Ryder said, smiling as he shook his head. "Matt got his dick out as usual."

I swirled the tablets around in the glass, watching them fizz and dissolve.

"Hey, Saw?" Ryder said nervously. "You're not pissed at me are you?"

We had a bit of a spat last night when I caught him smoking pot in the house. I'm not against that shit if that's what you're into, I just don't want it stinking my condo out.

"Look, I overreacted last night, Ry. I shouldn't have yelled the way I did. You know it doesn't bother me what you do. Just not in the house, 'kay?"

"Got it. I'm still sorry. You know I really appreciate you letting me stay here."

"I know you do, man. Let's just forget last night." Ryder nodded, his slightly hunched postured suggesting he still felt uneasy. "I'm heading back to bed," I announced, sipping my aspirin as I walked.

"Sure. Say mornin' to Jake for me."

That made me smile as I made my way back to the bedroom. Back to Jake, who was in my bed. I can't understand now how I ever thought keeping him hidden was for the best. I don't think, fuck that, I *know*, I have never been so happy. So content.

"Hey," Jake mumbled sleepily when I crawled in beside him. "What were you doing up." He turned over to face me, yawning groggily.

"Couldn't sleep," I replied, resting my hand on his hip. "Headache."

"You've done a thousand interviews, Sawyer," he tried to soothe.

"Yeah, and I've hated every single one of them."

"That's because you've always had to *lie*. Today you get to be yourself, babe. Embrace it. Show the world who Sawyer Knight really is."

Being Sawyer Knight

"Truth is, I'm not even sure who Sawyer Knight is anymore."

"What do you mean" he asked, apprehension forcing his eyebrows together. "You're not having regrets?"

"No," I answered quickly. "Not about us if that's what you're thinking. I just… I'm tired, Jake. This life – being on parade all the damn time, having things expected of me. I keep thinking back to when we were in The Lakes. It was so peaceful, so quiet. We could do what we wanted, when we wanted. Just *us*. You and me. I *want* that for us, Jake."

"Are you saying you want to leave the band?"

"I don't know what I'm saying. I just know I want more than this. Or less, depending on how you see it."

"Sawyer," he breathed, reaching over and cupping my face in his palm. "Music is your whole life. It always has been."

"No, Jake. Music *was* my whole life. Now I have *you*."

"I wouldn't be able to count the amount of times I used to dream of you saying those words to me," he admitted, shuffling closer, torso to torso. "Sometimes I have to look twice because I can't believe you're really here, that you're really *mine*."

"I'll be yours for the rest of forever, Jake."

"How's your headache?"

"Um, easing off a little."

"Good. Because I'm going to fuck you now." Smiling, I willingly rolled onto my back, laughing as he pounced on top of me. "You're so fucking beautiful," were the last words he said, before devouring every inch of my body.

By the time morning rolled fully around, I just couldn't think straight. I didn't even know what I planned to say, but I called an emergency meeting with Claire and the guys anyway. They turned up at my house just after midday, looking like death reheated.

"This better be good, Saw," Matt complained. "I feel like shit, I should be in fucking bed."

"Is this to do with what happened in Australia?" Claire asked. "Have the police been in touch?"

"No, not since Thursday."

Jerry tried to apply for extradition to the UK but was refused. He committed the crime in Australia and he will pay the price for it there too. Laurelin however, *has* been sent back to the UK to stand trial for conspiracy to murder. I haven't seen nor spoken to her and I don't plan to. After seeing Jerry, I realised I don't need answers anymore. There aren't any that I would understand or accept, so what's the point?

"Guys…" I trailed off, sinking back into the white leather couch. "I'm not even sure what it is I want to say here."

"So you got me out of bed with Belle for nothing? Fuck you, man."

Being Sawyer Knight

Matt and Belle have been inseparable since they met. He flew her out here with us when we returned and so far, in his words, he can't imagine another pussy tasting sweeter than hers.

"This is serious," I said, causing Claire's eyes to widen. "I've been thinking. In fact, I've been doing nothing else. "I think… I think I'm *done*, guys."

"*Done?*" Claire repeated. "What do you mean you're 'done'?"

"I've reached the end of the road. We've had ten *amazing* years together, but I don't think I want another ten."

"You're not serious!" Claire snapped. "You're being irrational. The last few months would test anyone, Sawyer. Once Jerry's been sentenced and this is all over you'll-"

"It's got nothing to do with that," I interjected. "I've had ten amazing years with you guys and I *love* every single one of you like my own family. We've spent year after year doing what we adore, we've experienced so much, *gained* so much… but I've always been kinda lost. Fame and music were the only things I lived for, I didn't know anything beyond that even existed for guys like us. But now… I've learned so much this last few months, about life, about myself. I'm tired, guys. Tired of living for the rest of the world. I'm sick of being on show. I just want to live at my own pace, enjoy the smaller things that we don't get to experience anymore."

"Like grocery shopping," Gavin said, smiling as if he understood. "Running for the paper. Getting' a dog because you know you'll be stickin' around the same place long enough. Yeah… I get it, man."

"You know," Daz chipped in. "I've been putting off saying but, well since I found out Dana was pregnant, I've kinda been thinking the same thing. She needs me, the kid's going to need me. This isn't the life I want for them."

"I think Kerry would be pleased," Gavin said. "Since I proposed she keeps dropping not so subtle hints about wanting kids."

"What about you, Matt. What do you think?"

"I think… I think I can't believe this is over." Emotion swelled inside my chest when I noticed the rims of Matt's eyes starting to redden. It was the first human emotion I'd ever seen him show. "We're… *us*. We're a team. You guys are my brothers. How the fuck are we supposed to go our separate ways?"

"We'll always be a family," I assured him. "Just with less travel and less chaos."

"Elle and I have discussed this recently too," Kip admitted, looking straight at me.

"Guys…" Claire practically whispered, her eyes glistening with tears that hadn't found the courage to fall yet. "You're… you're really serious, aren't you?"

"Yeah," I answered. "Yeah I think we are."

"So what next?" Matt questioned. "We talk to Pete?"

"Um, well," Claire stuttered, her face pale with shock. "Y-yes. Of course we'll need to talk to Pete. There's a lot to sort through, a lot to plan. You can't just bow out, you know that right?"

"Of course," I agreed.

"We'll need to finish this album, make it a farewell one. Plan a final tour. Talk about your futures, arrange appearances and announcements."

"Sooo, this is it?" Kip said, exhaling a long sigh. "Souls of the Knight are no more."

"No," I disagreed. "We'll *always* be a band. You guys are my life, that will never change."

"Well," Claire began. "I suppose I'd best start making some calls," she added, sighing dejectedly. "And for the record, guys, you're *my* family too." She walked out of the room, heading towards the outside pool area, before any of us could respond.

Guilt simmered in my veins. She'd dedicated the last nine years of her life to us since joining the team a year after our first hit. In many ways she's like our surrogate mother. She's bossy, condescending but she always looks out for us. She'd never married, had kids, spending every waking hour managing us or sorting out our shit. Now we were quitting, moving on with new people, who would she have?

She'll have us, that's who. I meant what I said. This band and everyone involved with us are a family, and I would give up my life before I'd let that change.

"Are we all okay?" I asked, addressing everyone.

"Feels kinda surreal," Gavin said, and I noticed the other guys nodding in understanding. "We've had a fucking blast though, haven't we?"

"Yeah," I nodded. "Even with Matt in the band," I joked. Matt threw a cushion my way, sulking as he missed me completely.

We spent the next hour or so swapping memories, laughing, insulting each other's past mistakes. Then, when it was time for me to get ready for my appearance on the Levi Davidson show, we all stood up in unison, gathering in the middle of the room. I opened my arms, my heart ballooning with love and awe for these four guys who have been with me through everything. One by one they followed my lead until we ended up in a scrum, arms locked together, heads down.

"I fuckin' love you guys," I said. "I wouldn't have wanted to share this life with anyone but you."

"Hear, hear," Kip chirped, breaking the scrum and offering his hand for a round of high fives.

In just a couple of hours the course of my future had been completely upturned. I was as afraid as I was excited, but when Jake entered the room, coming up behind me and pressing a kiss to my shoulder, I knew whatever was in store for me would be fucking amazing.

After showering and changing I called Elle, filling her in about our decision. Of course she questioned it, made sure it wasn't impulsive, but after explaining like I did to the guys she was behind me one hundred percent. She's flying out next week, after some hairdressing awards ceremony she'd been banging on about for months, and for the first time she was bringing her sister Kylie out with her.

Being Sawyer Knight

She's just finished school for the summer and has been having a hard time with their mum. Elle thinks showing her a bit of the world will show her that there's a whole life ahead of her, where she can achieve anything she sets her mind to. Elle and I have both been in Kylie's position, living with a parent who doesn't give a shit about you. It's easy to believe that's all life has to offer, especially when most people on the estate stay there, getting pissed, procreating and sponging off the state until they die.

The topic of conversation led me to my own mother. As soon as I knew Jake had pulled through after the shooting, I tried to contact her, tell her what was happening before she saw it on the news. I can only assume I was too late seeing as she never took any of my calls and hasn't attempted to get in touch herself.

I asked if Elle had seen her, if she knew how she was. All she could offer me was an apology, which clearly translated to the fact my mother has given up on me. It hurts, possibly more than she deserves, but she's still my mother. When you're a kid there's no one more important than your mum. I still remember her singing me lullabies and kissing my grazed knees.

"You ready to head off?" Jake asked, entering the bedroom. "Neil's outside."

"Sure," I replied, although I don't think I'd ever been quite so un-ready in my life.

We travelled to the TV studio with Neil and Claire sitting up front, while Jake held my hand in his, sitting with me in the back. On arrival, we were met with a sea of screaming fans. I took my time walking past the crowd, stopping for autographs and photos and for the first time spending a little extra time to chat with some of them. I'd miss this… the knowledge that our music brought so many people together. I absorbed every second of the crazy atmosphere as studio staff escorted us into the building.

From this moment on, I would appreciate every single moment of this lifestyle, knowing it was coming to an end.

Once inside I was taken through to makeup where two women fussed with my hair and layered my face in powder. Soon enough I was taken through to the studio, pausing outside the door until the recording light flashed red. I heard Levi announce my name, and then I was given the go ahead by a guy wearing a headset to go on through.

"Ladies and gentlemen, the one and only, Sawyer Knight!" he called out to the audience. They clapped and cheered for me as I made my way onto the set, offering them a smile and a wave before sitting down on the couch adjacent to Levi's desk.

Levi broke me in slowly, asking me the usual list of questions about the band and our plans, many of which I was forced to dodge after our meeting this morning.

"So," Levi started, his face turning serious. I guessed now we were getting to the reason I was actually here. "You've had quite a tough couple of months. There's been a lot of press, a lot of rumours surrounding you and your sexuality. Would you like to share your side of the story with us?"

"I've fallen in love, that's really all there is to tell," I admitted, feeling unexpectedly proud. "Yes, I've fallen in love with another man. He's been my best friend since we were kids, he knows me absolutely, my best parts and my worse. If loving him makes people turn away from me, so be it. He makes me happy, end of story. End of rumours."

"You talk of people turning away from you, are you referring to your mother?"

What the hell?

"We've actually been given an advanced copy of tomorrow's Daily Record, which has an interview with your mother inside."

I saw Claire appear at the side of the stage, off camera and out of view of the audience. She was slicing her throat with her flattened hand, silently signalling them to cease filming. Clearly, this revelation was as much of a surprise to her as it was to me, and that she was most certainly *not* happy about. She looked directly at me, assessing my reaction with her eyes. I nodded once, ensuring her that I was okay to continue. It was evident from the scowl on her face though, that someone would be getting some serious shit off her very soon.

"Are you aware of what it says?" Levi continued.

"No," I stated, taking a deep breath in preparation.

"She calls you and your lifestyle an abomination. She says that she has disowned you, that you are no longer her son. How would you like to respond to that?"

"If she's watching, I would like to say..." I turned to the camera facing me, talking directly to her. "I'm sorry. I'm sorry you can't bring yourself to understand, or accept me. I'm sorry I'm not enough for you, but I will never be sorry for falling in love, for finding the kind of connection some people spend their whole lives trying to find without success. I might no longer be a son to you, but you will always be my mum."

The audience clapped and Levi smiled encouragingly at me. When I looked to the back of the set I saw Jake standing there, dressed in a crisp black suit, as usual, leaning against one of the prop walls. I smiled unconsciously, tears pricking the back of my eyes. Levi's voice brought my attention back to him as he asked his final question.

"So, tell me. What's it like being Sawyer Knight?"

"Awesome. Of course it is. I'm a very lucky guy."

I gave the same robotic answer I'd been trained to give a thousand times, but for the very first time in my existence, I meant every single world.

You've just met Ryder Richardson in Being Sawyer Knight. Stay tuned for his story – Taming Ryder - with special guest appearances from the rest of the gang, coming Summer 2014!

Acknowledgements

This is the hardest part of writing a book. I'm always scared I'm going to forget to mention someone important! If I do, then it's because I'm a noob, and I still love you!

Okay, pull up a chair and pour yourself a drink… this could be a long one.

I'd like to start with my oldest, gayest, most fabulous friend, Paul Horrocks, also known as Luap, Poel, mofo, wabbit…Don't ask me why. He's just one of those crazy people you learn to accept! Thank you for all the tips and advice, you know, seeing as I don't have my own cock ;-)

Next I'd like to thank my amazing friend Emma Clark. She is one of the reasons being in this game is so worth it. She read one of my books, stalked me a little (yep, I'm cool enough to be stalked! Go me!) and we got chatting and realised we lived pretty close to each other. A day hasn't gone by since where we haven't spoken – usually about utter filth ☺ Thank you for your friendship, taking me on hot dates, your help promoting me, making my teasers, brainstorming with me… You have helped me so much since we met and when I'm with you EVERYTHING IS AWESOME! ;-)

Now I need to thank my beta readers. Thank you for lending me your keen eyes, catching my mistakes and being honest with me. Keeley Wall, Karen Peacock, Emma Clark, Heather Reed, Autumn Thibault, Caroline Lindkvist, Claire Pengelly, Stacey Mosteller, Vanessa

Morse – I love you guys! You're all exactly my brand of awesomeness ☺

I'd like to thank all the amazing bloggers of the world now. I truly believe I would be nothing and nowhere without their support. They read, review, pimp, recommend, and work bloody hard to support authors and spread their name for no other reason than they're awesome! Emthebookbabe's Book Blog, Holly's Hot Reads, The Book Trollop, The Book Enthusiast, Mia's Point of View, Rumpled Sheets Book Blog, Tanya - The Book Obsessed Momma, A Pair of Oakies, I Dare You to Read…thank you for your support, pimping and amazing words! I'm sure there are so many more, and this is the part I hate! If I haven't mentioned you, that *doesn't* mean I don't love and appreciate everything you do. Oh, and Kristy Louise from Book Addict Mumma – thank you for your info about Sydney!

I HAVE to thank my fantabulous street team – Nicola Haken ~ Dirty Dolls! Thank you for reading and loving my books, for sharing, pimping and joining in the fun! You guys are the reason I write and you have no idea how much I appreciate you ☺

Time to thank my favourite group on Facebook now – Nicola's CockyBitches! I made this group for the dirtier members of my street team ☺ I don't think I have *ever* laughed so much, drooled so much, or discussed so much filth in my life before I created this group. It's FANTASTIC and so much fun! Slowly but surely, I am converting my members to gay porn, particular CockyBoys, addicts like myself, and I can share my love of Jake Bass with them until my heart's content without them wanting to punch me in the face. At least I don't think they do… CockyBitches if you're reading, do you want to punch me in the face? If I waffle on about Jake too much just tell me and I'll stop. KIDDING! That is *never* going to happen! So thank you, girls… oh and Luap, our resident gay! Thank you for all the fun, friendship and downright FILTHY pictures! ☺

Thank You to Debra at Book Enthusiast Promotions for all your hard work and support. You've been amazing organizing my tours, cover reveals and all that promotional shizz from the beginning. You're also a pretty damn awesome friend and I love being your Queen Bitch!

Kelly Micklefield – also known as – Kelly with the jelly belly who walks around in smelly wellies – thank you for bringing fun to my evenings (when I should be writing!). No one knows how to talk shit (literally) like you ;-)

Now for my wonderful family – my husband and my four children. Thank you for your love, support and encouragement. You guys are my world and I adore you so much. Big hugs and sloppy kisses for all of you!

Holly Baker – my fantabulous new editor! Not only do you have a fab eye for detail and have helped me make this book the best it can be, but you're also a great friend – even when you're threatening me with violence ;-) I can't thank you enough for all your support these last few months. I love you!

Last but not least, my readers – old and new – THANK YOU from the bottom of my heart. This being an author shizzle wouldn't be possible with you. I thank you for every book you've read, every review, every rating, every kind word, every everything! Whenever I hear back from one of my readers it never fails to surprise me and put a huge grin on my face (unless they're slating me of course, then I just think 'fuck off, you nob'). Sometimes I genuinely have to take a moment to compose myself. It's like, whooooa…

someone has actually read *my* book. It's an amazing feeling and one I will never get used to, nor tire of. So thank you, thank you, thank you!

When I published my first book just over a year ago, I never could've imagined what an amazing journey I was about to embark on. It's so much more than just the writing. The book world is an incredible place to be a part of and I have made so many new, genuine and lifelong friends along the way. Authors, bloggers, readers…so many of them have become such important people in my life, and I feel truly honoured to be where I am right now.

So, thank you. If we've ever spoken, exchanged a message, comment, tweet, or even if you've just given me a 'like'… thank you. You make this experience incredible, and I love and appreciate every single one of you.

Big hugs and saucy licks for all ;-)

About the Author

Okay, let's get the boring stuff out of the way first. I live in Rochdale, UK, with my husband and four little shi- um, I mean angels. We have two pretty mean looking, but adorable rescue dogs – Gio and Pippa, and I kind of want a cat but I've not told the hubs that yet ☺

Now for the things that make me me! I like to do things a little different, so instead of boring you with a tonne of paragraphs – here's some fun facts instead!

1. I am a tattoo-a-holic
2. I am a Pepsi Max-a-holic
3. I am a CockyBoys-a-holic
4. I am a Jake Bass-a-holic
5. I am a potato-a-holic – mashed, chipped, baked, roasted, boiled…I NEED them in my life
6. I like saying a-holic
7. I don't like even numbers
8. I can't eat with metal spoons. Not for a medical reason, just because I'm weird.
9. I have a filthy mind and an even filthier mouth (make of that what you will ☺)
10. I want a penis of my very own
11. I am a Twihard and PROUD
12. I am a Gleek and PROUD
13. I love One Direction and I am not so proud
14. Music makes me happy
15. I swear way too fucking much
16. My favourite colour is purple

17. Haken is my maiden name. My married name is Wall, and let's face it, that's a shit name
18. For a fat chick, I'm incredibly flexible ;-)
19. I like making lists
20. I'm crazy awesome!

So there you go. That's me ☺

Nicola Haken

If you want to keep up with my crazy world, you can do that by following me here:

http://www.facebook.com/nicolahaken

http://www.twitter.com/NicolaHaken

https://www.goodreads.com/author/show/7094294.Nicola_Haken

http://www.pinterest.com/nicolahaken/

Follow my Tumblr at your own risk!

http://nicolahaken.tumblr.com

Instagram - @nicolahaken

Being Sawyer Knight

Other titles by Nicola Haken

New Adult/Contemporary

Saving Amy
Missing Pieces
Take My Hand
Hold On Tight (Take My Hand #2)
Lean On Me (Take My Hand #3)
Never Let Go (Take My Hand #4)

CPSIA information can be obtained at www.ICGtesting.com
Printed in the USA
LVOW12s1924050415

433370LV00010B/632/P

9 781499 670028